Between Darkness and Light

Between Darkness and Light

Roy Peachey

Eyrie Press

First published in 2019 by Eyrie Press

The moral right of the author has been asserted.

Cover image by Anjalee Burrows.

ISBN 978-1-913149-02-4

A catalogue record of this book is available
from the British Library.

This book is dedicated to the memory of the
Chinese Labour Corps. We will remember them.

Through the dense din, I say, we heard him shout
'I see your lights!' But ours had long died out.

'The Sentry' – Wilfred Owen

不 识 庐 山 真 面 目, 只 缘 身 在 此 山 中
苏轼

The reason we do not know the true face of
Mount Lu is because we have no distance from it.

Su Shi

Shanghai, 1900

Chapter 1

As the white devils celebrate the coming of their twentieth century, Wang Weijun is sitting upright in a doctor's chair, scrunching two paper balls into his fists in anticipation of the horror to come. His mother and third aunt are holding his head firm.

'And now we shall irrigate the remains of the eye,' the doctor says. 'Ah Qing has drawn fresh water from the well so that we can wash away any fatty substances that may have accumulated since ... er, since your last visit.'

Wang squirms in his chair, but his mother simply grips his neck more tightly.

'It is vital that the patient remain in a static position,' the doctor continues. 'A movement during cool fixation of the eyeball will merely result in the spillage of water, but a movement— even the slightest movement—during the operation itself could produce, er, unfortunate results.'

'Little Jun, you hear what the doctor says? You must stay still.'

The boy rolls his eyes upwards, but his mother is out of sight, anonymous, only a felt presence at his neck. He looks back at the doctor who, after hawking onto the floor, glances at the window to check the light and then pushes his spectacles onto the bridge of his nose. Satisfied that everything is ready for the procedure, he sniffs twice, opens the boy's right eye with the thumb and index finger of his left hand, and presses slightly backwards to prevent the eyeball from moving around. When his assistant hands him what appears to be a teacup, he carefully pours water into the eye socket. Wang's feet bang involuntarily on the earthen floor, but the doctor does not release his grip. Again, and a third time, he flushes the fatty substances from the eye socket, leans in close to check that the last of the viscous material has been washed away, and then stands tall with a satisfied snort.

'Do you need to do anything else?' Third Aunt asks hopefully.

The doctor ignores her, beckons to his assistant and takes a golden needle from him. Murmuring a prayer to Guanyin, he leans back towards the boy, whose left eye dilates in fear. The right eye remains as it has been for the last three days—pierced and swollen.

'Now the patient must take care to look to the right if the bridge of his nose is not to impede the progress of the operation. The head must be held in absolute stillness.'

The doctor clamps his knees over the child's and examines the tip of the needle.

'I shall be swift. Once all extraneous matter has been removed, true healing can begin. When the needle has done its work, I shall take a piece of bamboo one *fen* wide and tie it so that it has the strength of a spring. I shall clip one end to the upper lid before threading the eyelid closed. The patient must then rest.'

Wang's mother nods rapidly, hoping that the doctor will just get on with the operation.

'It is particularly important during this time that he does not eat fish, fried noodle, chicken, goose, donkey, horse, pork, dog, onions or garlic. He should eat congee, so as to avoid the use of teeth in chewing, and extreme care should be taken when evacuating the bowels. Do you understand?'

Wang's mother nods again.

'I tell you now,' the doctor continues, 'in case of distraction later. It is my experience that disturbed times sometimes follow operations like these.'

The boy thrashes around in the chair. He moans in terror and begins to drool.

'Ah Qing!' the doctor barks.

The assistant steps forward and thrusts a piece of wood between the patient's teeth. Wang bites hard onto it and the soft moan of fear is thrust down into his throat.

'Now, maybe, we can begin,' the doctor says.

He lifts the needle to the light and then pushes it slowly through the lens. Observing where extraneous matter—small shards of bamboo and particles of dust—have entered the silver sea, he attempts to puncture the prolapsed iris. He withdraws the needle and probes again.

Dislodging the wood from his mouth, Wang screams. He screams for his father, the only protector he knows against such pain. Then, forcing his head out of his mother's trembling hands, he screams again, begging for help, demanding release. As the doctor struggles to hold him in his place and his mother and aunt try to pinion his arms, he calls again for his father and, to everyone's surprise, his father runs into the dingy room. As he does so, the gold chain of his watch flies out of his top pocket, and the expensive timepiece catches Ah Qing squarely on the side of his head.

'My son, my son,' he cries. 'What are they doing to you?'

He grabs the doctor, who has ripped the boy's already mutilated eyeball in his panic, and tosses him into the display cabinet that Third Aunt has spent so long admiring, sending spectacles (made in Shanghai), opium (grown in Imperial India), and rhinoceros horn (smuggled from God knows where) across the filthy floor of this den of superstition, this torture chamber into which his son has been dragged.

'They told me that he'd got a bloody arrow in his eye. An arrow!' he shouts. 'And then I find this dumb egg having another go.'

His wife and sister move as far back in the room as they can, while the boy throws himself into his father's arms, something he cannot remember ever having done before.

'What have they done to you?' his father repeats, as he begins to sob, something he cannot remember ever having done before either. 'We must get you to the hospital.'

Wiping the blood from his son's eye with the sleeve of his suit, he hauls him onto his back. He runs to the door, then stops, steps back into the room and faces the doctor.

'*Niaoren*,' he says, 'you have blinded my son.'

The rickshaw rushes and bumps its way through the streets of western Shanghai, carrying the boy and his parents to St Luke's Hospital on North Szechuan Road. Third Aunt has been left to find another rickshaw and is soon forgotten. Wang Weijun closes his eyes, the one that works and the one that feels like a shredded pork bun, and leans against his father, who stiffens. The time for open demonstrations of feeling being past, he pulls away so that his son is forced to turn and rest his head against his mother's soft breast. The pain—the sharp, fierce pain that the native doctor inflicted—has now subsided, but the horror is still there. He slumps against her and recalls the moment, three days earlier, when, taking advantage of his father's absence on a business trip, he talked her into letting him go out to play with Zhou Lianke.

* * *

'What shall we play?' Zhou asked as they climbed the wall that separated Wang's two-storey, stone-arched house from the yard where the poorer children played.

'William Tell,' Wang replied.

'Weilian who?' Zhou asked. 'Sounds like a white devil.'

'That's because he was a white devil. He was a hero who shot an apple off his son's head and then drove out the Japanese.'

He tried to remember the rest of the story his uncle had told him, but the details were hazy. His uncle had never stuck simply to the plot. He had jumped from Yuan Dynasty Switzerland to Qing Dynasty China, from Habsburg oppression to British imperialism. He had harangued his nephew about the horrors of unequal treaties and foreign control. He had spoken of dignity and honour and national self-determination. But Wang was eight—he just wanted to hear about the arrow and the apple.

'Nah, let's play Zhuge Liang instead,' said Zhou. Being a whole six months older than his friend, he was used to getting his own way.

Wang opened negotiations. 'You can be Zhuge Liang as long as we play William Tell first.'

Zhou hesitated.

'You can make the arrows too,' Wang added.

'Then I agree,' Zhou said and immediately started hacking at a piece of bamboo. When he had a piece the right length, he tied the two ends together with a cord from round his waist. 'Come on, hold this,' he demanded. 'If it whips me in the face I'll be blinded for life.'

While Wang did as he was told, Zhou pushed with all the strength that a boy of eight years and six months possesses and bent the bamboo into something resembling the shape of a bow.

'Now for some arrows,' he said, brandishing the weapon above his head.

With the knife Zhou had stolen from his parents' kitchen, they whittled ends sharp enough to pierce every apple in Shanghai. Zhou was so impressed by his handiwork that he strode about the yard, stabbing at birds, crickets, and imaginary enemies.

'Die, die, die,' he yelled. 'I am Weilian Tell, bow-master, rebel-flayer, apple-piercer. And this is my son, a fool who has let himself be captured by the Japanese vermin. I will put this arrow through the apple on his head and so free all China from the imperialist running dogs.'

'Shall we practise first?' Wang asked.

'I am Weilian. I never miss.'

You are Zhou Lianke. You never hit, Wang thought, remembering their many unsuccessful attempts to reduce Shanghai's sparrow population. 'Just a short practice,' he suggested.

'I'm not wasting arrows,' Zhou said proudly. 'Like Hou Yi, I only need one shot.'

For the first time that afternoon, Wang felt scared.

'I have to go back now,' he said.

Zhou fitted an arrow to the string of the bow. 'Pick up an apple,' he said.

'My mother will be expecting me.'

Zhou ignored him. 'Pick up an apple and stick it on your head. Weilian's son wasn't afraid to have his father shoot arrows at him. I will tell your father that you are a coward, and no one will ever speak to you again.'

'He won't believe you.'

'Of course he'll believe me. He thinks you're as weak as a woman.'

Wang knew that Zhou was right. His father did not approve of him. He wanted a son who was stronger, cleverer, more open to the West. Wang put his arrows down, bowed his head, and walked towards the yard wall. When he got there he stopped, turned to face his friend, and tried to shut his mother's voice out of his head—the voice that told him to be careful, the voice that told him she was always there if he needed her. Zhou prepared himself to shoot.

The silence of the afternoon gathered as Zhou lifted the makeshift bamboo arrow to his bow. Holding his left elbow taut, he stared at Wang, peering, rather short-sightedly Wang thought, along the line of the arrow towards the apple balanced precariously on his friend's head. It was Zhou's stillness that unnerved him—that and the slipshod weapon. He watched his friend stare impassively at him, saw the sheer strength of those eight-and-a-half-year-old arms, closed his eyes, and prayed to any god that would listen.

Then he felt the apple begin to move and, resisting the temptation to steady it with his hand, opened his eyes and tilted his head. But too far. The apple started to slip. He jerked his head upwards as Zhou's fingers relaxed and the arrow flew. A shape flew towards him, blurred and uncertain, and then the terror of anticipation was driven out by pain and horror. Weilian Tell missed the apple. The arrow's sharp, bright tip pierced his eyeball.

The rickshaw passes along Chapoo Road. The driver is having to fight the crowd now, heaving his passengers through a sea that stubbornly refuses to be parted. Wang Weijun lifts his head and looks out of the window. Shanghai has been shattered. It fades in and out of focus. Shadows swirl and flicker. The dark rises. He shuts his right eye and tries again. The city coalesces. Now he can see that they are on Bubbling Well Road. The Cricket Club pavilion and the Country Club drift past, bold buildings from a world that has floated across the oceans to this bustling port and dumped itself on the seafront.

'It's just like Harold Godwin,' his father says, interrupting his thoughts. He looks incredulous.

Wang leans back. He does not know who Harold Godwin is. The name seems odd, foreign, threatening. Maybe he is one of the missionaries or western bankers his father spends time with. Closing his eyes, while his father chides his wife yet again for letting the boy out of the house, he burrows into himself, though he knows already that he has nothing that will dispel his agony. Or his loss. There is no longer any pain to speak of, only a tremendous ache and an irremediable confusion of vision, the sharpness of the neon lights refracting into shapes so jagged, so linear, that he senses they will never bend again. It feels as though he is falling off the edge of a world he never had time to examine. The sense of something gone forever—this is what hurts.

When they arrive at St Luke's Hospital, his father has an argument with the rickshaw man, as though a rickshaw fare could ever matter again. Wang is embarrassed; his mother is resigned. Eventually his father flings a few coins at the man's feet. He picks them up and shouts a terrible insult after them.

Refusing to look back, his father places his hand on his son's shoulder and steers him through the crowd of sniffing beggars and helpless amputees that are milling around the front doors. Wang holds back, horrified by the disfigured old men who peer at him and terrified by the prospect of the operation that he knows is still to come. His mother takes his hand, while his father berates one of the women at the reception desk, then waves them on. They follow him up a back staircase to a consultation room where a Chinese doctor is besieged by a mob of patients, most of whom are speaking Shanghaihua. The doctor is answering, stubbornly, in English.

'I am Wang Zhebu,' his father announces as he pushes his way to the front of the mob. 'I know Dr Peters. We have dined together at the International Institute.'

The doctor, who is sitting with his legs splayed and his waistcoat unbuttoned, looks at him warily.

'My son needs treatment. Some damn *jianghu* has been poking around in his eye.'

He pulls the boy forward and thrusts him in front of the doctor.

'Dr Peters is extremely busy.'

'And my son is extremely injured.'

'Maybe there are others who could examine the difficulty?'

'I don't need him examined. I need him operated on.'

Wang begins to whimper. His father clumps him round the back of the head and the doctor races to different corners of the room before slowly, incompletely, reassembling himself.

'I will see what I can do,' he promises.

An hour later, Wang is lying on a bed, its sheets white, its pillows luxurious. Dr Peters is looming over him with a powerful lens attached to his forehead. He is an impassive man who seems to blink only when his implausibly long hair tumbles into his line of sight. Though he doesn't blink much, he does frown a lot, and he is frowning now as he sighs and straightens up. Wang's father plays with his collar. His mother and third aunt, who has just arrived, stand in the corner and listen. Someone whistles Beethoven in another room.

'I do wish they wouldn't do this,' the doctor says. 'It makes our job so much more difficult.'

'What can you do?' Wang's father asks.

'Oh, there are a few procedures,' the doctor replies, 'though I doubt we'll save the eye. It's probably too far gone.'

Third Aunt begins to cry. Dr Peters looks irritated.

'If you'd come to us straightaway . . .' he says.

Wang's mother starts to sob as well. The boy is bewildered. He is not used to unseemly displays of emotion.

The doctor sidles up to the boy's father. 'Do try to control the women,' he says. 'It makes our lives easier.'

It is another five hours before an operating theatre becomes free, and they are all tired. Even Dr Peters has difficulty suppressing a yawn. He doesn't enjoy these operations. On arriving in China he specialised in eye surgery mainly because the results were so spectacular. He could carry out comparatively simple operations and have his Chinese clients fall over themselves with amazement. But operations like this, days after the event, when others have already stuck their oar in—they are no fun. He looks at Wang's father and curses the day he made his acquaintance at the institute.

Wang's father keeps his head down. Now that he realises just how little his influence buys, he is deeply troubled.

'You'll do your best, won't you?' he asks, suddenly unsure whether he has done the right thing in bringing his only son here.

'Of course we will,' the doctor snaps. 'Now, if you don't mind just waiting here, we'll get the show underway.' He opens the operating theatre door and, as Wang's father seems about to follow him in, shuts it firmly behind him.

Wang is already asleep on the couch, chloroform and atropine for dilation of the pupil having been applied a few minutes earlier. Dr Peters washes his hands, takes an ophthalmoscope from the trolley and examines the patient. The eye is a mess. It looks like a spotted dick, but a spotted dick that is dotted with shards of bamboo rather than raisins.

Clamping a spring speculum onto the boy's head, Dr Peters waits until a nurse has prised the eyelids apart. Then he examines the mutilated eyeball and, holding his forceps like his mother used to hold her pair of tweezers, tries to remove pieces of bamboo from deep within the damaged organ. He probes and pokes, but when it becomes clear that he is merely forcing the fragments deeper into the anterior chamber he stops, wipes his brow, and hands the forceps back to the nurse. He tries again, this time with a bistoury, and again he fails. Muttering to himself, he throws the bistoury back into the tray, knowing that he is going to have to do what he feared would end up happening anyway. He removes his jacket and leaves the operating theatre.

The nurse cannot hear the conversation that is being held just outside the door, but he scrubs the forceps and washes the scissors just in case. As the wailing starts, he checks the spring speculum. When Dr Peters comes back in, haggard and visibly annoyed, the theatre is ready for him. He turns back to the patient and does what he has to do.

The eyeball is so enlarged with all the trauma it has suffered that he is forced to cut along the line where the eyelids meet. He snips at the skin, carefully lifts the conjunctival fold, and starts cutting into the membrane as though it were a piece of expensive cloth. As the women's ululations grow in intensity, he eases the forceps through the gap he has created, pulls the eyeball forward, rolls it inwards, and reveals the fibrous tissues that bind it to the optic nerves. Then, as the nurse hovers at his elbow waiting for instructions, he cuts through bands of areolar tissue and watches as the wound fills with the darkness of blood. There is nothing now to be done but to finish the job Zhou Lianke began. He pulls the severed eyeball from its socket, drops it into a bowl on the trolley, and places his finger on the wound until the haemorrhaging stops.

Wang Zhebu cannot see the blood-darkened socket where his son's eye used to be; in fact, he can see very little as he strains to make out what is happening inside the operating theatre, but he sees enough to make him pound on the door in distress. The doctor turns away in embarrassment, snaps his fingers at the nurse, takes the lint-covered pad of cloth he is belatedly offered and packs it into the cavity. When he leaves the room, he finds Wang Zhebu sitting with his head in his hands, his wife pacing nervously, and Third Aunt whimpering in a corner. He tries to put on an affable smile.

'The operation was a success,' he says.

Third Aunt wipes her eyes with her sleeve. Wang Zhebu looks away. His wife seems confused.

'I have removed the damaged organ and have applied a compress. When the bleeding stops I will stitch the wound shut but, even so, the bandage will require changing every day.' He looks hard at them all. 'It is vital that this be done in as sanitary a fashion as possible so that infection does not set in. I trust that you will take all necessary precautions.'

Wang's mother nods hesitantly. She has not followed all the doctor has said in his strange, foreign tongue.

'When the boy feels ready,' the doctor continues, 'and if you should consider it helpful, we can fit an artificial eye.'

As Third Aunt reshapes the words for her, Wang's mother rolls her eyes upwards and collapses, hitting her head hard on the floor as she falls. Dr Peters jumps to her aid while Third Aunt gives way to grief and Wang Zhebu lifts his head from his hands. As the doctor tries to haul her up into a sitting position, he shouts for the nurse to bring a cloth, then wipes the blood from her face and drags her out of the corridor. Third Aunt stops in front of Wang Zhebu for a moment and, when he continues to ignore her, follows them out.

When they have gone, Wang Zhebu pulls himself to his feet, bangs his hand against the wall in frustration, walks to the door of the operating theatre, pushes it open, and slowly approaches his sleeping son. As the lingering tang of formaldehyde assails him, he reaches out to stroke his son's hair, then picks up a cloth and gently wipes his face. He feels nothing, but knows that as soon as he starts thinking he will feel too much.

With a sudden burst of anger, he knocks the metal tray containing his son's shattered eyeball onto the floor. The metal rings dreadfully across the empty theatre; the eye squelches where it falls. Scarcely believing that the world can be so harsh and that doctors can be so useless, Wang Zhebu stares at what he has done, before turning and walking slowly back to the theatre door. It is only as he pushes it open that he notices the blood on his hands.

Chapter 2

'It's expensive to keep a lot in stock,' the oculist says ruefully.

Wang Weijun looks at the enamel balls, two rows of them, beautifully arranged in gradations of colour.

'It's mostly Europeans we treat here,' the oculist adds with a touch of embarrassment, 'but I suppose we should keep a few more brown ones, just in case.'

Running his finger along the line, Wang considers each of the eyes in turn, until he alights on an incongruous red sphere.

'Er, yes. That's someone's idea of a joke,' the oculist says. 'I'm sorry.'

Wang looks up to see his father's lips pursed in annoyance. Turning back to the eyeballs, which are nestling in wooden trays, he is reminded suddenly of childhood trips to the confectioners with his second aunt, of stuffing so many sweets into his mouth that he always felt sick. Now that he is faced with so many balls staring up at him, silently begging to be chosen, now that he is expected to pop one into his empty socket, he feels no better. It has been two months since his accident, and he has not yet come close to accepting the dull blank where his eye had always been. His mother has removed all mirrors from the house, but he has secreted one away and, when he is alone, he stares at the hole, at the hideous beast he has become. Simultaneously fascinated and appalled by the gap that appears when his stitches are removed, he tries to make sense of his loss.

Picking up one of the enamel balls, he rolls it across the table. It is not quite the right shade of brown, but he accepts this as part of his punishment for having failed to face the arrow without fear. He glances at the oculist.

'Do you want a hand?' the man says.

Wang nods gratefully but shudders as the oculist, who smells improbably of peppermint, pulls out a cushion and beckons him over to the table.

'Better stick your head down here,' he says, 'just in case we drop it. They're terribly expensive, you know.'

Wang nods again and does as he is told.

'Now then,' the oculist continues, 'you need to continue looking downwards whatever I'm doing. But don't worry because all I'll be doing is lifting up your lid so that I can pop this little beauty in for you. Nothing to worry about, eh?'

Wang is about to nod again when the man sticks the ball in his mouth and smears it with saliva. Spitting it back out into his palm, he lays a hand on Wang's shoulder, pushes him down onto the cushion, folds back his eyelid and slips the eyeball into place.

'Perhaps not quite the right shade,' the oculist says, 'but you'll never get the perfect match.'

He looks a touch embarrassed, but Wang doesn't mind—he quite likes the eyeball he has chosen. Staring into the mirror that the man holds up, he watches his good eye moving naturally from side to side while the new one stares squarely back at him.

'It'll take a little practice before you can manoeuvre it around, but it'll come,' the oculist says, walking over to the sink and giving his hands a good scrub. 'Just a few things to remember. If you need to give your eye a wipe, do it towards the nose or you'll end up twisting the whole thing round. I know we all want eyes in the back of our head but … well, you know what I'm driving at. Another thing is, be careful not to rub your lower lid. It's the surest way of popping the bally thing out. Come to think of it, we always advise having a spare eyeball just in case. If you crack one you can always slip another in before too many people notice. And it's really important that you keep your new eye clean, so take it out every night and give it a good wipe. Every now and again dip it in whisky or cologne to wash off any extraneous animal substances. That way it'll last you a year at least.'

Wang's father, who still doesn't want to acknowledge what has happened to his only son, drags himself away from the window. 'Haven't you got anything better?' he asks.

'I can have a look out the back,' the oculist replies, 'but I'm pretty certain this is about it.'

As he disappears and Wang Zhebu goes back to looking distractedly out of the window, Wang continues to finger the balls. He thinks about what the westerner said about having a spare ball and begins to consider other colours. Picking up a globe, its lens as blue as the oculist's, he holds it up to his socket.

'I'll try this one as well,' he says when the man returns. 'You know, as a spare.'

'Well, you could do, I suppose,' the oculist says, glancing at the boy's father, 'but I'm not quite sure—'

'This is the one I'd like,' Wang says decisively, laying his head on the cushion.

His father seems distracted so, in the absence of any contradiction, the oculist sighs, flicks back the eyelid, pulls the first eyeball out, gives the blue one a quick suck and puts it in.

'Young boys and their jokes,' he says, half to himself and half to Wang's father, who cannot bear to look.

'I can't see,' Wang says.

'What?'

'I need to look in the mirror.'

The oculist lifts up the mirror so that Wang can peer at his reflection. Seeing a brown eye and a blue one look back at him, Wang takes a moment to consider his newly exotic look.

'I'll take it,' he says decisively.

'Well, it's up to you, of course, but I'd have to advise against it.' He turns to Wang's father in silent appeal. 'I'm not sure what your father will make of it.'

Finally, Wang Zhebu joins the conversation. 'What's it cost?' he asks.

'I really wouldn't advise—'

'I want the blue one as well,' Wang interrupts.

'I hardly think—'

'I want the blue one,' he repeats louder.

The oculist turns to Wang Zhebu.

'Give the boy what he wants,' his father says.

'But—'

Wang Zhebu pulls out his wallet and the argument ends.

When Wang's mother finds out, she is furious. She sobs and wails and beats her husband helplessly with her fists.

'It's not enough that he's blind? And now you want him humiliated as well?'

She throws herself at him until he throws her to the floor and shouts at her to pull herself together. But she doesn't pull herself together. She slumps in a corner and refuses to work.

No meal is prepared that evening and Wang hears the argument continue in his parents' room late into the night. He looks at his blue eyeball, strangely distorted and magnified in its glass of water, and knows that he doesn't want to let it go. It reminds him of the doctor who shook his hand when he left the hospital, of the foreign glamour he has seen on posters all over Shanghai. It seems to offer a glimpse into a world he has never been part of before.

Even so, it takes him some time to get over his squeamishness. As simple a task as pulling back his lid so that he can insert the ball in its proper resting place is too much for him at first. He tries asking his mother but, while he refuses to hand over the blue eyeball, she refuses to help him, so as the weeks pass he gets slowly used to manipulating the eyeballs himself, cleaning them thoroughly, wiping the socket, everting the eyelid and then slipping one or other into place. He cares enough for family peace to choose the brown one most of the time, but he keeps the blue one for special occasions.

Neither Wang nor his parents have ever thought about vision before. Sight always came like breath and was no more to be valued than the groceries that were delivered to the back door every other day. The sensational, the spectacular, was what nature was expected to give as of right. But now that its supplies have been disrupted—now that the very notion of clarity has become blurred and uncertain—they are forced to consider the visual world afresh.

Wang finds himself and his sight a topic of conversation. Aunts and uncles talk about compensation, which his father takes in a monetary sense and his mother understands to refer to her son's other senses. Relatives who have never previously shown any concern for his needs insist that furniture be moved to allow him to track his way through the house now that his peripheral vision is gone. All perspective is lost. As advice and arguments swirl over his head, Wang himself sits silently and nods whenever a question is thrown in his direction. He itches to be let outside again and longs for the freedom that he seems to have lost through sheer carelessness. As a distraction, and partly because he knows it annoys his elderly relatives, he fingers his enamel eyeball whenever they look at him.

Back in his room, his only true place of refuge, he digs the ball out of its socket and, tipping it reverently onto his bed, rolls it up and down to convince himself that it is still in his power to fix the shifting contours of the world. Encouraged by the sense of calm that this ritual spilling seems to bring, he shuns the light and sticks close to what he knows—his games and his books.

When Third Aunt drags him to the market, he is repelled by the sheer profusion of uselessness the traders thrust in their faces—shimmering reproductions of famous paintings, brightly glazed vases, jade bracelets, lucky charms, ivory earrings, clocks and barometers. None of these luxuries has the power to lift him out of the uncertainty that losing an eye has brought, so he clings instead to the mundane, hoarding objects he already has in abundance—marbles, cigarette cards, even small pieces of food smuggled from the dinner table. With half the world in darkness, he searches for glamour in the objects around him.

Collecting the ordinary becomes something of an obsession, as if laying out his life in a box could restore the simplicity and wonder of the world. As he crams the city's transitory detritus into a cupboard that is forbidden territory to his parents, he exercises his new eye, rolling it from left to right until he almost believes that it is no different from the other, the one that works, that makes sense of light and shade, that sees what other people see.

Alone in his room at night, he fingers his hoarded goods until their shape and texture become as familiar to him as their look. By day he is less mournful and more tenacious. He becomes proud of his artificial eye, especially when he realises that he can turn disfigurement to his advantage. If he cannot have his vision whole and unimpaired, then he can at least stand out in a crowd. No longer burdened by an eyepatch or humiliated by an empty socket, he discovers, when back at school with his two-eyed friends, that he can bring his class to a standstill by everting his lower eyelid and flicking his enamel eye onto his desk. When his artificial eye becomes a prop in an ongoing piece of popular theatre, with Wang as impresario, producer and star, he begins to live a new kind of life.

'It's literature next,' his classmate Li Ma tells him. 'Do your eyeball trick.'

The rest of the class laughs, knowing that Teacher Su is particularly easy to distract. Wang waits until the teacher is explaining the difference between *wuyan lüshi* and *qiyan lüshi* before he lets the enamel grenade drop.

'*Laoshi*, Wang Weijun's eye's fallen out again.'

'Shall I help him stick it back in again, *laoshi*?'

'Shall I take him to the washstand, *laoshi*? He can only find his way halfway there with one eye.'

Teacher Su becomes flustered. He is used to ill-mannered boys but struggles to maintain composure when eyeballs roll across his classroom floor.

Other teachers are less sympathetic and less easily upset, as Wang discovers when he makes the mistake of popping his eye out while Teacher Yan is giving an arithmetic lesson. The whole class watches as, at a pre-arranged signal, it drops softly onto the *Jiuzhang Suanshu*, gathers pace on the inclined cover, tips over the desk's precipice and rolls down the aisle to where their teacher is standing, his hands behind his back, his feet planted firmly in front of the blackboard. Without missing a beat he leans down, picks up the eye and slips it into his waistcoat pocket. It is only at the very end of the lesson, almost as an afterthought, that he addresses Wang from the doorway.

'If you require your belongings, Wang, come and collect them from my office at the end of the day.'

Wang learns to choose his victims more carefully after that misjudgement. Away from school, he turns his attention to his parents' friends. Removing his eyeball, popping it in his mouth to cover it with saliva, and then sticking it back into the empty socket always causes a most agreeable stir. The more saliva he applies, the more easily the eyeball returns to its place and the greater the adult reaction. When he visits his many cousins and their friends, it is easier still to make an impression. One minute he has two brown eyes, the next he has mysteriously acquired a blue one. With small children—and there are many small children in his family—he can keep the entertainment going for hours. In fact, he practises for so long that eventually he develops a patter.

'Now then, girls and boys, draw closer and see sights that have never been seen before. Stay still. Watch closely. Observe ... Whoops, sorry, I'll just pop him back in. He does like to have a quick look around before we start. Just to check who's here, you know.'

The young cousins draw back, appalled that an organ so fixed and permanent should leave its appointed place.

'Wah, here he comes again. What's the problem now?'

He holds the tiny enamel ball to his ear. 'I can't hear you.' He tries again. 'You'll have to speak up. What? I know you're an eye. I can see that.'

The audience comes closer. One of them, a shaven-headed

boy who looks like he might be trouble, has edged closer than the others.

'Watch what you're doing,' Wang shouts suddenly. 'I've got my eye on you.' He waves the eyeball over the impudent boy's head, watches him scurry back to his place, and then continues with the show.

'Now, let's try again. What was it you were saying? You're an eye? Yes, I know you're an eye. You haven't got a voice box? Well, I suppose not. So I'm going to have to do all the talking? Yes, if I must.'

He shrugs, gives the eyeball a quick lick and sticks it back in. His young audience squeals. Some of the girls snuggle up to the shaven-headed boy, whose reputation has risen immeasurably since the eyeball was waved over his head. A few of the other boys—jealous, emboldened—edge forward to where Wang is preparing his next trick. He has been expecting them.

'Too close, too close!'

He turns sharply, drops the black, silk handkerchief he is holding, and allows a dozen cheap glass eyeballs, which he bought at the market especially for occasions like this, to roll across the floor like marbles. The room is filled with screams, the boys scuttle back, and Wang smiles broadly. He has found his vocation.

His parents are simultaneously dismayed and proud of the turn their son has taken.

'But he's so amusing,' their friends say. 'So jolly. You'd never know he's suffered so much.'

His parents smile and half believe what is said, but then, when the friends leave, disappointment and anger set in. They draw no consolation from their son's growing confidence, from the development of his performance to include card tricks and simple illusions. They want an undamaged son, a boy who has not been denied a future.

In order to protect him from further injury and the dangers of the outside world, his mother decides that she must draw him back into a Chinese world, into a secure past in which children

30

are protected from stray arrows and threats from across the seas. Appalled that he should still be able to shed tears from his dead eye, she tells him stories from the classics—*The Water Margin*, *The Dream of the Red Chamber*—but turns them into warnings, into morality tales. The outlaws of the marsh rebel against legitimate authority and are crushed; dissolute families fall from grace; the Han Dynasty is rebuilt according to solid Confucian values.

Wang listens, half fascinated and half repelled, knowing that it is a story—albeit a western one—that has grabbed him with its violent hand, dragged him into the dark alleyway of the twentieth century and beaten him about the face. He fights against his mother's desperate backward glance and reads western books surreptitiously, holding stories closer to his face than most boys of his age.

His father tries to distract him with tales of his own, stories drawn from the great word hoard of the West. Collaring him during twilight hours, he forces tales of heroism onto him— Beowulf and Arthur, Alfred and Robin Hood. He rewrites the great western myths, ignoring reversals and defeats, erasing irony wherever he senses it. Don Quixote becomes a second Lancelot, Mandeville outsails Columbus, the Ancient Mariner becomes a reincarnation of Marco Polo. Wang finds himself entranced. Revolving his enamel eyepiece, he lets the strong, foreign stories burrow beneath his imagination's paltry defences.

Not content with the power of stories, his father hires tutors to keep his son busy during the little free time he has. If the boy is to travel through life with only one eye then he should have every other benefit, and chiefly the benefit that European languages bring. None of these tutors inspire devotion, but Wang does not need hero-worship when he has the languages they teach. There is something alluring about syllables that do not rise and fall as they do in his native tongue, something fascinating about languages which do not rely upon corrupted pictograms, something mysteriously tempting about grammar that is based upon the strange notion of tense. As he learns English, and slowly gets to grips with French, he discovers that there are other ways of making sense of the world.

To Wang Zhebu's great surprise, the extra lessons slowly come between him and his son. He tries to keep pace with the boy but soon gives up the unequal struggle. His mother doesn't even try—seeing anything that comes from Europe as a threat to the family's stability, she has no interest in learning foreign words. Rarely letting him out of her sight and refusing him permission to play outside unless under strict adult supervision, she keeps him from other children. But, to his own surprise, Wang rarely feels resentful. The external world of activity and children's games seems distant, designed for others, trivial. Language matters more to him now. It is a form of reassurance, a solid, almost tangible thing. Now that he has words, now that he can stretch across the oceans on a bridge of books, he tries to convince himself that he has no need of the eye that Zhou Lianke snatched from him.

The only time the family comes together with a single purpose is on Wang's birthday. Without ever consciously choosing to do so, they develop a ritual, a compensatory journey of return that is part expiation and part pilgrimage, rising early, eating a celebratory breakfast, and then taking a rickshaw to the oculist's.

The city is a machine in perpetual motion. Pedestrians, rickshaws, carts, and the occasional car surge like an electrical current through its streets. Clutching the grey, drawstring bag in which he keeps his spare eyeballs, Wang sits with his mother on his left and his father on his right, feeling an outsider in this place where he has always lived. Each year he insists on entering the oculist's showroom alone. Each year he is overruled. They enter as a family and quickly argue as a family. But, however intense the argument, however great the loss of face, Wang always comes away with one brown eyeball and one blue.

Chapter 3

Wang Zhebu's study is dark and intimidating. Oak-panelled, desk-dominated and weighed down by shelf-loads of books—everything from legal journals to the writings of Liang Qichao—it has a solid presence not dissimilar to that possessed by Wang Zhebu himself. When Wang receives a summons on his thirteenth birthday, it is the study as much as the inevitable and inevitably interminable interview that he dreads. As he stands and waits with his head bowed and his arms by his side, he realises that he has never seen his father take any of the books from the shelves to read; perhaps that is not their purpose.

'We are ruled by an effete and self-serving elite that no longer obeys the dictates of Heaven or cares for the needs of men,' his father says, without any preamble. 'The Dowager Empress has brought disaster upon our country. If she had built a modern army instead of giving herself over to the pursuit of pleasure and the rebuilding of the Summer Palace, then we would now be able to lift our heads high in the community of nations.'

'Yes, father,' Wang replies listlessly.

'Look at the chaos that terrible woman has created! We have been mired in the past while the Japanese have been garnering the best of western learning. We who have given printing, gunpowder, paper and the compass to the world, have fallen into a technological torpor and been swept away by the winds of modernity.'

'The winds of modernity, father?'

'The winds that blow across the East China Sea—the divine winds, the forces of change.'

'Yes, father.'

'Do you know what I resolved when the Treaty of Shimonoseki was signed?'

'No, father.'

'I resolved that I would do all that was in my power to ensure such a disaster should never again be visited upon our nation.'

'Yes, father. I mean, no, father.'

Wang Zhebu stares at his son.

'But change is now coming,' he continues quietly. 'At last the reforms we have longed for are on their way.'

'Which reforms, father?' Wang asks anxiously. He is no longer so keen on change.

'The examination system is being swept away. There will be no more eight-legged essays to torment China's young men. The Japanese are printing new textbooks, with pictures as well as text. And there is more to come. Maybe one day we will simplify or scrap these absurd characters. Maybe we will write from left to right like the most advanced nations. Maybe. But first we have to overcome the obscurantist, obstructionist elements at court. And that may take some time.'

He falls back in his chair with a sigh.

'Which is why I am enrolling you in the School of Foreign Languages. I am sending you to school to perfect your French and your English. Without them you will be nothing. With them, perhaps, you might help make something of our great country.'

Wang's ears feel as though they have been thrust underneath a running tap. In his excitement he cannot fully make out the rest of his father's words.

'You will be following in the illustrious footsteps of Rong Hong, the first of our citizens to graduate from an American university; Dr Zhan Tianyou, the designer and engineer of the Beijing-Zhangjiakou Railway; and the diplomatists Wang Fengxiang and Lu Zhengxiang. You will not let me or our country down.'

Wang bows and thanks his father. He realises that, by being sent across Shanghai to a western school, he is being removed from his mother's sphere of influence, and he is delighted. The prospect of a new start, a fresh set of teachers to torment with his eyeball and, above all, the chance to make English truly his own, is tremendously exciting.

'And one last thing,' his father says as Wang reaches the door. 'We'll have no more of these tricks with cards and spare eyeballs. You are a man now. Wang Weijun, my son, we are putting these childish things away.'

As Wang prepares for school, he imagines himself into the streets of Shanghai, mapping in his mind the new territory he is going to inhabit. Drawing out his box of hoarded objects, he sets aside his earliest compulsions—broken toys, playing cards, magazine articles. Now that he is on the threshold of a fully-fledged education, he prefers the liminal: books that are suitable for neither children nor adults, half-smoked cigars, French magazines—grimy reminders of the world into which he is due to emerge.

Maps are a particular obsession. When he is not reading foreign novels in translation, he is poring over any atlas he can lay his hands on. Maps of Europe are what he prefers but, if he has no other option, he makes do with reproductions of ancient maps of China drawn by meticulous Jesuits, or even the shoddy, garish maps they sell in back street bookstores. Fascinated by their equivalence to, and distance from, a reality he cannot reach, he walks across them with his fingers, as if determined to discover the one path that the arrow in his eye has denied him.

He knows that travelling across Shanghai to school will take him into new territory, a fact that simultaneously excites and appals him because, even though he craves a guide, he knows that he needs to be alone when he plunges into the broad chaos of the city's streets. He is acutely aware that his wound has made him an outsider, that being kept from the life and bustle of the city since the day of his disaster has made him a foreigner. He knows this, resents it, and is determined to undo the damage that has been done as quickly as he can.

When he learns that his father is going away on business the day before the new school year begins, he tells his mother that she is not to accompany him. Realising that her battle is lost, she reluctantly agrees.

As soon as he is out of the house, he knows that he was right to insist, though such knowledge does not protect him from a deeper anxiety that comes from not having ventured out alone for almost five years. He wants to be the man his father has demanded he become, but he cannot escape the reality of confinement that has been forced upon him. His life has been curtailed.

Confronted by a river of people, he throws himself into the turbulence and shudders at the shock to his system. He has never been caught up in such movement before, never been part of so much commotion. Without the consoling presence of his parents, he feels fragile and insignificant, but he also senses the glamour of possibility. Hawkers spit slogans from roadside stalls, strangely intense traders stand by upturned umbrellas and thrust obscene prints into his hands, hunchbacked women dangle bright yellow ribbons from fishing rods, a dark boy no older than himself sits on a pile of redwood coffins while picking his teeth. Every sight, sound, smell and sensation takes physical form before him—the roofs of the houses buck and dip like wild horses, strange plumes of incense fume before his face, the hawkers' cries dance alongside the red lanterns in unbridled celebration.

Consciously slowing himself down so that he can assimilate the strange sounds that assail him—dialects from every part of China, rhythmic chants he doesn't understand, the song of an eerie wind instrument snatched from the breeze that eddies across the crowd's faces—he tries to feel himself into his native city. But, however hard he tries, he knows that he is still out of place, that his wound and all his parents have kept from him since the day of his disaster have made him a foreigner in his own land.

Sensing straightaway that he is a fruit ripe for plucking, beggars no older than he rush forwards with their hands outstretched and lash him with their demands. He fights back with puny fists but, like pigeons, they flutter back into their roadside roosts only to emerge once more with their fingers grasping and their eyes staring. When a passing stranger rescues him, he turns and runs until he is surging downhill with the sweet taste of freedom in his mouth.

As he pulls up a long, steep hill on the edge of the French quarter, he notices the river bellying its way through the city deep in the distance. Broad bridges straddle its path while small black dots fleck their way up and down its course. He tries to make out the boats' contents but can no more distinguish goods from people than he can tell the difference between the fantastical figures of his mother's bedtime stories and the people of Shanghai. All he knows is that the people he is now pushing his way through, and the black dots on the distant boats, are the people from whom he has been kept during the long years of childhood—the people whose destiny he is now determined to yoke to his own.

When he arrives at school and lessons begin, he begins to appreciate just how difficult that yoking might be. His first class, history, lifts him out of the Shanghainese present and dumps him across the ages into sixteenth-century Scotland. His teacher, Mr Davis, who is a tall, stooped mumbler of a man, might as well be from the same era for all the sense Wang can make of him.

'What is history?' he mutters as the boys file in. 'I'll tell you what it is—it is the delights and disasters of the past. And what is a teacher?' he continues once they have taken up position behind their battered wooden desks. 'A teacher is a guide. No more, but certainly no less. You will learn no lessons from me. You will learn to learn for yourselves.'

Mr Davis's lessons are messy affairs. His pupils arrive when they are ready and listen on their own terms. Mr Davis remains unconcerned.

'History teaches us nothing,' he says, 'other than a respect for facts. Find the facts, and the rest will look after itself. The past is dead—there is no learning from it. What Mary, Queen of Scots said to Lord Darnley has no bearing on the Qing Empire.'

'What did Mary, Queen of Scots say to Lord Darnley, sir?' Wang asks. It has not taken him many lessons to establish that Mr Davis is prone to distraction. If he poses the right questions, he ensures that no work is done and so gains his classmates' admiration and respect.

'Not a great deal. They didn't get on terribly well.'

'I don't get on terribly well with Yan, sir, but it doesn't bother either of us.'

'But, Wang, you're not married to Yan.'

'Mary, Queen of Scots was married to Lord Darnley, sir?'

'If you had been paying the slightest bit of attention in this week's lessons, you would have known that, Wang.'

'I'm sorry, sir. So did she divorce him?'

With Henry VIII's matrimonial affairs the ostensible topic of study, Wang hopes that he is on safe ground. Divorce seems so impossibly daring and *modeng* that he returns to the topic whenever he can.

'Oh no, she went one step further,' Mr Davis replies. 'She had him murdered.'

'Can you act it out, sir?' Cai Yuanping interrupts. Wang scowls at him. He has introduced the idea too soon—there is always the chance that Mr Davis will cotton onto their ploy. The teacher thinks for a moment.

'I have to tell you about Rizzio first.'

Wang sits back in his chair. There will be no more work today because Mr Davis is not merely a mumbler and a teacher— he is also an actor. The past may be dead, but there is no aspect of the past that cannot be resurrected in his one-man show. He drapes his jacket over his head and, adopting an incomprehensible Scottish accent, becomes Queen Mary. Then, hanging the same jacket on his hat stand and slipping one arm through the sleeve, he becomes the amorous Rizzio. Finally, and most dramatically of all, he seizes his board rubber and becomes a blood-crazed Lord Darnley, advancing on the unsuspecting lovers and (chalk dust flying everywhere) plunging his naked weapon into the secretary's defenceless body. Leaping into the role of the secretary once more, he staggers, falls against the desk, pulls himself up and then falls again. Finally, after dragging himself to the door, he collapses in the corridor, where he is spotted by Principal Yang who summons the nearest doctor, discovers his mistake too late, and threatens Mr Davis with dismissal if he ever dares repeat such foolishness in his school again. Wang has never enjoyed a lesson more.

'Tell me about your lessons,' Wang Zhebu demands when he returns from his business trip.

'I am working hard, father,' Wang replies.

'I don't want you working hard. I want you working like a coolie—flat out like all the hounds of empire are at your back.'

'Mr Davis says we shouldn't use words like coolie.'

His father looks at him until Wang drops his eye. He has grown tall, unusually tall, and there are times when his father thinks he takes advantage of his height.

'And why did he say that?' he asks quietly.

'He said it was demeaning. He said that there is a nobility in labour that the thinking classes ignore at their peril.'

'Did he indeed?'

'Yes, and he also said there's a man in Germany who says that property is theft and what he means by that is that—'

'Enough of this nonsense. You learn your books and leave property to those who deserve it. I am not sending you to a prestigious western school to pick up such communitarian nonsense.'

Wang bows and leaves as quickly as he can. He is not surprised to see his father emerging from Principal Yang's office the next day, nor is he surprised to discover that Mr Davis's lessons become noticeably apolitical. Apolitical and rather dull, he thinks. For his part, Wang Zhebu is so shocked to discover that his son and his son's ideas are no longer under his control that he decides to take action.

'It is time that your education began,' he announces.

'But, father, my education has already begun. I'm working hard at school. I will not let you down.'

'I am not talking about school. I am talking about something much more important. I tolerated your mother's nonsense for too long; I'm not going to make the same mistake with school. I want to hear no more about the nobility of labour—we are going to learn about chivalry, about honour, about obedience. We are going to study Shakespeare.'

'Sha Weng?' Wang repeats incredulously.

'Not Sha Weng—Shakespeare. We'll have nothing to do with Lin Shu's ridiculous translation. Every evening—at least, every evening I can spare—you are going to read Shakespeare's English with me.'

Wang bows again.

'And we are starting today with *Richard III*, a noble king who fought the French and overcame great odds. Here.'

He hands his son one of the books from his desk.

'Repeat after me. *Now is the winter of our discontent ...*'

It is during these painful, half-poetic evenings, when meaning appears in the darkness only to scuttle away when challenged, that Wang first learns what it is to be a translator. Sha Weng's translation may be banned from his father's study, but Wang is certain it can be no more ponderous than the words he heaves onto the page. Compelled to look up every word, he steps warily across the play. Cut free from the architectural glories of syntax, the western alphabet becomes dust and rubble in his hands. He tries to haul letters into order, but what he creates is, as often as not, fit only for destruction—a fact his father recognises and goes some way towards effecting with his heavy red pen.

Wang perseveres. He has no choice. He fights the words, refusing to accept intractability, bending and shaping them until they yield. But, as meaning begins to gain a recognisable shape, he discovers that the translator's task has barely begun. With no guide but his own partial success, he finds that there is more to the translator's craft than dragging words from one language to the next. He comes to grasp that it is in the interplay of the two languages—Shakespeare's and his—that meaning is to be found. His father, by contrast, demands obedience to the words on the page and refuses to stop until the two of them have slowly battered Shakespeare into submission.

Lessons continue at school but, to Wang's great surprise, it is the end of the school day that draws him on, not simply because he can linger in the Zhang Gardens on his way home to watch jugglers and illusionists perform, nor because he can spend his hoarded coins on the daring peep shows that have begun to spring up across Shanghai. He looks forward to the end of school because he knows that when he gets home his father will be waiting to read Shakespeare with him.

His mother is baffled—she cannot understand what is wrong with the stories China has produced; she cannot make sense of this obsession with incomprehensible characters speaking a long-dead, foreign language. When Wang tries to explain the nobility of the characters, the complexity of the drama, the excitement the fighting generates—when he attempts to convince her that the mechanics of the plot are matched only by the drama of the language, that the Englishman's words reach beyond themselves to a place where poetry and music combine—she simply talks over him.

Henry V is the first Shakespearean king to inspire him. Reliving the anguish of the plot at Southampton and the rage at Harfleur, Wang pines for the days when men fought on horseback and chants the eve of Agincourt speech as he tumbles into sleep. He cannot imagine a more perfect experience than reading the play, but in early spring his father provides it by buying two tickets for a performance at the Shanghai Municipal Theatre.

On the evening of the show, as Shanghai's stonework glows neon, Wang hopes that the performance will enable him to transgress every boundary that has been laid before him. Feeling himself lifted above his city's towering buildings, towards a place which is more dream than reality and yet more real than the travesty he sees all around him, he enters the theatre, where

41

the world of early twentieth-century Shanghai seems to merge with that of Shakespearean London. The smell of the crowds, the darkness of the theatre, the softness of the seats—these simple, apparently inconsequential, components of the theatrical experience combine to create a sense of possibility that he has never experienced before. Lights are dimmed, heavy curtains are pulled back, and words roll across the auditorium until they are lost in the pulse of the play. Maybe it is more than that; maybe the words are vehicles that take him beyond language to a place where pure emotion resides. The more he hears, the more he loses his ability to explain, and the more he sees, the more the words seem invested with meaning and yet terribly insignificant.

There are two scenes he never forgets. The first comes when Henry is attempting to rally the troops. *Once more unto the breach, dear friends, once more*, he cries. He is looking not at the other actors, Wang realises with a sudden stomach-twisting pang of understanding, but at the audience. Hearing the call, he half rises from his seat. *Or close the wall up with our English dead.* The actors raise their swords above their heads and charge at the amateurishly painted backdrop. Then Henry—King Henry—stops, looks back, and realises that all his hopes have failed, because neither Wang nor anyone else in the auditorium has followed him into battle. Wang sinks back into his seat and resolves to do better next time.

But there is a scene more powerful, an episode that sinks almost as deep as shards of bamboo into his memory. The king crying *God for Harry, England, and St George* fades, as do the tennis balls, the betrayals, and those baffling scenes with the French princess. What Wang remembers through the years is the desolation after the battle, the moment when the French seek permission to bury their dead. *O, give us leave, great king, to view the field in safety, and dispose of their dead bodies*, they say, and Wang says it with them.

That night, with the play over, his life seems to fragment, like slim rays of light refracted through a pierced lens. He sits up in his bed, hugging his knees with one hand and fingering his eye socket with the other, trying to remember what it was like to have peripheral vision, to judge distances, to see without having to think about seeing. He tries not to look at the enamel eyeball that keeps him company in a small glass of water by his bed. He tries not to recall the moment when the apple moved and his head jerked upwards, that moment when the unalterable future altered. Now that the play is over, he tries not to think about the horrors of battle. Instead, he attempts to stave off the sense that he is fraying, the fine silk of his life torn and devalued. But, as tears run down the side of his empty socket, he gives up on the attempt and wallows in sorrow instead.

He longs to read but cannot risk waking his parents by fetching a light, so he drifts in and out of a state that is neither wakefulness nor oblivion, neither sight nor blindness, but something less than either. His thoughts merge into nightmares and back into dreams, taking on the luminosity of the imagination and the unfathomable power of the subconscious mind.

He dreams that he is back in the Shanghai Theatre, but this time he is not watching but performing. He scans the faces in front of him, picking out their eyes and marvelling at their power. He closes his own and concentrates on his opening routine. Pulling handkerchiefs from his pocket, he everts his eyelid and rolls eyeball after eyeball across the stage. When he opens his eyes again the audience is waiting, so he works mechanically through his act and waits for the silence of rejection. He closes his eyes again until he hears the slow thud of applause and then is gratified to see a member of the audience rise to his feet. With a start he realises that it is Zhou Lianke and that he has a bow in his hand. He smiles, roars his approval, and lets the arrow fly.

Chapter 4

Making his way home from school through the Zhang Gardens, Wang looks into the kinetoscopes and crams their improbable and improper visions into his one good eye. A shrivelled old man who has set up his stall at the garden's entrance pulls red beans out of thin air, swallows needles, and breathes fire; musicians saw at strange western instruments until they fill the air with their dark music; an illusionist tumbles across the grass, producing a bowl of unspilt water from out of nowhere when he lands on his feet; a group of puppeteers manipulate a small red boat across an artificial pond.

Wang stops to watch as a horde of unruly wooden children tumble out of the boat onto the shore. Fat ones and thin ones; misshapen men and lank, tall women; puppets with wild, unwieldy hair and long, itchy fingers—the puppeteer leads them one by one across the grass. A tall, thin puppet dressed in a long, black jacket leads the way, wringing his hands as he walks, pausing for breath where the incline grows too steep, darting in front of elegant young women to remove stray pieces of paper from their path. Behind him skips a mischievous wooden boy who runs into the crowds whenever he sees the slightest sign of food. Wang watches him grab a pork bun, which the puppeteer promptly knocks from his grasp, only for him to snatch a half-eaten dumpling from a startled child. Another puppet—a sallow-looking creature with long, knobbly fingers—is distracted by pretty girls in the crowd. Whenever he sees one, he stretches out his neck and swivels his head until his eyes pop out on elongated stalks. Bringing up the rear is a curious old woman with one eye, who limps along in a vain effort to keep up with the others. Among all the other oddballs and misfits—and all of the puppets are oddballs and misfits in one way or another—she alone seems comfortable among the crowds. As she limps back to her puppet boat she turns and looks directly at Wang, who fancies that there is a glimmer of recognition in her eye, even though he knows there is nothing more to it than a round piece of wood painted black and brown.

When he gets back home, Wang begs his mother to tell him about the Shandong magicians and puppeteers of her youth.

'Your father would not approve,' she says.

'Father will never know.'

'Well, if he does, you mustn't tell him that I told you.'

Examining the back of her hands, as though embarrassed to be sharing occult knowledge, his mother tells him about itinerant showmen who sloped into the village on market days accompanied by mangy dogs or stick-wielding, snub-nosed monkeys—how they stumbled over knowledge as they read the cracks in tortoise shells heated on makeshift braziers; how their monkeys kept guard over black wooden boxes that were always opened to the accompaniment of firecrackers and smoke-darkened erhus; how they cut themselves with swords when divining the future. As she picks at the loose skin on her fleshy hands, she speaks about ghost-catching and penetrating walls, about gnarled wooden puppets that dangled from improbably long strings and others that seemed to have their own motive force. For a moment, as she tries to explain the intricacies of some long-forgotten card trick, Wang forgets that he is listening to the woman who has kept him enclosed and prevented him from feeling the dirty excitement of precisely such secrets.

When she has told him all she can remember, Wang runs to his room, pulls his box from under the bed and, scrabbling through maps and pages ripped from western novels, digs out his first set of playing cards. When he returns to school the next day, he takes them with him as if they will somehow harden him for the

45

struggle with another kind of learning—mathematical symbols that seem to manoeuvre numbers out of reach; experiments that yield nothing but confusion and broken petri dishes; facts that demand to be learned. On one side is the glory that card tricks and Shakespeare appear to promise, on the other is the sheer intractability of knowledge.

As one year of schooling slides into another, he learns the piano, wrestles with history, and slugs it out with the capitals of the world. His own world is widened by books and distinguished alumni, who throw ideas out to their captive audiences like bread to starving prisoners. The diplomatist Lu Zhengxiang, who impresses Wang as much with his green waistcoat and waxed moustache as with his arguments, speaks carefully and earnestly on a rare return to the country, explaining the duties of the citizen in the light of Confucian thought and the pressing need for young men educated in foreign languages and according to western principles. Stirred by Lu Zhengxiang's words, Wang finds renewed purpose in the only two subjects which truly inspire him—English and French.

Even when the sheer drudgery of school threatens to overwhelm him, he never loses his love of languages or his ability to work them into new shapes, because his memory is good and words come easily. Not that words much matter. As he grapples with grammar and experiments with semantics, language becomes more than symbols on the page—it is the gateway to a place where he can remould himself. Half-blind, he sees ideas and concepts with a radical clarity when speaking foreign languages. His Chinese self has been disfigured beyond all hope of healing and a new man has emerged—a hideous European monster, if his mother is to be believed; a mysterious golem, his father thinks; a figure of immense possibility, Wang himself sometimes dares to hope. As he chips fragments from the half-formed statue his parents have long since given up hope of perfecting, he comes to believe that he will also be able to reshape the Chinese world into a place worthy of the modern age. Peppering his dialect with words and phrases garnered from the West, he picks up the *delufeng* when he wants to speak to a distant friend. When he goes for a walk he puts on his hat and picks up a *sidike*. He loves being young and *modeng* and despises all those who are not.

By the time he enters his nineteenth year, and his final year of school, he no longer resembles the diffident boy he was when he joined. He is brash, self-confident, and determined to be transformed by the full force of western learning. The Qing dynasty must do the same, he believes, and if it refuses to do so, if it struggles to maintain its authority in the face of political and economic challenges, then it will not be long before it is swept away. Hoping that his country's troubles will be a catalyst for revolution, he becomes an ardent republican, debating the failings of the imperial household with his schoolmates, reading *Shenbao*, *Xinwenbao*, *Dongfang Zazhi* and any other radical journal he can lay his hands on.

But political enthusiasms cannot entirely dispel youthful distractions. When provincial rebellions create political instability that the old regime clearly cannot manage, Wang throws himself into Shakespeare's history plays, hoping to find parallels that will help him and his fellow young radicals to cast aside the old regime. A great performance is being played out on the Beijing stage for the benefit of a non-paying audience, and he is anxious to get hold of a ticket.

The bitterest casualties in this long, drawn-out battle for identity are his parents. His father is reduced to hectoring, while his mother gnaws at her distress from the safe prison of home. Like the Qing dynasty itself, they are increasingly irrelevant. In an era that belongs to the young, when the new dominates the political and cultural scene, anyone over the age of thirty becomes less than irrelevant—they are impostors. When his father suggests that they go to the theatre together to celebrate his birthday, Wang simply doesn't know what to say. Age and politics have so distanced him from his parents that he lacks the ability to translate what he now believes into words they will understand.

47

In his confusion he remembers a poster he has seen advertising an evening of mystery and magic at the *Daying Xiguan*, featuring a great American magician. Tentatively he suggests that they get tickets but, when pressed for further details, hears himself telling his father about William Mozart Nicol, an artist from the West. Unable to use Nichol's nom de plume (Nicola) or to describe the nature of the performance, he lurches into a conversation that is out of control from the moment it begins.

'Mozart's coming to Shanghai?' his father asks incredulously.

'That's right, father. I saw the poster.'

'To the Great British Theatre? Are you sure?'

'W. Mozart. That's what it said.'

His father walks up and down his study. If he suspects that the Mozart his western friends are so fond of is long dead, he gives no indication of the fact to his son.

'I am not sure it will assist your studies.'

He hesitates.

'But if I rearrange a couple of meetings, I may be able to make that day. It will do us good to visit the theatre together and there may be some interesting people there. It is time we considered the work you will do when your schooling is finished.'

'What am I going to do?' Wang asks his schoolfriend Hong Bo disconsolately when the enormity of his mistake breaks through.

'Why not tell him that the tickets have already sold out?'

'He's not going to believe that,' Wang says. 'And even if he did, he'd just use some of his connections to bypass the box office.'

'In that case, you'd better find someone who is performing Mozart somewhere else in Shanghai and say you got muddled about the theatre.'

'What are the chances of that?' Wang asks, banging his head on the desk.

'What other option have you got?' Hong replies. 'It's either that or you'll just have to buy the tickets. You never know, he might like the show.'

'Would *your* father like it?' Wang asks.

'My father doesn't like anything apart from making money. He's not a good comparison. You're in trouble either way. You might as well take what's coming to you and get to see the show.'

Wang gets up, sweeps his hair from his fringe and trudges to the door. 'Goodbye, my friend,' he says. 'This could be the last time we meet.'

'You are so melodramatic, Wang,' Hong replies. 'You were made for the theatre.'

In his desperation, Wang turns to Mr Davis.

'Sounds like a load of nonsense to me,' the teacher says.

'Have you ever seen him perform?' Wang asks.

'Of course I haven't. The man's American and I've been stuck in Shanghai for the last ten years.'

'But you must have read about him?' Wang insists.

'Oh yes, I've read about him. He's a complete charlatan.'

'Sir, I don't like to beg, but you've got to help me out here. Can't you organise a school trip?'

'I couldn't justify it on educational grounds.'

'You don't need to justify it on educational grounds,' Wang tells him rather more boldly than he anticipated. 'It's artistic.'

Mr Davis smiles. 'It's that all right.'

'So what do you think, sir? Could you get me out of a hole?'

Mr Davis smiles again, though ruefully this time.

'No, Wang, I don't think I can. You'll have to sort this one out on your own.'

Pacing along Shanghai's busy streets towards the theatre with his father beside him reminds Wang of his annual visits to the oculist's. There is the same sense of doom, of arguments about to erupt, of tension that no show or purchase will ever be able to dissipate. As they approach the theatre, Wang Zhebu runs into a business acquaintance called Jia Minsi. As they talk, Wang hangs back and hopes that their conversation will prove sufficient distraction from the inevitable revelation that their arrival at the theatre will provide. Watching warily, he sees his father's shoulders tense, from which he surmises that Jia Minsi has provided the first of the evening's *coups de théâtre*, but since there is no possibility of giving way without losing face, his father continues walking. With judgment delayed, Wang falls in with the rest of the crowd and keeps his head down.

As he settles into one of the theatre's plush red seats, Wang spots Jia Minsi a couple of rows away and lifts his hand in greeting or farewell. It is a futile gesture but, given the circumstances, it seems apt. When the lights finally go down, he steals a glance at his father, who looks grimly determined and then fixes his attention on the stage as the curtains swing open and the great Nicola himself sweeps forward in his black cape, wearing his trademark red horns and with his face painted green.

In the theatrical dark, a certain nostalgia for the arts of illusion that helped see him through semi-blindness sweeps over Wang. Chinese magicians are all very well, but there is something about the allure of the foreign—the language, the colour, the sheer otherness—that always wins out over the ingenuity of native showmen. And Nicola is the greatest foreign magician of them all—an American who has performed in Paris and Berlin, tramped and triumphed across half of Asia, and been given an elephant by a grateful Maharajah in India. And now he is in Shanghai, hypnotizing a staid businessman and playing card tricks on a pretty young schoolgirl.

'Enough is enough,' his father growls, leaning across him. 'Let's go.'

Deeply ashamed, Wang does as he is told, edging as unobtrusively as he can along the row with his father pushing close behind, drawing complaints and embarrassed smiles from the rest of the audience. They are almost at the aisle when Nicola's voice reaches across the audience.

'Gee, someone's keen to get on stage,' he calls.

Wang tries to look in the other direction and considers just turning and running, but when he sees Jia Minsi looking straight at him and feels his father's hand on his shoulder he forces a strained smile.

'Won't you come up?' Nicola calls again. 'I could do with an assistant for my next trick.'

Wang nods politely and starts walking again as he feels his father's grip tighten.

'Come on, won't you?' Nicola calls again. 'These ladies and gentlemen want the next part of the show.'

Conscious that the eyes of the whole audience are on them, Wang Zhebu lets his hand fall from his son's shoulder. He tries to edge away, but the audience, mistaking the movement for acquiescence, starts applauding enthusiastically. With seemingly no other choice, Wang is compelled to make his way onto the stage. He dares not look round to see his father's reaction.

'What's your name, young man?'

'Wang, sir.'

'Well there's a surprise—a Chinaman called Wang! Now just you stand there, young Wang and ... what's this? A coin behind your ear! And a pack of cards in your pocket! So that's where they got to.'

Nicola works his way through a few routine card tricks before getting Wang to lock him in a metal cabinet.

'Don't worry, old fellow,' he whispers as he steps inside. 'I've checked out the locking mechanism already. You're not going to get into trouble for suffocating America's greatest magician.'

Wang nods, pushes the door closed and pockets the key as he has been asked. With strict instructions not to unlock it whatever noises or pleas he hears, he is dutiful enough to do as he is told, even when the great magician starts banging from within. What he has not been prepared for are the eyes of the audience upon him. He looks up at the gallery, as much to avoid catching his father's eye as to take in the view, and is taken aback by row after row of eager faces smiling down on him. Taking a step or two back under the intensity of the examination, he is startled out of his thoughts by a tap on his shoulder. He jumps and turns to find the great Nicola himself standing behind him. Rapturous applause sweeps across the stage and, despite the sick feeling in his stomach, Wang feels the vicarious thrill of success.

As they leave the theatre, Wang prepares for a confrontation of Shakespearean dimensions but, if his father was planning to speak, his words are swept away by a series of thunderous explosions that pull the night apart. When the sky is almost simultaneously lit with a violent spectrum of colours that could have graced any New Year celebrations, Wang realises that the moment of his and China's redemption has finally arrived.

As the theatre crowds merge into greater, wilder groups of ecstatic, slogan-chanting, *baijiu*-drinking young men, Wang and his father are swept along to the waterfront where, as fireworks punch holes in the complacent night sky, copies of *Xinwenbao* are passed from hand to triumphant hand. Hastily printed and badly written, they confirm what Wang has long known to be inevitable—the emperor has been forced to abdicate and the republic is now a reality. Forced further along the riverfront, he looks back in the hope that his father's expression has changed but can no longer see him at his back. He cannot tell whether they have been separated by the extravagant crowds, or whether his father has fought his way out of the confusion. With time enough to find out, he lingers on the Bund, letting off firecrackers and hugging strangers. By the time he gets home, he has made a resolution not to watch from the sidelines any more.

'Shanghai is being left behind,' he tells his parents the next day. 'Yuan Shikai is leading the republic into the glorious future you have always dreamt about.'

His father doesn't answer at first. Picking up the copy of *Xinwenbao* that his son has left on the reception room table, he skims through the account of the previous day's events in Beijing.

'Yuan Shikai is certainly leading the way,' he admits eventually, 'though whether the future will be glorious is yet to be seen.'

Wang turns to his mother. 'Beijing is where I have to be,' he tells her.

'What can you do in that terrible city,' she says, 'that you can't do here?'

'I can study, mother. I can perfect my English and French. I can help nurse the new order into health and strength.'

Decisively laying *Xinwenbao* back down on the table to signal that he will be the one to reply, Wang's father delivers the lecture Wang has been expecting ever since they stepped into the theatre the previous evening.

'I cannot deny that part of me is pleased with the turn of events, but nor can I fail to express my displeasure at your peremptoriness. I would not expect a decision of such magnitude to be made without reference to me, without discussion. There is much to be done here in Shanghai.'

His wife tries to intervene but is silenced with a wave of the hand.

'There is much to be done,' her husband repeats, 'which can only be done from a position of stability that having a career provides. When you finish your schooling, we will establish you in business or possibly in the law—there are people I can speak to—and then, but only then, will you be able to effect the sort of changes we all desire for this nation of ours.'

'But father, can't you see?' Wang interrupts. 'All the action is happening in Beijing. The new government is already being formed. The republic needs to be established. I can't stay here and take some inconsequential job while the world races by.'

His father frowns. 'You cannot stay here because the action is all happening in Beijing?' he asks incredulously. 'Do they have superior magicians there?'

'Your father is right,' Wang's mother says, as Wang Zhebu walks out of the room as though ending a business meeting. 'How can we save you from guns and violence when you are so far away?'

Collapsing into a chair, Wang waves her fears aside. In attempting to convince her that a new era has begun—an era in

53

which all men are brothers—and that the only danger he now faces is the danger of being left behind, he realises that he is also trying to convince himself. He tells her that the greatest Chinese minds of the age will flock to Beijing. Exiles will return home. The bold will turn north. Only those who are timid will remain where accidents of birth have placed them. When she is unable to reply—quieted by the force of his argument or by grief—he takes her silence for agreement and leaves the room as well.

Somehow it doesn't seem so simple when he lies sleepless on his bed that night. An exile in his own home, he cannot quite convince himself that Beijing is really where he belongs either. He knows that he has been sheltered but secure in Shanghai, and he is not entirely certain that he has enough of what his father calls moral steel for the journey he is still determined to make. But when, in the morning, his father doesn't even look up when he enters the room, Wang decides that he has to get himself a place at one of Beijing's universities whatever his parents think.

The agony of the wait is dissipated only by the news that Lu Zhengxiang, the alumnus he admires above all others, has been appointed prime minister of the fledgling republic, though his disastrous first speech to the national assembly and precipitous resignation scarcely bodes well for the future. With some of his confidence dented, Wang concentrates instead on improving his language skills and learns to wait. When eventually he learns that he has been offered a place at Peking University, he thrusts doubt deep within him and confronts his parents with the news.

With that unpleasantness over, he decides that he must make one final journey to the oculist's before he shakes the Shanghai dust from his feet. As he fights the traffic in an antiquated rickshaw pulled by a man at least four times his age, he calls to mind his first visit—enamel eyeballs laid out like sweets, his father's heavy disapproval, the white-coated westerner's unexpectedly minty breath. The memories are blurred and uncertain, reminders of an age that no longer contains him, but the sight of the oculist's now faded facade reminds him that he cannot wholly escape his own history. Now that he has stopped growing he doesn't need regular eyeball replacements, but he cannot break a habit as deeply embedded as shards of bamboo in the eye's anterior chamber. Recoiling from the day he was first taken to the display room, helpless and naïve, a young boy lost in a violent adult world, he cannot help but remember what it was like to be two-eyed and ordinary as he fingers the balls he is offered. He opens his grubby, drawstring bag, drops the brown and blue enamel balls in and takes the rickshaw back to the station to buy himself a one-way ticket to Beijing.

However hard he tries in the years that follow, he finds it hard to recall the rest of that day. Even when far from home, he can picture the expression on the oculist's face, the rickshaw's grubby curtain, and the exact wording of the advertisements that pulsed up and down his street. But he cannot remember how he and his parents travelled into the centre of Shanghai, nor what they said when he got there. All he can grasp are tatters of feelings and an overwhelming sense of dependency—knowing that he needs his parents' money and his father's approval—and not wanting to feel indebted any more. Only one sentence survives his amnesia, a sentence that he tries wholly unsuccessfully to forget over the years of separation, for the past cannot be expunged any more than words can be unsaid.

'The forces of history are greater than the ties of blood.'

That is what he tells his parents as he steps onto the train, but as he settles into his seat in the first-class carriage and watches his parents fade from sight, his father standing with his right hand raised and his mother turning away in grief, he knows that it simply isn't true.

Chapter 5

Unable to secure a rickshaw among the crowds, Wang walks from Beijing's station, along the river front, past wharves and piers, until he reaches a jetty where, despite the freezing conditions, fish traders have set up their stalls.

Where a smell of frying vegetables and pungent spices mingles with the pervasive aroma of fish and the inescapable tang of the river, he walks uphill towards the university, following the map he has been sent. Small children peer from upper windows and throw orange peel at him as he passes, housemaids wring out their washing in the streets, and dark, unfriendly men heave impossibly large loads onto their shoulders and teeter through the streets like women wearing glamorous new shoes.

After walking for close to an hour, Wang hears the city change its tune. Heaving his bag onto his shoulder, he struggles up another hill towards the noise—traders shouting and laughing, wooden poles thudding dully as they are dropped, a market being packed away for the night.

He struggles towards what he cannot yet see, while crowds of Beijingers—always constant, always changing—merge into one another in the street's stream. Gangs of beggars swim towards him, pulling alongside with their strong strokes, but, as they hold out their hands, Wang pushes them away in disgust. On every snow-burdened corner there are soldiers, but none of them intervenes. He doesn't care any more because on the far side of the market square he can see what he has come for. Putting all doubts about the capital to one side, he fights his way towards the entrance of the university building and, pausing to savour the moment, pushes his way inside.

The first person he meets, dressed in a padded jacket that might once have been blue, is Bao Weihe, an engineer from Nanning.

'So you're Wang Weijun,' he says peremptorily when Wang introduces himself. 'The Shanghaier I'm forced to share a room with.'

'Pleased to meet you,' Wang replies, holding out a hand, which Bao ignores.

Dropping his head like a threatened animal, Bao pushes his way through the crowds instead. 'This way,' he calls back. 'And keep up, because I'm not waiting.'

The hostel is grubbier than Wang has been expecting, and the room pokier, but, doing his best to maintain a tone of cheerful confidence, he attempts to engage his surly roommate in conversation as he unpacks.

'We are living in heady days,' he says.

'We are living in dangerous times,' Bao replies. 'Thousands of years swept away like dust from a neglected shrine. I fear the next few months. The looting hasn't started yet, but it will.'

'Yuan Shikai will never allow it.'

'Yuan Shikai will be leading it.'

'But he's a great servant of the republic.'

'He's a *lao piao*.'

Without stopping to think, Wang lashes out. Bao falls over in surprise.

'Yuan Shikai is the protector of the republic,' Wang says with as much menace as he can muster. 'Never speak of him like that in my presence again.'

Wang and Bao live separate lives after their first encounter, ignoring each other as far as is possible in such an enclosed space— Bao working, drinking, and cursing every political change, while Wang tries to get to grips with his studies. As if afraid that Beijing might escape him as soon as he turns his back, he tries to impose himself on the city by collecting it. The box into which as a child he stuffed maps, book covers, and playing cards is now, along with his drawstring bag of eyeballs, his strongest connection to home. As he struggles to shape what he is learning into coherence, as he acclimatises to the city's bland food, bold architecture and harsh climate, he gathers what he can from the streets and hopes that northern ephemera will anchor him in his new home. Newspaper cuttings, torn posters, and free samples from upmarket shops all find their way into his box, which he hides not under his bed where Bao Weihe might find it, but in the backpack he carries with him everywhere. In a burst of unregulated enthusiasm, he even tears the last page of *Walden* from the library's only copy and stuffs it in among the rest of his papers, though the anxiety such an act of desecration provokes is enough to ensure that he never tries anything like it again.

Ignoring Bao as much as possible in their confined living conditions, he makes a determined effort to make new connections and find new friends—Jiang Tao, a radical student of Economics from rural Jiangxi; Chen Da, a bookish Beijinger who fancies himself China's Ibsen; Yan Yangchu, a Sichuanese student who has already spent three years studying in Japan. None of them find his company as congenial as he finds theirs, but Wang is untroubled. Finding that his mind cannot expand fast enough to take in what has happened to his country, he is engrossed in nursing the new order into maturity, joining political societies and supporting radical causes.

With a bewildering variety of groups jostling for his time, attention and money, he cannot keep pace with the changes that are threatening to carry his country away—Lu Zhengxiang returning as foreign minister after his disastrous term as prime minister, Yuan Shikai being chosen as President, the confusion of national elections, the assassination of Song Jiaoren in Shanghai, only a few yards from his father's office. The speed and scope of the revolution constantly catches him by surprise, but when Jiang Tao arrives for class without his queue, he realises that he has barely begun to respond to the revolution that has swept the old order away.

'What have you done?' he asks.

'I've rid myself of a symbol of Manchu domination,' Jiang replies.

'But what will your parents say?'

'What can they say? I'm hardly going to tie it back on, am I?'

Wang agonises for weeks. There are limits to his rebelliousness and boundaries over which he is not yet prepared to step. But when Jiang Tao mocks him for his timidity, he comes to a decision. Already grown used to being at the heart of student politics, he cannot bear the thought of being pushed to the fringes. He kneels down in the university's central courtyard, bows his head, and demands that Jiang cut his hair. When he returns to his room, Bao is dismissive.

'It's just what I'd expect from a Shanghai peasant,' he says.

'That's some statement coming from a Nanning pig farmer,' Wang replies.

But Bao is not alone. For every student who welcomes the revolution, there are two or three who are deeply troubled by it. Wang ignores them and reads himself into greater radicalism. Longing for a cultural revolution as much as a dynastic one, he looks for salvation in foreign books.

'I have made a resolution,' he tells Jiang Tao, the day he finishes reading Emerson's essay on 'Self-reliance'. 'I am no longer going to rely on my parents for support.'

Jiang, who is only able to pay for his studies by taking two jobs, neither of which pays enough, merely rolls his eyes.

'What is more, I am going to choose whom I marry.'

'Who'd have you?' Jiang asks.

Wang ignores him. 'She must be educated and beautiful. We will be equals.'

'Do you have anyone in mind?' Jiang asks.

'Well ...' Wang replies.

'I thought not,' Jiang says.

Slowly, as the new republic establishes its legitimacy, Beijing achieves a degree of stability, which allows Wang to become more adventurous. He visits the Zhonghua Gate on Tiananmen Square, makes a pilgrimage to the remains of the *Yuan Ming Yuan*, and walks up and down Yongdingmen, Qianmen, Tiananmen, and Wumen until he knows them as well as Bubbling Well Road and the Bund. For the first time in his life he feels free, not only of his parents' influence, but also of the need to follow the example of others. Now that he is away from home, alone among millions, he can find his own way, and that way leads him inexorably towards the West.

It takes him only a few classes to discover that his proficiency with languages is not merely the result of his early exposure to English and French but the product of some innate ability that sets him apart from all but the very brightest of his fellow students, which leads him to immerse himself in language studies at the expense of all else. Freed from his parents' control, he loses his Shanghai accent, his unsophisticated habits, and his attachment to old-fashioned ways of living; regarding himself now as a Beijinger and a modish intellectual, he sees no need ever to revisit the burdensome past.

In his spare time, Wang writes for one of the new English-language literary magazines and ploughs a sizeable proportion of his monthly allowance into the venture, even though he is not certain he will ever see a financial return on his investment. He studies hard and passes his examinations but, as he comes to the end of his second year at the university, he finds that his publishing interests are gaining ascendancy over his academic ones. Under his direction, the magazine concentrates increasingly on North American and European affairs—literature, arts and, sometimes, politics—which means that he is drawn inexorably towards a decision. As he struggles over an article on the greatest North American universities and their first Chinese graduates, he decides that there is no longer any need for him to gain his western experiences second-hand.

'You want to do what?' his father bellows, when Wang pays one of his fleeting visits home.

'I want to study abroad,' Wang replies. 'Maybe Yale, maybe Harvard.'

'You're going to abandon our country and your family?'

'I'm not abandoning anything or anyone,' Wang shouts back. It is the first time he has ever raised his voice to his father. 'And don't forget it was you who wanted me to be forward-looking.'

'I wanted you to free our country from imperial oppression. I wanted you to have the opportunities I never had, not to run away when your country needs you.'

Wang storms from the room. His mother seeks him out and hugs him like she did all those years before when he came running into the house with an arrow in his eye.

'Little Jun, Little Jun,' she says.

'I'm doing what I think for the best.'

'I know, I know,' she says, 'but why do you want to go to America? I just can't understand why you'd want to go to America.'

'I'm going to apply to Cambridge and to the Sorbonne as well,' he says.

'Is that in Japan?' she asks hopefully.

He tears himself from her desperate embrace.

'There's more to the world than China and Japan, mother.'

The division between them has become so deep that he no longer sees himself in any meaningful sense as his parents' son. He has become a child of modernity, reborn into a China that is changing, into a world that can survive only by turning from its past. He has crossed the threshold that separates the new world from the dark Chinese past and can no longer look back. In his imagination he is already on his way to America and not even the outbreak of the European war dampens his enthusiasm. Most of his fellow students see the Siege of Qingdao as a mere sideshow, but to Wang this European intrusion into China's already chaotic world offers a foretaste of freedoms yet to be won. He writes frenetically about current affairs and follows the progress of the Japanese onslaught on the German garrison with mounting excitement.

A week after the siege begins, he attends a party thrown by one of the political economy professors and his elegant young wife in their beautifully furnished house. Four huge scrolls dominate the walls, and the red lacquered furniture is more finely crafted than any Wang has ever seen. Intricate clocks, leather-bound books, and a wrought iron bird cage perched on top of a Ming-era cabinet impose themselves on the room, offering a reassuring solidity to the otherwise vacuous discussions around the Japanese navy's chances of success.

'You are a very intense young man,' the professor's wife says, interrupting him as he lambasts a younger student with an explanation of East Asian political difficulties.

Wang bows his head, not knowing how he is expected to reply. 'I was talking about the war,' he says.

The professor's wife smiles. 'Which war would that be?' she asks.

'The war of liberation,' he answers. 'The battle for those parts of Shandong that have been so unjustly wrestled from us. Qingdao is going to be freed any day now.'

'Oh, I hope not,' she replies. 'The Japanese are sure to be worse tyrants than the Germans ever were.'

Wang is taken aback. The younger student takes his chance to back away. 'But it's not just the Japanese,' he says. 'The British are lending their support as well. They will moderate any Japanese excesses.'

'Just as they did in 1895,' she replies.

'I ... I don't remember 1895.'

She laughs. 'No, nor do I, but I read, and what I read tells me that we cannot trust the British to save our country for us.'

Wang senses that the conversation is not going well and so attempts to change tack. 'What is it that you read?' he asks.

'That the fittest survive, that nature is red in tooth and claw.'

'Tennyson?' he says, surprised.

'Very good,' she says. 'It was Tennyson first, but it was Darwin after. Tennyson only sensed what Darwin was able to prove.'

'So you do admire the British?'

'I admire their writers and their scientists. Their soldiers, their merchants, and their missionaries I can happily live without.'

Wang is taken aback. 'But if it weren't for their merchants and soldiers,' he says tentatively, 'Qingdao would not be the city it is today. And nor would Shanghai.'

She smiles again. 'Oh yes, Shanghai.' She turns her head away. 'I thought I detected the glimmer of an accent.'

With the conversation slipping away from him, Wang looks for a way to save face and finds it in the deck of cards that is lying on the table beside them ready for a late evening poker session.

'Would you please pick one of these?' he says, picking them up.

'Whatever for?'

'I can create illusions,' he says.

'An illusionist?' She raises one of her pretty eyebrows. 'Like Jin Lingfu?'

'Not like Jin Lingfu,' Wang assures her. 'I am better read, better bred, and I am studying at Peking University.'

'Then I should be impressed,' she says smiling, and chooses a card from his hand.

'If you would be so kind as to look at it before returning it to the pack.'

She does so, stubs out her cigarette and smiles again. Wang tries to concentrate on the trick but, never having met such a glamorous intellectual before, struggles to keep his thoughts in order.

'Now I will shuffle the cards,' he says, 'turn the pack three times, and ask my assistant to help me.'

'Your assistant?' she asks, looking round.

'My assistant,' he confirms, walking across the room to the canary in its cage. He opens the door and gently takes the bird in his hand. 'Now then, my little friend, if you could choose the lady's card for her, we would be most grateful.'

He spreads his hand wide and waits for the creature to do as it has been asked. Eventually it raises a foot, grips one of the cards and hands it to Wang, who pauses for effect. He looks at the professor's wife and then at the card.

'Now then, don't be foolish,' he says to the bird. 'You know full well that's not the one the lady picked.'

He lets the bird hop onto his arm and, turning slightly away, reaches out to one of the plates that is being carried across the room by a waiter.

'Here's a little snack to encourage you,' he says.

The bird steps onto his hand and, as it does so, the professor's wife realises that it isn't food but a card, the very card she chose, that it has in its beak. Wang smiles and returns the bird to its cage. His performance having gone as well as he could have wished, he decides to leave his eyeball where it is for the time being.

Chapter 6

Wang is in Beijing's largest department store three months after the fall of Qingdao when he next sees the professor's wife. He is trying to find a fashionable suit when she slips her arm through his and leads him only half-protesting away from the obsequious shop assistant who had been trying to persuade him to buy Parisian rather than Chinese.

'So, it's the tall illusionist,' she says. 'The man with the intriguing eyes. I'm surprised to find you in this den of iniquity.'

'I was trying to find a—'

She puts a finger to his lips.

'I don't care,' she interrupts.

She leads him through a pair of double doors into the heart of the store, where skins of tigers, panthers, leopards, and wildcats hang from the walls, and immaculately-dressed women emerge from the drift of cigarette smoke. Keeping her arm firmly through his, she leads him towards a huge stove that provides enough heat, it seems, not just for the room but for the whole store. She takes a cigarette from a shop assistant and glides towards a pile of silks that slip and slide from a table in apparently casual distress. Choosing the brightest scarf she can find, she smiles delicately at the young man whose job it is to maintain the display's nonchalance, and then leads Wang on to a display of red dresses.

A young Englishman, oblivious of Wang's presence, approaches her as she flicks through them. He looks her up and down, rather too obviously for Wang's liking, and then lifts a hanger out of her way so that she can look along the rest of the rail without fear of distraction. She smiles benignly over his head and continues with her search. The Englishman, whose pale, pink shirt and green cravat seem desperately mannered to Wang, coughs discreetly as though about to speak, but she cuts him off by sweeping one of the garments from the rail. Laying her bag on the floor, she holds the dress up, sways over to a full-length mirror and, turning to find her best angle, looks back over her shoulder to where the Englishman is hovering expectantly.

'Come on, Weijun,' she calls out seductively, 'the servant can bring our bag.'

Wang pulls himself away from the wall against which he has been rather disconsolately leaning and hurries after her, pausing only to grin in triumph at the spurned foreigner.

Realising what a risk he is taking, he lets her take him on a circuit of Beijing's most fashionable cafés and galleries. At first, he finds it almost impossible to maintain concentration as they discuss literature and politics but, eventually, calmed by her manner and impelled by a determination he scarcely knows he possesses, he begins to talk freely. Amused by his enthusiasm, the professor's wife takes his hand and tries to get him to look at her directly.

'I have a name, you know,' she tells him. 'I'm not just a wife.'

Wang keeps silent.

'It's Rong Meifan,' she continues, 'and I don't mind if you use it.'

They meet often, exploring the city together and taking only the most superficial precautions to keep their relationship hidden. Rong Meifan is intrigued by Wang, his eyes so peculiar and his manners such a strange combination of the sophisticated and the innocently childish. She finds his voice and his strength of feeling appealing. She enjoys being the object of his tongue-tied confusion. Wang is constantly surprised by the views she holds, by her ambivalent love of the West and her utter contempt for westerners. As his attitudes are questioned and his silent prejudices rebuked, he finds it difficult to believe he ever managed to survive in Beijing without her. She takes him to restaurants hidden away in bleak *hutongs*, to parks that none but the most ancient of rickshaw men know, to department stores run by the Chinese and not by faded Parisians. Coaxing him away from his studies, she teaches him how to read the city.

A small geological museum, which opens with a flurry of intellectual excitement in 1916 and retains its aura of fashionable intellectuality even when Beijingers' interest in fossils dissipates, becomes one of their favourite retreats. Playing on Rong Meifan's interest in evolutionary theories, Wang takes her to an exhibition and contrives to guide her towards the museum's furthest and darkest cabinets. Safe from prying eyes, he takes her hand while she is trying to make sense of a series of geological drawings that have been labelled only in Latin.

'I need to see you more often,' he says briskly. 'When can we meet again?'

'It's an archaeopteryx,' she replies. 'What do you think that means? Has it got anything to do with arches or archaeologists?'

'That's not what I asked,' he says, as she walks around to the other side of the cabinet.

'I know it's not what you asked, but it's what I want to know.'

Wang tries to take her hand again.

'If only I had someone with me who knew something about language,' she continues.

Relaxing, he moves round to join her. 'Are we supposed to feel fragile here?' he asks as they promenade around the rest of the exhibition. 'Fleeting? Ephemeral? Do you think the scale of this place is meant to be such that we quail before it? Do you think that—'

Rong Meifan squeezes his hand. 'No, I don't.'

Wang steps back from the display cabinet and tries again, speaking less frenetically this time. 'Think about what all this geological time is doing to us. You've read Darwin. You know what it's like to be a mere link in the evolutionary chain. A flash in the dark, a moth burning in a gas lamp—that's what we are. Ephemeral. It is the word. If being here doesn't make you feel ephemeral, then what else can?'

Rong Meifan turns away. 'I don't believe in the ephemeral,' she says. 'I believe in the moment.'

'How can the moment matter in a place like this?'

'The moment matters here,' she says, 'as much as it matters anywhere else. Maybe you're too young to appreciate that yet.'

Wang frowns. He hates it when she reminds them of their respective ages.

Rong Meifan laughs. 'Young and full of life—that's what I like about you.'

Wang forces himself not to show annoyance. 'Is that all?' he says.

Rong Meifan looks up at him. 'Oh no, that's certainly not all,' she says.

Their assignations become no more frequent or glamorous as their affair progresses, but even a trip to the market can be an intensely sensual experience with Rong Meifan. Brightness is such an essential part of her life that when Wang sees only fruit and vegetables she experiences visions—apples, pears, lemons and peaches glisten in pyramidal splendour; dragon fruit, their black seeds sitting like pebbles in snow, perch cheek by jowl with pomegranates and oranges; strings of sea kale and sorrel are only marginally less metaphysical than bundles of *gai choi*, *xian cai* and *jie lan*. With Rong Meifan at his side, Wang sees what he has only looked at before.

It is not just the brightness of the colours that delights Rong Meifan but the dazzle and dance of sound as it bounces off market stalls. Fishmongers slap thrashing garoupa and snapper onto their slabs, dispatch them with the flat of their choppers and fling them to their assistants to be sliced and descaled, while simultaneously shouting greetings, warnings, and prices to the women who mill around their stalls shouting back their own well-considered advice. Small birds in finely-crafted cages sing as they hop from peg to pole, while old men stand, their heads slightly to one side, and listen. Children laugh and shout encouragement as they fly their delicate red flags across the faces of the buildings. As Rong Meifan revels in the bounce and sparkle of life that she finds among the market traders' stalls, Wang learns to revel with her.

But even when they are together, he never stops following political developments. Ever since the Japanese issued their Twenty-One Demands it has become clear to everyone but the government itself that the republic is powerless. Feeling powerless too, Wang attempts to seize control of what he still can, which amounts to little more than his daily life. At the corner of his street he buys noodles from the vendor whom he has previously ignored, chats to the toothless rickshaw man who waits at the entrance to his building, and reads every English and French newspaper he can lay his hands on. As the Japanese grow progressively more arrogant, Yuan Shikai acts less like the protector of the nation and more like the emperor he has declared himself to be. It is painful to lose faith in one on whom such great hopes have been placed but Wang still has faith in others, like Liang Shiyi, who have greater moral credibility even if they have less political power. He reads Liang's speeches with pride and imagines him standing before the country's political elite to fulminate against Japan's act of betrayal and to demand redress for the wrongs that have been done. Stuffing copies of the speeches into his box of hoarded detritus, which is now too full to be carried everywhere he goes, he longs for the day when Qingdao will be retaken and China's treacherous neighbours driven out of the country.

Convinced that his country must join the European conflict, or world war as the newspapers are now calling it, and so win itself a place at any future peace conference, he rejoices when he hears that troops have already been offered but sinks back into despair when it emerges that the Allies have turned them down. He clings onto the slim hope that Liang Shiyi's Labourers as Soldiers strategy holds out, and shouts for joy when he hears that the British have begun to recruit Chinese workers to help relieve

69

their hard-pressed manual labourers. But when he speaks to Rong Meifan about whether the Japanese will be expelled once and for all from Chinese soil so that the era of semi-colonial control can finally be brought to an end, he is disconcerted to discover that, though she is the wife of a professor of political economy, or perhaps because she is the wife of a professor of political economy, she sees no prospect of a political solution to China's political difficulties.

'I've heard enough about New China. There's no more truth in it than there is in patriarchal concepts of the New Woman. We still dance to Japanese tunes and copy Japanese books. There's nothing new in China apart from a lust after novelty, and that's not going to free women from their families or cure the country of its illness.'

'So you're going to accept slavery and humiliation?' Wang asks, annoyed despite himself.

Rong Meifan smiles, though not at him. 'There are more ways for women to get what they want than politicians or writers have ever thought of,' she replies.

As the European war gets bogged down in European mud, and Wang's final examinations draw closer, it occurs to him that the conflict might scupper his plan to study abroad too. As foreign travel becomes difficult and visas become harder to obtain, both the Europeans and the Americans become less willing to hand out scholarships to foreigners. Neglecting the revision he knows he should be doing, he concentrates all his efforts on writing applications while there is still any chance of success.

Aware that the days are dark for his country, he is more immediately aware of the dangers that attend him should Rong Meifan's husband find out about their affair. Now that his relationship with her is less carefree and more furtive, their meetings become more infrequent and are usually limited to hasty meals in Beijing's less salubrious neighbourhoods, places where they are unlikely to be seen by any of her many acquaintances. When they aren't together, he hangs around in the shadows at the end of her street, trying to catch a glimpse of her as she leaves her house. He sees nothing except, one day, someone who looks a great deal like her with her arm through another student's.

Despite these anxieties, he cannot shake off a sense of hopeful impatience, knowing that all he needs is one chance to escape his moribund country so that he will eventually be able to return in triumph. Sending a few more scholarship applications, he resumes his studies and prepares feverishly for his final examinations. He hopes that he has not left it too late.

When he goes to register formally for his final examinations, he tries to keep his mind off his latest scholarship application but to little effect, until the university official tells him that his name has been removed from the list of final year students. Wang protests vigorously, but the official politely shakes his head and replies that there is nothing he can do now that disciplinary proceedings are underway.

'Disciplinary proceedings?' Wang yells. 'What disciplinary proceedings?'

The official hands him a copy of the letter he has extracted from Wang's file, most of which Wang fails to understand because it is couched in quasi-legal terms. But when he gets to the bottom of the page he understands enough. The signature is Rong Meifan's husband's. He hands the letter back to the official in silence and walks quietly away.

Beijing is emptied of meaning from that moment. Pacing along Yongdingmen, Wang tries to pound himself back to life, but Beijing's contours have been flattened, the map of the city shredded until it is whisked from him by the slightest of mental breezes. He revisits Tiananmen Square and stands silent before the Gugong. He thinks about walking round the outer walls but the dust of its history chokes him out of further exploration. Neither Qianmen, Tiananmen, nor Wumen are any better—crowded beyond any reasonable bounds of comfort, they force solitariness upon him. In a city of so many hundreds of thousands of people, he cannot escape the realisation that he is utterly alone.

When he bumps into one of his English colleagues from the literary magazine, he keeps his head down, but cannot avoid a confrontation.

'How are you feeling, old chap?' the earnest young man asks, but the truth is that he isn't feeling anything at all.

Chapter 7

When his humiliation becomes public, Wang moves out of his student hostel into a small, barely-furnished room in the north of the city. Avoiding familiar teahouses and all company, he sits alone in the dark, listens for Rong Meifan's knock, and chokes back the fear that she may be gone for good. Finally, when he can no longer bear to be alone, he goes out in search of her.

He revisits all the places that have mattered to them, the cafés, galleries and stores they have spent time in, but she is nowhere to be found. Hoping to catch at least a glimpse or, even better, a word with her, he lingers outside her house until the winter's snow drives him back to the solitary darkness of his room. He props himself up against his desk and shreds paper after paper, knowing that with no prospect of a degree he has no chance of winning a scholarship to a foreign university either. Having staked all on his break from home, he knows that, like his country, he cannot now go back.

There is a teahouse fifty yards from his lodgings, a seedy place where there are more mice than customers. Left free to roam over the tables and counters, they scurry from surface to surface, eating crumbs and scraps, leaving their own distinctive deposits in lieu of payment.

Everything about the place disgusts Wang—its mouldy cane chairs, its dusty tea, the picture of the Xuantong Emperor which, inexplicably, still hangs above the serving hatch, where a figure of indeterminate gender has the distinctive habit of hawking onto the floor with each cup of tea that is served. It disgusts him, but it is where he spends most of his time now that the more fashionable teahouses and restaurants are closed to him. Students never come here, for it is neither cheap nor trendy enough to attract them, which means that the place has been abandoned to the elderly, who slump over the tables, moving only to spit seed shells onto the floor and pick their teeth.

There is nothing to draw Wang here but its obscurity and the displaced piano that has been jammed into the corner of the room between a couple of round tables. A piano so old and out of tune that it is only fit for service as an extra table, which is what the proprietor has been using it for until Wang tries to coax a tune out of the broken beast. Sensing a novel way to attract business, the old man (or woman) encourages Wang to play on by means of a complicated but largely untranslatable series of hand gestures and grunts. Wang obliges until the grunts increase in volume and intensity, when it occurs to him that maybe the old woman (or man) is unhappy with some aspect of his playing.

'The keys are so sticky,' Wang complains. 'You need to look after pianos. Get them tuned every once in a while. Have it serviced. You know, show it a little care.'

One of the elderly tea-drinkers lifts his head from the table. 'It's not the piano,' he rasps. 'It's that foreign shit you're playing he's not happy about. Why can't you play Poor Butterfly or something from The Peony Pavilion?'

'It's not foreign shit,' Wang replies angrily. 'It's Chopin!'

'Don't know what that means,' the old man mutters. 'One shit smells like another, especially when it's been dumped from a foreign arse.'

Wang slams the piano lid shut, but a few days later he returns chastened. With no other piano available now that he has lost his place at the university, he has no choice but to swallow his musical pride if he wants to console himself with preludes and nocturnes. Day after featureless day he drinks the establishment's foul tea and imposes his musical tastes on the regulars, only occasionally giving way to their demands for something more authentically Chinese. When the complaints grow too vociferous, he returns through snow and rain to his lodgings.

As Beijing works its way through the predictable disaster of another dark winter, it occurs to him that the war might not be an unmitigated calamity, that it might provide him with the opportunity he has been looking for. Light seeps back into the dark places of his mind. Hope grabs him with its grubby hands and starts to heave him out of the gloom. With no chance of now winning a scholarship, he begins to think about securing a place in the Chinese Labour Corps. He is under no illusions about his ability to dig trenches, unload ships, or build tanks, but it occurs to him that he has skills the Allies value. He can leap from language to language. He can speak in tongues. He can translate. As the slow ache of feeling returns, he dares to hope again. The shadows shorten. The city recovers its purpose.

As he makes enquiries, Wang also makes a systematic effort to read all he can about the progress of the war, becoming cautiously optimistic when Lloyd George becomes British prime minister, losing heart when Trepov resigns in Russia, and finding himself utterly confused by the rapidly changing situation in America. With the snow still thick on the ground, he puts papers and dark thoughts to one side and makes an appointment to see Mr Henry Williams, the Chinese Labour Corps' British representative in Beijing.

When the week of his appointment finally arrives, he has his hair cut and gets his smartest western suit cleaned. Searching out the toothless rickshaw man, he explains in the clearest terms that he has a meeting for which he must not be late, that the rickshaw must be spotlessly clean, and that no one else must be allowed to hire it. The old man nods excitedly and mutters a response of such incomprehensibility that Wang just claps him on the shoulder, gives him some money and walks off while he is still talking.

As the rickshaw bumps its way through Beijing's crowds and the terrible snow, spraying vagrants and beggars as it goes,

Wang cannot help but remember the terrible day when, wedged between his parents, he was hauled by a rickshaw through the streets of western Shanghai. He closes his eyes and sees what he saw all those years before—a confusion of lights, his mother sobbing, shadows swirling in Chapoo Road as the overwhelming dark rose against him.

'Stop! Stop here!' he shouts.

When the rickshaw man skids to a halt, Wang leans out of the side and vomits into the gutter. Feeling a second wave of nausea coming, he tries to control himself but then vomits again. When he has finished wiping himself clean, he drops his handkerchief into the road and decides to walk the rest of the way, even though it means trudging through the snow and arriving at the offices of the British delegation with his shoes and trousers soaked.

Climbing the narrow staircase that leads to the strangely unassuming headquarters of the Chinese Labour Corps in Beijing, Wang contemplates turning back before his interview has even begun, but a western voice stops him in his tracks.

'Enter!' it bawls.

Wang knocks demurely and enters to find a middle-aged Englishman with brown hair and a red face sitting on a leather chair and with his feet on the desk.

'Come in, come in,' the man greets him in execrable Chinese. 'If you're looking for a job then you've come to the right place.'

Wang feels a curious mixture of amusement and embarrassment at the Englishman's attempt to speak his language. Looking around, he sees a grandfather clock in the corner of the room and a picture of King George V hanging on the wall behind the desk. The room smells musty and foreign.

'So, you want to join the Chinese Labour Corps?' the Englishman continues in Chinese, removing his feet from the desk.

Wang replies slowly in the same language. 'No, sir. I am an educated man and believe that I can be of more use to your government in other fields.'

The Englishman looks up from his papers.

'In what way could someone like you possibly be of use to the British government?' he demands.

'I have knowledge of both English and French,' Wang replies.

'Look, my man,' the Englishman says, 'we have Chinese in here all the time asking for work because they claim a facility with the language that they clearly do not possess. Half-educated Chinese are of no use to the British army.'

He has slipped back into English, but Wang, keeping his powder dry, replies in Chinese. 'I think you will find that I have a facility with the language, as you put it, that may be of some assistance to you in the field of battle, sir,' he says.

This time the Englishman doesn't even deign to speak so Wang widens his stance and, shifting to English, begins to declaim:

And you, good yeomen,
Whose limbs were made in England, show us here
The mettle of your pasture; let us swear
That you are worth your breeding; which I doubt not;
For there is none of you so mean and base,
That hath not noble lustre in your eyes.
I see you stand like greyhounds in the slips,
Straining upon the start. The game's afoot:
Follow your spirit, and upon this charge
Cry 'God for Harry, England, and Saint George!'

'Well I'll be jiggered,' the Englishman says.

Wang inclines his head and smiles. 'Jiggered' is not a term with which he is familiar, and he doesn't want to lose the advantage he has so suddenly gained.

'You don't happen to know it in French too, do you?'

'*Le gibier se prépare. Suivez donc votre ardeur et quand vous chargerez—*'

'Stop, stop! I get the picture! Now look,' the Englishman says, furiously scribbling something on the paper in front of him,

'I can promise nothing, but if you leave your details here, I will make some enquiries and contact you directly.'

'You have been most understanding,' Wang replies in English, 'and it has been a pleasure to make your acquaintance.'

The Englishman looks as if he is going to reply but finally just waves him out of the room without another word.

Wang lives in a state of nervous tension as he waits for a decision from the recruiting office. Every morning he checks his post and his 'box of rubbish', as Rong Meifan called it. Now that he is alone, he finds comfort and distraction in simple repetitive acts—rolling his spare eyeball from one palm to the other, unfolding faded magazine articles, re-reading outdated advertisements and pages ripped from books whose plots he can no longer remember.

When he has exhausted the words on their ephemeral pages, or they have exhausted him, he turns to his collection of maps, tracing continents with his fingers and journeying vicariously through the power of sight. He ditches the few Chinese maps he has kept in the bottom of the box and pores over western ones instead, maps that place Europe or America at the centre, that displace the Middle Kingdom to the bottom right corner, where, merging with Indo-China, Sumatra and Siam, it becomes no more than an exotic curiosity.

The mere act of looking seems to unblock other channels—remapping the world is, for Wang, a deeply poetic experience. Poems that he committed to memory years earlier return with fresh vigour, until he floats crane-like above the reach of language. The only sound that is capable of rousing him from this catatonic state is the thud of the street door, a sound that ought to announce the arrival of the yearned for telegram, but which, day after relentless day, is a sign of nothing more than a Beijinger rushing out to work or returning with a flurry. Time flows, Mr Davis once told him, but Wang thinks that it swirls, with a fixed centre that can be perceived only by those outside the rush and pull of motion.

When a telegram finally arrives, it throws him into a place where disturbance is all, where the gravitational pull of time has no meaning, but the message it gives is not the one he has been expecting. His mother has died, and he is required to return to Shanghai.

Huddled in his seat on the Shanghai train, Wang is grateful for the cold which keeps him from thinking or feeling. Every time the train stops, moisture condenses on the axles, forming icicles which faceless railway workers scrape away as he sits and watches. Although he refuses to admit it, he knows that he is an alien presence in the fleeting landscape, but what confronts him inside the train is no easier to make sense of than what he sees outside.

Though he has not wholly discarded his republican views, he recoils from the poverty he finds onboard—chickens in baskets, sacks of turnips, peasants sprawled across their goods. Walking to the restaurant car, he struggles past suitcases, boxes of pickled vegetables, and bottles of *baijiu*, but however hard he tries to clear a space in his mind he finds it difficult to wrestle his thoughts into order. For years he has been an exile in his own country, but now, as he watches waves of people beat against the implacable rocks of his grief, guilt and loneliness, he thinks that even exiles are more rooted than he. He remembers being told that when cities and hopes collide it is always hopes that are destroyed. He remembers and tries hard to forget.

By the time he reaches Shanghai the whole family has gathered. Save for a cursory greeting, his father refuses to talk to him—Wang has the impression that he is being blamed for his mother's death or, at least, for being away when it happened—and the silence that lies between them is thick and impenetrable. Nevertheless, he behaves as he is expected to behave, goes where he is expected to go, and follows the path of the dutiful son. His mother has gone, but she has been gone for years, ever since she allowed her husband to send him to the School of Foreign

Languages, ever since she abandoned him to the influence of others.

He tries to recall the years of comfort, the times when it was only natural that he should turn to her warm embrace when all other comforts failed, when he longed for her stories of rural Shandong, when, reaching further back, he was cradled in milk and warmth, with food, cuddles, and wiped tears. But he cannot touch the dead past. Instead, he finds himself confronted by a distant father who expects nothing more than unthinking obedience to pseudo-feudal traditions. Torn between repugnance for these effete traditions and disgust at his father's hypocrisy, he nurses his grievance, keeps his mouth shut, and follows the hollow customs that are forced upon him.

A tent has been erected in the yard for the coffin, and gifts of cloth are already hanging from the rooftop. Like all his other relatives, Wang wears a headband and outer garments made of hemp, but to him they feel like the clothes of the dead. He tries to explain to an uncle why he has rid himself of his queue, but such is the old man's incomprehension that he gives up and resolves to do what he has to do in silence. The spirit tablet already having been prepared, he joins in the opening of the altar ritual without another word. It is difficult, though, standing in front of Dizang, god of the underworld, and listening to the musicians' long, tuneless drone. It is hard to act as he is expected to act while dusk falls and the kitchen is ritually pacified. He accepts tea when it is brought to him and picks at the simple meal of *doufu*, vegetables and bread, but all the while he wishes that he were back in Beijing where the air is not sodden with the sea's damp or infected by its dank smell.

Bidding farewell to his mother's spirit, he kowtows to the coffin and burns paper money along with the rest of his relations, but, however hard he tries to concentrate on his loss, on the mother who gave him life, he cannot escape the conviction that he is taking part in a dreadful superstition, a superstition presided over by the father who first encouraged him to rid himself of such feudal relics. He walks in the rain and feels a deeper cold penetrate him, a chill that will not be driven off by strong fire or the power of a metal stove. As soon as he can, he slips away into the darkness.

The next few days are no easier. During the burial procession he takes the soul tablet and soul banner and, kowtowing every few minutes, follows the coffin to its palanquin. Once he has watched it being loaded into position, he is held up by his father and his first uncle, as though unable to support himself in his distress, and slowly, so slowly he cannot imagine how they will ever reach their destination, they make their way to the family's plot in a cemetery further along the coast. He is not sure which is worse— the ritual wailing from the women in the cart who bring up the back of the procession, or his father's tears—but he does what he has to do to ensure that his mother's spirit is safely dismissed. Then, disregarding all further expectations and ignoring what is generally regarded as seemly, he leaves his angry family behind and returns to the station, knowing that he has to get back to Beijing, that he has to collect his escape pass from the country.

Chapter 8

To the astonishment of the old woman who is sweeping the stairs, Wang sinks down onto his knees as he reads the one letter he finds in his mailbox on his return—a letter written in English, a letter that re-establishes time and restores the familiar world. He is to be a translator with the Chinese Labour Corps and is to report to the recruiting sergeant at Qingdao by the end of the month. Crying with joy, he gives the startled cleaner a hug and rushes into the street but, even as he throws himself into the welter of traffic, he knows that he is utterly alone, that there is no one with whom he can share his news.

Nonetheless, as he struggles to pack up his Chinese life, Wang drives his family from his mind. He sends a letter to Shanghai, outlining his success and expressing his hope that his father will be proud of what he is about to achieve for their country, and then, not knowing how easy it will be to find replacement eyeballs in France, pulls out his grey drawstring bag and pays a return visit to Beijing's best, and most expensive, oculist.

Shopping for eyes has become almost as familiar as shopping for clothes, but he cannot help but think that this time must be different—so different, in fact, that when the white-jacketed, short-sighted old man asks him whether he wants the usual, he rolls the blue and brown balls he has been offered in his hand and shakes his head.

'I'll take two blue ones instead,' he says.

As he trudges back to his lodgings, he senses that the city has battled on without him. Rickshaws, bicycles and pedestrians pound the streets like blinkered racehorses intent only on the next fence. Feeling in his pocket for the letter he tried earlier to dash off with a note of disdain, he turns up the side road he has spent the last few months avoiding and, keeping his head down, delivers his simple farewell to Rong Meifan's house. Then, spurning the lingering glance, the final farewell to his adopted city, he collects his few belongings and takes the night train to Qingdao.

He arrives as a sea mist is infiltrating the city and choking the remnants of its Germanic grandeur—a red brick post office on the sea front, a church's steeple on the hillside, a distant villa where the city ends and the view begins. He is met at the British legation's headquarters by a cheerful former missionary.

'Weijun Wang? Ah yes, here it is. We're sending you to Weihaiwei. It's a great place—looks like a cross between an industrial plant and a prison camp. Roberts here is just about to take some other chap so you might as well hop in with him.'

He introduces Wang to Second Lieutenant Roberts then shakes his hand and wishes him all the luck in the world. Roberts throws Wang's pack into the car he has been leaning against and swings himself into the driver's seat. Wang pulls a back door open and slides in alongside a nervous-looking southerner who tells him that his name is Fan and that he too is an interpreter.

'I'm glad you two are here,' Roberts says as they pull out into the street. 'Don't speak any Chinese myself to speak of. The best officers don't.'

Fan gets his dictionary out and starts scribbling notes.

'You see, in the army there has to be an unbridgeable gulf between an officer and his men. Not that you're joining the army as such. Don't get me wrong—all these silly rumours about coolies being sent off to fight on the western front are just a load of codswallop.'

'Excuse me, sir,' Fan politely interrupts as they hit a pothole. 'How do you spell codswallop?'

'Cods and wallop. But you won't find it in that dictionary

of yours. A dictionary's one thing—really knowing the lingo's another.'

'Lingo?' Fan asks.

'The language, the language! An officer's got to understand his men, of course he does. But it's a basic sympathy that's required. There's no place for pals in the army. No room for conversations. The only Chinese an officer needs is *yi*, *er*, *san* and *lizheng*. That usually does the job. For all the rest, that's where you lot come in. The nitty gritty, the details, the letters home, the petty complaints. We leave all that to you while we deal with the real business of war.'

As Fan writes 'nitty gritty' on his pad, Wang looks out at the mountainous Shandong countryside. He feels out of place. He is so used to living in the city that he cannot stretch his imagination wide enough to take in the long view, to see the rough and tumble of the landscape. Having been brought up in Shanghai and having lived in Beijing, the countryside through which they are now driving is almost wholly alien to him; he has no experience or understanding of this liminal space where sea and mountains meet in an explosion of the sublime. Aware suddenly that these might be the last weeks he ever spends in his homeland, he watches as one battered village after another is dragged in and out of view. As Roberts talks, he thinks about his mother and about death. Somehow he has never connected what he is about to do with the notion that he might die. Both the British and the Chinese authorities have gone to such lengths to reassure the public that the Chinese Labour Corps will not be working in the front line, that the labourers are not soldiers, that it has scarcely occurred to him that there might be any risk involved in his great adventure.

'I'm not one of those little Englanders who subscribes to fashionable views about this country of yours,' Roberts is saying. 'I have no truck with the idea that both Cain and coolies were murderers from the beginning. No, there's a strange nobility about most coolies, as well as a simplicity and openness that I've come to appreciate. I expect you chaps, with all your education, know about as much of the coolie as I once did, but I'm sure you'll come to feel the same way too.'

As the road cuts back towards the coast and the mountains seem to fall directly into the sea, Wang struggles to keep his thoughts from turning towards the old gods who are shrouded on the hill tops, sacred in the mist, but forcing them from his mind, he finds himself thinking about Rong Meifan instead. Roberts and Fan, by contrast, seem entirely oblivious to the world around them. The car is all. That and the shallow words the Englishman spews into the empty air.

It is an immense relief when they eventually arrive at the training camp which is tucked away in its own protective valley not far from the sea, even though it is, as Wang has been warned, a grim place. There is no Germanic solidity here and no Chinese gracefulness, only grey prefabrication. A few nondescript buildings huddle around a central parade ground where a sea wind buffets the spindly trees.

'Good morning, sir,' Roberts says, as a broad-shouldered man in a western suit steps out of a battered building by the entrance to greet them. 'May I introduce the interpreters, fresh from their journey and ready to muck in?'

'Very good, Roberts. Stand easy.' He turns to the two interpreters. 'We're frightfully pleased you're here. I can't tell you how much I've missed having top-notch translators, ones who can actually speak the language. You can speak the language, can't you?'

Wang and Fan confirm that they can.

'Well, that's a start. Come on then, let's show you around.'

He starts walking before he has finished speaking, leaving the two interpreters to jog after him. Roberts gives a quick wave of the hand, jumps back into the car, and speeds off.

'Should have said who I am, I suppose,' the broad-shouldered man says as he walks. 'The name's Maxwell, Lieutenant Maxwell, and I'm in charge here. For the time being anyway. But I can tell you, I'm as keen to get going as you are. For a start, we might actually be given a bloody uniform when we get to France.'

He marches them round a dormitory block that is sparse to the point of emptiness and points out where the officer's mess is, while explaining the history of the camp and the job he expects them to do. Every now and again he stops in his tracks, throws out a question, and waits until either Wang or Fan gives a decent response. Then, with a quick glance at his watch, he comes to an abrupt halt and claps Wang on the shoulder.

'You'll do,' he says. 'Both of you, though you'll have to speak up a bit, Fan, if you're going to make yourself heard over the bloody rabble we have to put up with here.'

'Yes, sir,' Fan mutters.

Maxwell looks at his watch again. 'But enough of my chuntering. I mustn't keep you from the formalities or I won't hear the last of it from the old women in admin. Line up over there for your medical, bath and haircut, and then you can get started.'

Fan bows and rushes off.

'Yes, sir,' Wang says and stays where he is.

Maxwell looks at him quizzically. 'Well run along then.'

Wang doesn't move. 'This medical, sir, it's—'

'It's a damned nuisance, I know, but it won't be a problem,' Maxwell interrupts. 'You educated fellows are almost always in tip-top physical condition. It's these coolies we have to worry about. You'd think the outdoor life would do them good, but they seem to pick up every damned disease known to the medical profession, and a good few that have passed them by. And that's without even taking the opium smokers into account. It's a miracle we end up with any damned recruits at all.'

Wang feels numb. 'I am sure you do a very thorough job, sir,' he says.

'Oh, it's thorough all right. Just don't be surprised when old McKay starts poking you about below decks. I'm not sure I fancy all those needles and tigers' teeth you fellows go in for, but

86

when you see what McKay's got up his sleeve you've got to wonder what's the more unpleasant.'

'I ... the problem is, sir ...' Wang says before finally losing the power of speech.

'Come on, man, what is it?'

Wang closes his eyes and recalls all he has suffered—the mockery of small children, the demands of his parents, the slow taunts of the past. He looks down at the dusty parade ground and tries to shut out the voices that hector him from every side. When he opens his eyes he sees Lieutenant Maxwell still staring at him so, with a sigh, he pops out his eyeball and holds it in his palm for the officer to inspect.

Maxwell leans forward and peers at it. Then he throws back his head and laughs.

'Well, there's a thing,' he says.

He strokes his chin and peers at Wang as if to check the veracity of the trick. Then he picks the eyeball up, twirls it in his hand, and clears his throat.

'We'd better not let the pettifoggers in there know what's what or they'll start quoting some bloody regulation or other. I'll just have a quiet word with the chief medical officer, and we'll have you through on the nod, all right? It's your voice we need, not your bloody eyeballs.'

'That's very kind, sir.'

'Just make sure you don't mutter like Fan there when you're talking to me, that's all,' Maxwell barks, 'or I'll change my bloody mind.'

He hands the enamel ball back and marches off without a backward glance.

Though he is spared the medical, Wang cannot escape a bath or a haircut. Ordered to strip naked, he sits in a chair while one of his countrymen, who is twirling a razor and a pair of scissors, throws a grimy white sheet around his neck and wordlessly removes what remains of his hair, nicking his scalp in two or three places as he does so.

'There's your first war wound,' he says. 'Now get out of my chair. I've got dozens more to do before I finish this evening.'

As Wang wipes a trickle of blood from his face, he notices a pile of queues at the barber's feet and feels a curious sense of nostalgia. Having taken weeks to steel himself to the act of rebellion that the loss of his queue represented, he discovers that scores, if not hundreds, of his countrymen are losing theirs without a moment's thought. One of the labourers, rising from another chair, picks up his severed queue and holds it out in front of him as if seeing it for the first time.

'Just look at that,' he says. 'I look like one of the white devils now.'

Wang has no chance to disillusion him because an orderly pushes him in the direction of a giant vat of hot water where half a dozen men are washing themselves clean of what appears to be half the Shandong countryside. Taking a group bath is not a prospect that fills him with a great deal of enthusiasm but, when the orderly encourages him with a shove, he climbs slowly into the vat, surmising that the alternative—standing naked and bleeding in the middle of the draughty room—is less pleasant than contact with the labourers he has come to help.

Emerging from the bath, he is handed a scratchy towel and a pile of clothes which are evidently meant to do service as a uniform until he collects the regulation one in Europe. He prods doubtfully at a blue padded jacket, a pair of stained trousers and a dark brown raincoat, before being pointed in the direction of a pile of shoes, most of which seem to be the same large size. He tries to find some that fit but, under pressure from one of the orderlies, grabs the nearest pair and resolves to swap them later if necessary.

Hobbling from the room, he is directed towards a wooden table, behind which is seated a British officer—the first he has seen since Lieutenant Maxwell wandered off—and a man Wang takes to be a translator. When he reaches the front of the line, a Chinese orderly clamps a brass identification tag onto his wrist and passes him onto the officer.

'Name?' the officer demands.

'*Xing shenme?*' the translator repeats.

'You're a translator?' Wang asks him.

'Name?' the officer repeats, this time with a note of irritation in his voice.

'*Xing shenme?*' the translator repeats.

'I'm an interpreter too,' Wang replies in Chinese.

'What's the problem here?' the officer interrupts. 'Does he know his own name or not?'

Wang shifts into English. 'My name is Wang Weijun. My address is Shanghai, 83a, *Da Ma Lu*. And, I warrant, I need the services of this translator no more than you.'

The officer stares at him for a few seconds. 'In that case, we might get this done in a decent amount of time for a change. Date of birth?'

'The fourteenth day of the First Moon in the year of *Renchen*.'

The officer looks up again. 'Don't get cocky with me, sonny,' he says.

Wang pauses to ensure he retains the upper hand. 'February the twelfth, 1892, sir.'

'Next of kin?'

'Wang Zhebu.'

'Put your thumbs in the ink.'

'You may already have worked it out for yourself, sir, but I am capable of signing my own name.'

'Put your thumbs in the ink.'

After another confrontational pause, Wang does so.

'I'm not wholly convinced you and I are going to get along, Wang.'

'I am sure I will be able to do you future service, sir,' Wang replies, inclining his head.

'That's what you're paid to do, buddy, so don't you bloody well forget it.'

Over the next two weeks, Wang grows used to the camp's routine. He spends most of his time drilling and finds, to his surprise, that he enjoys the discipline. He comes quickly to appreciate all the camp's rituals, including the wholly useless translation work that he is given to do. Caught in a place that is neither wholly Chinese nor wholly British, he keeps himself to himself as much as he can and reads to stave off boredom. Sharing a dormitory with a translator from Luoyang who, despite his profession, is uncommunicative to the point of sullenness, he spends such free time as he is able to garner attempting to learn the language of the army. Until he arrived in Weihaiwei, his knowledge of western warfare was based almost entirely on Shakespeare—if the war had been fought by tribunes in Rome he would have been the happiest of interpreters—which means that he has now to work his way through every handbook he can find to enlarge his working military vocabulary.

He is pacing the parade ground with a manual in his hands, declaiming each tricky word to the distant Shandong mountains, when he is confronted by one of the more talkative British officers.

'What the devil are you doing, Wang?'

Wang looks up from his book to see Captain Seymour, a former accountant, looking at him with what appears to be a mixture of amusement and bemusement.

'Learning some vocabulary, sir.'

'Aren't there more comfortable places to study?'

'More comfortable, but not quieter, sir.'

'A fair point, Wang. Mind if I walk with you?'

Having little choice in the matter, Wang lets Seymour distract him from his vocabulary building. As grasshoppers creak and a dog barks at a sentry, Seymour talks about Shanghai, about books of which Wang has never heard, and about his hopes for a new China. It isn't clear whether Wang is expected to join in or not, so he keeps quiet until Seymour starts quoting Chinese poetry.

'You know the poetry of Li Yu, sir?'

'A little,' Seymour admits. 'Just a few anthologised pieces. Li Yu made a particular impression.'

'I didn't know that Englishmen read our poetry.'

'Most don't,' Seymour says. 'And even if they did they wouldn't understand a bloody word of it.'

Wang smiles, thinking of the Chinese he has been translating for. He can't imagine any of them reading Li Yu's poetry either. They are more interested in the state of the harvest, the amount of money they can extract from the Europeans, and the number of concubines they can procure in France.

As Seymour continues to enthuse, Wang senses that his time at Weihaiwei has the potential to be more than an interruption in the business of life. The Europe of which he has spent so long dreaming is not being realised in the cursory conversations he has extracted from the few British officers who can bear speaking to him, but it takes only a few minutes of listening to realise that Seymour is as unfulfilled as Wang. He has no interest in the conversations about football, commissions, and wives that swill around the mess. He too is longing for action in some other foreign field.

'You'd be surprised how much we have in common,' Seymour tells him. 'My fellow officers are forever complaining about the coolies' gambling habits, but they complain over games of poker. We smoke and drink as much as any of your lot, and I've no doubt, from what some of the others say, that we share a taste for the same women too.'

'I couldn't say what taste the labourers have in women,' Wang replies, 'but it is true that wherever soldiers or coolies congregate there is bound to be a plentiful supply of both nicotine and alcohol.'

'And praise the Lord for that, I say,' Seymour grins. 'But praise the Lord too for a literary companion. If I have to hear one more account of Jones's amatory conquests I'm not going to be responsible for my actions.'

They spend two months in the camp at Weihaiwei, the labourers drilling, gambling, and occasionally trying to break out, the interpreters ambling between jobs, and the British largely keeping to themselves. The European war seems as it is—a long way off. Wang and Seymour meet for what the Englishman insists on calling 'a literary chat' whenever they can, but time still passes slowly. There is only so much boredom a mind prepared for military action can bear, and the days drag slow with waiting.

Even so, when the movement order finally comes, Wang feels divided—part of him would like to stay in Weihaiwei with Seymour and part of him is desperate to get to where the action really is. Finding a place by the outer fence, he stares out at the alien countryside.

'It has a bleak sort of beauty about it, I suppose.'

Wang turns to find Seymour standing behind him.

'Here, I've got a present for you, Wang.' He pulls an eye patch and a toy parrot out of his bag. 'You might need it on the journey,' he explains.

Wang laughs. 'You've got a month at sea to show me how it works.'

'I'm afraid not, old chap. They've divided us into different companies and my lot's got to wait for the next ship. It's a right bugger, but there it is.'

Wang tries to speak but he cannot.

'Don't worry, old fellow,' Seymour says, clapping him on the back. 'We'll all get to France soon enough, and then we'll probably wish we were back here.'

'I find that very hard to believe,' Wang replies.

'Well, we shall see. In the meantime, you've got to keep your pecker up. You've an important job of work to do.'

Wang nods, unconvinced that he will ever fully master the strange, mongrel language Seymour and the other officers speak.

'And you've got to report to Maxwell. He's in a terrible mood, so if I were you I'd agree with whatever he says before he's finished saying it.'

Walking away, he throws out one last comment which Wang struggles to catch.

'If you come across any decent poetry on your travels, make

a note of it, because I'm going to come bothering you as soon as we're back in China.'

Returning to his quarters, Wang stacks his army-issue provisions and tries to decide what else to stuff into his knapsack, the only bag he is allowed to take with him to Europe. As an interpreter, he is a man apart, with no need of tools or weapons. A dictionary and a glaringly inaccurate glossary of British military vocabulary are all he is required to bring—a uniform, he hopes, will be waiting for him in France.

Slumping onto his bed, he pulls out his wooden box and flicks through the maps, torn pages, and cigarette cards. If these fragments are meant to root him in China, if they represent the quintessence of five thousand years of civilisation, then they have failed in their task. Quintessence of dust is closer to the mark, he thinks bitterly, seeing the box's contents for the first time as the few others who know of their existence see them—as rubbish, waste, symptoms of a diseased mind. Bundling them back into what is no longer a box but a coffin, he resolves to bury them or throw them into the sea, whichever is easier.

His grey drawstring bag of eyeballs is another matter. Briefly he considers adding it to the bonfire of his personal vanities but quickly rejects the idea and pushes the bag into the bottom of the knapsack. If anything of his Chinese past is to accompany him to the West then it has to be these fragile, man-made balls.

Chapter 9

During his time at Weihaiwei, Wang is lulled into believing that his knowledge of idiomatic English and his education have set him apart from the rest of the Chinese Labour Corps, but it takes only a day at sea and a terrible bout of seasickness to remind him how vulnerable he is. There is only so much a knowledge of English can do for a man when he is retching at the start of a long ocean crossing. For the first four days of their journey across the East China Sea he lies on his bunk feeling sorry for himself, without even a pillow to prop up his head. A canvas-covered slab of cork, which a gruff labourer tells him is his life-belt, is all he has. He watches the labourers strip the strings from theirs and put them to better use as washing lines, but he leaves his attached—he may not fear death in France, but he has no desire to die at sea.

'Ah, there you are at last, Wang,' Maxwell booms, when he eventually clambers up on deck. 'Where the hell have you been?'

Wang tries to stand to attention, but his legs are weak; the ship is swaying in a most alarming fashion.

'I am terribly sorry, sir. I have been confined to quarters with a bout of sea-illness.'

'Good God, man, you've had days to get over that. It's time to get to work.'

As he attempts to translate for the lieutenant, it becomes increasingly clear just how far Wang's world has been disturbed. On the *Empress of Russia* he enjoys none of the privileges he had in the camp at Weihaiwei. He is just one more Chinaman, his only distinction being that he is still required to work while most of his three thousand travelling companions lie on their bunks, eating nuts, playing cards, and singing Beijing opera arias as they cross the Pacific. When he is released from his translating duties he joins his shipmates in games of *Bashi Fen* and swaps stories from the *Laozhai Zhiyi*. Some of the labourers even listen to his tales from Shakespeare, but he can never hold their attention for long, so he often throws in a few card tricks to keep them on his side.

He never grows used to the terrible seasickness or the inadequate conditions on the ship. Since they never have enough water for washing, the labourers resort to tapping the scupper hydrants which are used for scouring the deck, and when the galleys fail to provide hot water for tea, they draw boiling water from the winches' cylinder boxes. Worse than the barely adequate provisions are the daily humiliations they are forced to witness—a Sichuanese labourer being beaten with a stick for smoking in the hold, one of the card-players having a refuse barrel strapped to his back for littering the floor, a labourer from Shanghai being handcuffed to a winch for stealing peanuts from the orderly room. Occasionally Wang tries to intervene, but the punishments are never changed. Lying alone in his bunk, with his eyeballs tucked underneath his lifebelt for safekeeping, he seriously doubts his wisdom in signing up.

'One of the labourers has pegged it,' an obviously irate Maxwell announces a few days into the crossing, 'and your lot are kicking up a bit of a fuss about the funeral ceremony. Captain Jones here has tried to reason with them, but matters seem to have come to a head. I don't know if it's his Chinese or their obduracy. Anyway, we need you to get along there, find out what's annoying them, and calm them down. I don't want to have to get heavy at this stage of the voyage.'

'I will do my best, sir,' Wang replies.

'I should damned well think so,' Maxwell says.

Wang finds the dead labourer and a group of his angry friends four floors below deck. The dead man is lying in an open-topped coffin, and a young man with a Jiangsu accent is the mourners' spokesman. Wang has Captain Jones to keep guard, but the Englishman's presence only serves to exacerbate the surging sense of grievance that powers towards them as they approach.

'Look what they've done to my uncle,' the angry young man shouts.

Wang opens his mouth to speak but, realising that he is about to be shouted down, clamps it quickly shut again.

'You need to tell our complaint to the foreign devils!' the young man demands.

'I will deliver any message when I know what the message is,' Wang replies.

The young man waves his hand to quieten the others.

'I am Jian Yushan and this is my second uncle. We were recruited together in Wuxi and came on board this death ship together too.'

'What happened to him?' Wang asks.

'Have a look for yourself,' Jian Yushan replies, drawing the shroud from his kinsman's face.

Wang understands the brutal realities of existence, but he hasn't looked so closely at a dead man before. Much of his face is dented out of recognition and the rest is still covered in blood. Looking down at the dead man's hands, Wang sees that, though they have been laid across his chest, they are clenched as though in anger.

'How did this happen?' he asks quietly.

'He fell from his bunk.'

'So it was an accident.'

'An accident!' Jian Yushan shouts. 'Look where the foreign devils made him sleep—on a flimsy piece of wood that wasn't even protected from the deck above.' He points to a broken piece of board hanging loose near the lattice ceiling. 'He lay on his bed at night and woke up covered with peanut shells, orange peel and rat shit. Until last night when the bed caved in and he was thrown to the floor.'

'He hit his head on the side on the way down,' another man interjects.

'On the way down and at the bottom.'

Wang nods slowly. He does not trust himself to say anything.

'So what are you going to do about it?' Jian Yushan says.

'I will take your complaint to the relevant authorities,' he replies.

'That's not good enough. The foreign devils can't bring Second Uncle back to life, but they can at least ensure that he's buried alongside his ancestors.'

'They want us to do what?' Maxwell asks incredulously when Wang reports back. 'Let me get this right—they want us to turn the ship around?'

'They want him sent back, sir.'

'We're in the middle of the bloody Pacific.'

'If I'm not mistaken, sir, we are close to the coast of Japan.'

'Don't try it on with me, Wang.'

'I was merely suggesting, sir, that it might well be possible to keep all sides happy in this unhappy dispute by having the body taken home from the nearest Japanese port.'

'And what are we supposed to do when someone dies in the middle of the Pacific?' Maxwell asks. 'Or in Canada? Or in France, for God's sake? We can't requisition a ship for every Johnny Chinaman whose number comes up outside Chinese territorial waters.'

'I am merely commenting on the current case, sir.'

'Well don't. It's impractical, and I simply won't have it. He can be buried at sea like everyone else.'

The man who fell from his bunk is the first to be buried at sea, but he is not the last. Several others fall prey to illness, accidents, or even in one case, Wang suspects, a premeditated attack. Each death provokes an argument, and each time Wang is called upon to interpret, negotiate and pacify.

It is something of a relief, therefore, when after three weeks

97

at sea rumours begin to circulate that they are nearing Canada. Hauling himself onto deck, Wang hangs onto the rails and peers out into the gloom, hoping to be the first to glimpse land. When the shout comes, three thousand men clamber onto deck to savour the sight.

'And jocund day stands tiptoe on the misty mountain tops, sir,' Wang bellows to Lieutenant Maxwell, who has come to join him at the rail.

Maxwell looks baffled. 'Jock and who?' he says.

'Jocund day, sir. It's a literary reference.'

Maxwell stares at him. 'You're a funny fish, Wang, and no mistake.'

Disembarkation at William Head takes many hours, and the longer Wang has to wait to get his feet onto solid North American ground the wilder the rumours become. The war is over and they are all to be shipped back home. The Austrians have come to Canada and a battle is imminent. Special trains have been constructed to convey the labourers across the vast Canadian wastelands so that they can pick up a different ship on the far Eastern coast.

Listening in on Maxwell's conversations when he is not called upon to translate, Wang attempts to peel truth from rumour. He establishes that they are to stay on Vancouver Island for as long as it takes *The Empress of Russia* to be reprovisioned, that they are to travel south, following the American coast to Panama, where they will strike out across the Atlantic for Liverpool. In the meantime, there is work to be done. A unit is moved to the other side of the river, a section of woodland is cleared, labourers are drilled in their thousands, orders are given, notices are written. Wang scarcely has the opportunity to take in the broad view, the forests, the mountains, the solidity of the West, with all the word work he is given to do.

'You've got to be careful, Wang,' Maxwell tells him on their third evening in the country. The sun is disappearing massively over the sound and the British are lounging around a tea urn, watching the waters turn red. 'I don't want you getting mournful on us once we set sail again.'

'Why would I do that, sir?' Wang asks, surprised. He picks up an enamel mug and shifts it from hand to hand.

'I've seen it before, Wang. Men like you—educated Chinese—become overactive when we're on the move. Rushing here and there, chopping and changing, making yourself useful. But it's a long journey and, from what I hear, it's going to be a long war. You've got to take it steady. Go slow so you can go strong.'

'Your advice is always appreciated, sir.'

'I don't see you reading so much these days, Wang. Get yourself a good book. It'll help take your mind off the war.'

'Well, I'll do my best, sir,' Wang replies with some regret, 'but there's not a ready supply of books around here.'

'I suppose not,' Maxwell agrees, draining the rest of his tea in a hurried gulp. 'I'll see what I can do.'

Wang very much doubts that he will ever be afflicted by mournfulness, given the intensity of his workload and the European prize that has been dangled in front of him. But when the movement order comes and thousands of men have to be packed back onto the ship, a sliver of doubt splits expectation and desire. As they leave Canada behind and follow the coast southwards, Wang stands at the rail and tries to make out the realities he has only ever read or dreamt about—the landscape of Thoreau and Twain, cities built with the best western technology, the unrestrained fashions of a country that has long learnt to be free—but all he can see is a blur of coastline, smeared across the surface of the waves.

Below decks, the atmosphere is muted. The ebullience of their Pacific journey has dissipated, leaving behind shorter tempers and emptier hearts. Feeling less inclined to while away his time in card games or to stare at the featureless sea, Wang turns inwards. The company he finds there being uncongenial, he decides to take up Maxwell's advice. He fishes his copy of *Henry V* out of his backpack and flicks listlessly through the first act, but

99

words seem a poor substitute for the reality he is yet to reach. When Maxwell summons him for some routine translation work, he takes the opportunity to ask for something else to read.

'Well, you could try this, I suppose,' Maxwell suggests hesitantly. 'I've been re-reading it.' He hands over a battered copy of *David Copperfield*. 'It reminds me of my childhood.'

Wang turns it over in his hands, handling it with the reverence due to an object of great age.

'Thank you very much, sir.'

'You might want to keep your eye in. Translate it into Chinese and then back into English. You know, see how Dickensian you can really be.' He takes the book back and flicks through the pages. 'Here's a bit I like: *Early in the morning, I sauntered through the dear old tranquil streets, and again mingled with the shadows of the venerable gateways and churches. The rooks were sailing about the Cathedral towers; and the towers themselves, overlooking many a long, unaltered mile of the rich country and its pleasant streams, were cutting the bright morning air, as if there was no such thing as change on earth.* That's what we're fighting for, Wang. That's what we're fighting for.'

Handing the book back, he walks off, leaving Wang alone with Dickens, David Copperfield, and Mr Micawber.

Finding a quiet place to work becomes increasingly difficult as the *Empress of Russia* steams south. The heat and the rumoured proximity of Europe bring labourers in their hundreds onto the deck, where they argue, gamble and fight. Clutching Maxwell's precious book and his own notebook close to his chest to prevent either of them from being lost, Wang walks the deck until he finds a place where he can rest his back against the bulkhead. Gathering his concentration, he works slowly, turning Dickens, phrase by careful phrase, into something worthy of Cao Xueqin or even Li Bai, keeping the balance and curl of the original, or rather transforming it into the precise musicality of his native language. Obsessively, he translates from English into Chinese and then back again, checking a word in the original novel only sporadically until at last the passage takes on an identity of its own, a character derived from Dickens but no longer dependent on him. As he reaches the final phrase of the final version, Wang becomes aware that his muscles have tensed, that his arms are bent as though ready for battle. He stretches them out and watches bemused as the ship resumes its unhurried journey, Chinese labourers and British officers re-emerging from his translator's fog. He hopes Maxwell will appreciate what he has done.

'Here it is, sir,' he announces proudly once he has tracked the officer down. 'My translation of a translation of the passage you liked in *David Copperfield*. I'm not sure who will read it though.'

'No one, I expect,' Maxwell replies breezily. 'But that's not the point really, is it?' He glances briefly at the page Wang has handed him. 'Not bad, not bad, though not a patch on the original.'

'I did the next part too, sir.'

Maxwell looks as though he is about to speak but stifles whatever it was he was going to say.

'I thought it was a very powerful section,' Wang continues. 'I can read it to you, if you like. It sounds better read aloud, I think. The rhetoric is strong.'

Taking Maxwell's struggle to express himself in words as permission to speak, Wang starts reading aloud. '*But when the bells tolled they spoke sadly of change in all things; they told me about old age and my pretty Dora's youth; they spoke about many men who had lived, loved and died without ever growing old, while the ringing of the bells hummed through the Black Prince's corroded armour, like dust in the depths of time, lost in air, as circles are in water.*'

Maxwell turns away. 'Rather cheerless to my way of thinking,' he says. 'Let's stick with the upbeat for the time being, shall we?'

Once through the Panama Canal, Wang rediscovers something of the sense of anticipation the long journey has ripped from his grasp. With Dickens having cleared the ground, he takes up *Henry V* again and half reads, half recites his way through the first two acts. Reading himself back into a state of equilibrium, he calms his mind but cannot control his body—his seasickness has subsided, but the achingly hot days and stifling nights are a constant trial. Unable wholly to reconcile himself to the tedium, the endless lifeboat drills, and the hours spent waiting for the emptiness of the ocean to become transformed by some strange western magic into their long-awaited destination, he tells himself that he is on the brink of some great adventure that will help to define the modern age. But, however much he congratulates himself on his success, he cannot completely overcome the worry that afflicts him.

His fellow travellers grow more restless too. The endless card games break up in petty fights, the interminable speculation becomes increasingly far-fetched, the long wait drags out. Feeling constrained by the talk and the narrow berths, Wang spends more and more time on deck. Attempting to put some darkness between himself and the labourers, he stays out in the open when the weather turns and harries his companions into submission.

One dull night, somewhere in the middle of the Atlantic, as a fierce blast of northern wind pummels him, he reaches into the dark and throws his voice against the elements.

'*Now all the youth of England are on fire,*' he shouts into the emptiness, '*and silken dalliance in the wardrobe lies. Now thrive the armourers, and honour's thought reigns solely in the breast of every man.*'

A labourer emerges from behind one of the ventilation shafts, the tip of his cigarette glowing faintly in the night. He looks curiously at Wang, who thought he was alone, and then disappears. There is nothing else to see. The thud and roar of the sea breaks through the dullness but offers nothing to heighten his sense of anticipation. Wang steadies himself, fixes his attention on an imaginary vanishing point and shouts again.

'*O England! model to thy inward greatness, like little body with a mighty heart, what mightst thou do, that honour would thee do, were all thy children kind and natural!'*

If the labourer is still there, he does not re-emerge. Wang is—and feels—alone, alone with the words of a long-dead Englishman who has helped break, shape and remake him. Saluting him through the spray and through the years, Wang turns away from the sea and climbs back down the ladder towards his berth.

As he draws closer to England, the nation of Shakespeare and Dickens, Wang worries that the reality may not live up to the power of his imagination. He explains his concerns to Fu Shengsan, one of the other translators, but Fu's estimation of the West, it transpires, is so low that the conversation subsides into incomprehension almost as soon as it begins. Seeking out Maxwell, who has grown increasingly irritable in recent days, Wang tries again with no more success.

'The place is a dump,' Maxwell opines. 'At least the bit I come from is. The day I waved the white cliffs goodbye was the day my life began.'

When eventually the clamour for land gives way to an actual sighting of dimmed dock lights, Wang rushes onto deck. Far fewer of his travelling companions join him this time. The more cynical of the British officers suggest that enthusiasm seems to have waned now that hard work is approaching. Wang ignores them all. He is desperate to arrive but is terribly disappointed by what he sees. After travelling for so long, all he can make out of the country of which he has read and dreamt so much are the sounds of disembarkation and a few shaded lights.

'Will we go straight from here to France, sir?' he asks when Maxwell joins him at the rail.

'You haven't thought about the logistics, have you, Wang? We can hardly take the *Empress of Russia* into the Channel for the enemy to take pot shots at. No, it's Liverpool for us and then, when they can arrange trains, it'll be a long haul down to the south coast and then across to France.'

'And how long might that all take, sir?' Wang asks, suddenly hopeful that he might get to stay in England for some substantial length of time.

'Well, with any luck the first trains will depart tonight. Some of us will have to go to the rest camp, of course, but I think it might be worth getting you on a train pronto so you can help establish some order once we get to Shorncliffe or wherever the hell it is they're sending us. I don't rate the chances of the billeting officers when three thousand Chinamen suddenly descend upon them.'

'That's ... that's good news, sir,' Wang replies. 'It will be good to get moving as soon as we can.'

'That's the spirit, Wang,' Maxwell enthuses. 'Up and at 'em, eh?'

It is midnight by the time they are tipped from the ship but, true to his word, Maxwell still arranges for Wang to be packed into the first train to leave. As he waits in line, Wang tries to get a sense of the country, but all he can he see in the darkness are hundreds of men marching unsteadily away from the docks and the enormous railway platform, all he can feel is the cold and an unreasonable sense of having been cheated.

Levering himself into an already-packed carriage, he finds himself separated from everyone he knows. The British have disappeared, and the labourers he is forced to mix with resent having to share their space with one more body. Forcing his way into the heart of the carriage, Wang finds a seat, which he guards jealously for the rest of the journey, watching in some dismay as the floor is gradually covered with fruit peel, nut shells, cigarette butts, matchsticks, saliva, and phlegm. When the train heaves its way slowly out of the station it is still dark, but Wang doesn't dare risk falling asleep. No one leaves the space they have grabbed. Men piss out of the windows or in corners of the carriage. The smell and the noise are overpowering.

As the miles accumulate and daylight comes, Wang tries to peer out of the window but, since the carriage is filled with the dense fog of Kuantung cigarettes, he can see neither the green and pleasant land nor the dark satanic mills. He stares anyway, but, other than the occasional flicker of a station or the smudged outline of a town, there is nothing to be seen. England has become a rumour, a destination that cannot be reached, a country that eludes the outstretched hand.

Jostling his neighbour in a vain attempt to get a clearer view, Wang is drawn back to China. Bleak train journeys from Shanghai to Beijing, from Beijing to Qingdao. His father's hand raised in farewell. He feels an acute jolt of anguish as he turns away from the window. Putting his hand into his pocket to check that his grey drawstring bag of eyeballs is safe, he pulls a couple of balls into his palm and rolls them round and round for reassurance. As the train maintains its rhythmic juddering and he feels the comfort of enamel against skin, he falls asleep where he is hunched. When eventually he wakes up, he sees two blue eyeballs on the floor by his feet and notices, to his irritation, that someone has stolen the laces from his boots.

They reach what he takes to be London late in the evening. As murky countryside gives way to grimy houses, Wang longs to catch a glimpse of Buckingham Palace, the Tower of London, or Westminster Abbey, but all he manages to see is the greyness of a capital overwhelmed by war and, as the train slows, a cavernous and unidentifiable station, where the corps is assigned new overseers who are less friendly and less tolerant than the former missionaries and teachers who travelled with them from China. Hoping that he might track down something more satisfying than the cold coffee and bland sandwiches that have been doled out on the journey south, he longs to get out and revive the circulation in his legs, but an officer who sticks his head briefly into their carriage leaves them in no doubt that everyone is to bloody well stay where they are or they'll have him to answer to. Wang doesn't trouble himself to translate for the others.

The next time a British officer appears in the carriage, Wang tries to engage him in conversation, watched curiously by the labourers who are squatting or sitting where they can, while chewing on what supplies of seeds they have managed to preserve.

'When are we due to arrive at our camp, sir?'

The overseer glances around to check that he hasn't made a mistake, and then calls over his shoulder to a colleague in the doorway of the next carriage.

'Here, Harry, come and have a listen to this. There's a Chink here speaks English like the Duke of Kent.' He looks Wang up and down as if trying to assess the mechanics of the operation and then, when his colleague pushes his way through, tells him to 'say it again'.

'I just wanted to know,' Wang says, more hesitantly this time, 'when the train was likely to arrive at the south coast.'

The second overseer whistles through his teeth. 'You know what? If I could talk like that I'd get myself a bleeding job at Buck House.'

The first man laughs a phlegmy laugh.

Wang looks from one to the other.

'I'm sorry if I wasn't clear,' he says, 'but do you know when we're due to arrive or not, sir?'

'We'll get there when we get there,' the second man says. 'In the meantime I'd get yourself some kip if I was you, otherwise you'll have the whole of South London badgering you for English lessons.'

As the train creaks slowly onwards, over what might conceivably be the Thames, Wang tries to take the overseer's advice but, hunched uncomfortably in his seat among dozens of irascible men, he finds that sleep is as elusive as a straight answer from the English. Sore, cold, and eager to arrive at any destination, he tries to find solace by pulling *Henry V* out of the back rooms of his memory but, even though the words come easily, they have lost their power. It isn't Henry but a solitary Roman, in a country turned alien, who comes to meet him. As he searches for some hint of the easy wonder that the West has always promised, it is

Mark Antony's words that reach out to him—*if any of you have tears, prepare to shed them now.*

When he wakes up several hours later, the train is approaching Shorncliffe. Wiping grime from the carriage window, Wang captures his first glimpse of the English Channel and a mark on the horizon which he thinks must be France. Having slept awkwardly upright, he feels too stiff to be exultant, but the sight of the sea reminds him that he still has one job to do before he starts active service—he must rid himself of the past by tipping the contents of his box of Chinese ephemera into the sea.

Reaching down to unbuckle his backpack, he senses that he is almost free. But, as he pulls the bag towards him, he notices that it is already open, and, plunging his hand inside, he finds that most of the contents have gone. The thief has left his dictionary and his copy of *Henry V* but everything else, including his box, has gone. Even Seymour's parrot and eye-patch have been taken. Throwing himself back into his seat in anger, he feels in his pocket for his grey drawstring bag of eyeballs. It, at least, is still there, the sole reminder of the day his westward journey began, of the moment Zhou Lianke's arrow robbed him of an eye. He keeps it firmly in his grasp. Whatever happens to him in France, he will never let it go.

France, 1917

Chapter 10

A troop train trundles along the northern French coast towards the Chinese Labour Corps' Base Camp at Noyelles, a place where the River Somme spits its dark brown water into the sea. When it comes to a halt, it feels more like a disruption of the natural order than an arrival to the troops onboard; for them journey and destination have merged into one. Having been enclosed, first in the *Empress of Russia* and then in a series of dark, dirty trains, they are overwhelmed by the sheer size of the camp as they pull themselves stiffly out of the carriages and look around.

Horses lumber along a grid of muddy roads, khaki lorries sound impatient horns, work parties march with shovels and picks slung over their shoulders. The hospital alone, into whose grounds the new arrivals are tipped, is spread over twelve acres and has enough beds for fifteen hundred men. Many of the new arrivals are citizens of Shanghai and Beijing, two of the most populous cities on earth, but the sight of so many men brought thousands of miles for so singular a purpose still catches at their throats.

As they line up in a muddy field and wait for medical clearance, they have many concerns, but it is only Wang Weijun who is worried about the lack of an eye. Surrounded by labourers shuffling forward towards two open-sided tents where a group of doctors poke, prod and peer, he dwells on his disability for the first time since leaving China. It is such a small lack, and yet he knows all too well that even such an unimportant absence could send him hurtling back towards the continent he has spent so long trying to leave. When he draws close to the unsmiling Canadian doctor into whose queue he is directed, he stands tall and prepares for a confrontation.

'Trousers!' the doctor orders without looking up.

'I beg your pardon, sir?'

'Drop your trousers.'

Wang looks around to see whether anyone else is affronted by this peremptory demand. Since everyone else is acquiescing, he reluctantly does as he is told. Without saying a word, the doctor lifts Wang's penis with his cane, pokes around in his mouth with a metal probe, prods and taps his chest with a finger then, without prior warning, everts his right eyelid. They both watch as Wang's enamel eyeball falls onto the ground and rolls into a depression. The doctor looks him square in the face for the first time.

'If you'd asked, I could have told you that would happen,' Wang says.

'You're here for a medical and you've only got one bloody eye?' the doctor says, screwing up his face in incredulity.

'I'm here to translate not to keep lookout, sir,' Wang says.

'Don't get funny with me, buster,' the doctor says.

'My surname is Wang and my given name is Weijun,' Wang replies.

'Your what is what?' The doctor has had a long day identifying cases of malignant trachoma and lifting infected scrota with his cane. He is not ready for a coolie who answers back.

'My name is Wang, not "Buster",' Wang explains in clipped English, enunciating perhaps more than is strictly necessary for the occasion. 'I'm here to translate.'

The doctor turns away. 'Jones!' he bawls.

'Sir?'

'Get here double quick. I want an explanation.'

When Jones arrives, he stares at Wang with his mouth open. The enamel eyeball remains where it landed at Wang's feet.

'Jones, who is this joker?'

'This joker, sir?'

'That's what I said, Jones. This one-eyed, dick-brained son of a bitch. Who is he?'

'I believe he's one of the new translators, sir. Lieutenant Maxwell says he seems very good, sir. Better English than most of the officers, sir.'

'He's got one fucking eye.'

'So I see, sir.'

Wang doesn't move. He continues to look straight at Jones as if challenging him to comment on his cavity.

'Get him out of here.'

'Is that really wise, sir? Captain Blyth seemed awfully keen on having a new translator, sir. Said all the others were worse than the bloody colonials, sir, begging your pardon, sir.'

'In that case,' the doctor says, pulling off his gloves and throwing them to the floor, 'he'll have to do the bloody medical himself. I'm finished here.'

Wang watches Jones watch him go and only stoops down to pick up his eyeball when the doctor is completely out of sight.

'I couldn't trouble you for a bowl of water, could I, sir?' he asks.

When Jones tracks Captain Blyth down outside one of the medical huts, he is caught up in conversation with two other medical officers, one British and one Chinese. Wang stands politely to one side and tries not to listen, which is perhaps why it takes him a minute or two to realise, with a start, that they are all speaking Chinese. When Jones eventually manages to catch Blyth's eye, the conversation is broken off, the Chinese doctor walks into the hut, and Blyth walks over to greet them.

'Sorry to keep you, Wang,' he says, thrusting out a hand to greet him. 'I'm afraid once Fell, Xi and I get jawing it takes a coolie with a crowbar to separate us.'

'Once he starts pontificating, he means,' the other man adds, holding out his hand. 'Dr David Fell. Pleased to make your acquaintance.'

113

'You'll get lots of advice over the next few days, Wang,' Captain Blyth says. 'The only piece I'll give you is to ignore everything you hear, especially if it comes from this man here.'

Fell rolls his eyes.

'I will do my best to listen to you both, sir,' Wang replies.

'Spoken with all the grace and tact we've come to expect of the Chinese,' Captain Blyth responds. 'But I'd still ignore him. Now, what's all this I hear about your having one eye?'

Wang shifts uncomfortably onto his other foot. 'Well, the thing is, sir, I lost an eye in a childhood accident, but the recruiting officer at Weihaiwei said it wouldn't get in the way of my work as a translator, sir.'

'Well I didn't like to say, Wang,' Blyth says, 'but your irises do rather stand out, being different colours. Professionally, you seemed very interesting.'

'And now, sir?' Wang asks hesitantly.

'Now, Wang, I realise you simply had a bloody awful optician.'

He looks so fierce for a moment that Wang's shoulders slump. Then the doctor laughs out loud and claps him on the back.

'Don't worry, old chap. I'm not going to have you sent back just because you've had an excision. But trachoma, that's another matter. So let's have a butcher's at that other eye.'

Unnerved by Blyth's choice of words, Wang stands straight while Blyth reaches up and holds his head still with his right hand before everting his left eyelid. Fell leans in close and has a look as well.

'A possible convergent strabismus, but nothing worse than that,' Blyth declares eventually.

'A possible what, sir?'

'A squint, in layman's terms. It may be that you had limited visual acuity in that eye at some point in the past, but I can't see anything that's going to give me great cause for alarm over here. Not when we've got more pressing problems anyway.'

Wang puffs out his cheeks and expels a relieved gust of air.

'Come on,' Blyth says, 'I'll give you a tour of the hospital while Lieutenant Fell here gets back to work. Or starts work, more likely.'

'So long, Wang. I'll catch up with you later when the old misery has bored you to death.'

As Fell gives a cheery wave of the arm and walks off whistling, Blyth leads Wang uphill towards a cluster of huts. A truck rattles past them, throwing up a spume of dirt. A group of mud-spattered labourers strolls along, waving their spades and mattocks in time to their chanting. Several British officers huddle by a hut door, smoking and laughing at what is written on a piece of paper that one of them is holding. They pass a bare-chested chef who is pounding at dough in an old crate. 'Stow Away from Engines and Boilers' it says on the side, but a makeshift earth stove is billowing smoke just a few feet away. The smell of steaming *mianbao* reminds Wang sharply of China, but far from being filled with longing or regret, his heart lifts. He breathes deeply and, remembering the pungency of the ship, gives silent thanks for European air and European space.

'They tell me that your command of English is exceptional,' Blyth says as Wang looks round.

'I do my best, sir.'

'And that your Chinese is pretty good too.'

'That requires less work, sir.'

'Not for me, sadly. But fortunately I got my posting here and so can practise my Chinese morning, noon and night. It pains me to admit it, but Fell's Chinese is far superior to mine. But you're still to ignore him, you hear me?'

'Loud and clear, sir.'

'I work in the ophthalmic department over there, but it's not on the guided tour, I'm afraid. Far too infectious a place for important interpreters like you. We have scores of men in there, though it was worse when we first started. Had whole wards stuffed full of trachomatous patients. A bloody pain in the arse, I can tell you.'

Wang nods politely.

'What I really want you to see is the electric lighting plant over here. It was all kerosene lamps when I arrived.'

Lighting plants are not of great interest to Wang, but it soon becomes apparent that Blyth's enthusiasms are rather unconventional. After the power plant, he takes Wang to see the water tanks and the pagoda, missing out the parade ground and the mess hut altogether.

'Nothing to do with me,' Blyth says when they reach the pagoda that straddles the camp's main entrance. 'It's our Chinese carpenters' pride and joy, made while they were recuperating from their injuries. It doubles up as fire station and clock tower. Who would have thought it, eh? That gong is struck for every hour of the day. Keeps me awake when I'm trying to get a bit of shut-eye between shifts. Bloody impressive, but bloody annoying too.'

He leads Wang to the camp's Chinese shrine, a simple affair where two men are burning incense. When Wang murmurs tactfully about the crudely painted door gods, Blyth seems pleased and leads him onto a compound where half a dozen men are bundling brushwood. One of them is sitting on the ground with a crutch next to him, but the others all look bodily sound.

'In here,' Blyth says, leading him into a well-equipped workshop. Four Chinese carpenters who are clearly used to being put on show for visitors salute him as he walks in.

'What are you working on today, Ling?' Blyth asks.

'Some more cabinets for the wards, sir,' one of the carpenters replies with a thick Hunanese accent. Wang tries not to stare at the man's wooden leg.

'Any hands to show our new interpreter here?'

'There's a couple on that table over there, sir. They still need a bit of smoothing off, though.'

Blyth turns to Wang with a mock serious look on his face.

'I'm sure he'll understand, won't you, Wang?'

'Of course, sir,' he replies, though he has no idea what Blyth is talking about.

Blyth takes him to the table, picks up a wooden model of a hand—a perfectly formed replica—and twirls it as Wang saw some of the officers do in Weihaiwei when they were poured a glass of wine.

'Just look at that!' he says. 'Exquisitely detailed, if a touch rough about the knuckles.' He puts it down and picks up another. 'But look at this one,' he says with a sense of awe in his voice. 'It's a little beauty.'

He pulls a lever at the base and, to Wang's surprise, the thumb moves. He does it again and again until the Hunanese carpenter begins to look twitchy.

'Isn't it wonderful?'

'Yes, sir.'

Rather reluctantly, Blyth puts the hand down, claps the carpenter on the back and leads Wang out.

'This isn't our only hospital, you know,' Blyth says. 'We have others in Calais, Boulogne, Dieppe and Rouen. That's where they make all our artificial legs. Glorious limbs they are too, but somehow I don't feel the same affection for them as I do for the hands we manufacture here. Men come to us from all over France, do you know that? Some have been gassed, some have been shot, and some are peppered with fragments of shell. But we see plenty more who have been involved in accidents. A few months ago we treated a man who'd been hit by a lorry while repairing the roads near Dunkerque. His pelvis was fractured in four places. The bone protruded through the skin near the top of his thigh, and, when we operated, we discovered that the urethra and all his perineal muscles were lacerated. We put him back together again, but then he developed general peritonitis so we performed a laparotomy and drained the purulent fluid from the peritoneal cavity. Net result—he's fit as a fiddle and back at work.'

Wang hasn't understood a word but does his best to sound impressed.

'Or let's take another example. A couple of months ago a patient was transferred to us from one of the field hospitals. He'd been caught in a revolving lathe and thrown across the factory floor, fracturing five different bones and sustaining a number of other injuries. He was sent to us as a hopeless case—his fractures had set in terrible positions—but we trimmed the overlapping fragments of bone and bone-plated them perfectly. That man too is back at work. In fact, when our patients leave us they are often in a better state than they were when they arrived in France.'

They walk past a group of men who are lounging around on the grass, chewing seeds and telling each other dirty jokes.

'Did you know we even have a convalescent company in Crécy Forest?' Blyth continues.

'Witness our too much memorable shame when Cressy battle fatally was struck,' Wang replies before he can stop himself. Blyth looks at him curiously. 'I'm sorry, sir. A bad habit of mine. It's Shakespeare. *Henry V*, sir.'

Blyth laughs. 'They said that you were a little unusual. I'm beginning to see what they meant. But do you know what? I think you're going to be good for me. Here I am talking to you like you're Fell or Astley or one of the other medicos, and all you're thinking about is bloody Shakespeare.'

'I'm sorry, sir.'

'Don't apologise, Wang. I shouldn't be surprised at your unusual talents. We do incredible things in this hospital, and when I say "we", I don't just mean the British. It's not just the shrine and the pagoda your chaps have created here. We have Chinese doctors and Chinese dressers too. Last year we even performed an entire Chinese opera. We run classes in English and French, in basic medicine, and elementary geography. We teach the illiterate how to read using Dr Wong's excellent phonetic shorthand. We have a hospital that is unsurpassed anywhere in the Chinese-speaking world. Men come to us broken and we fix them. They come to us as labourers and, when they can labour no longer, we get them going again. I had no desire to leave the mission field, but we have created something remarkable here at the mouth of the Somme. You may not have known it, but you are now in the largest Chinese hospital in the world.'

'I didn't realise that, sir.'

'The largest in the world,' Blyth confirms. 'We have almost everything we need—our own power plant, x-ray machines, well-trained doctors, an abundant supply of medicines. But we're still looking for more.'

'Is that right, sir?'

'It is. Come and look at one of our wards.'

He leads Wang past a group of Nissen huts, newly erected and decorated with the flags of three nations, into another of the low-slung buildings. It is neat, clean, and occupied by some thirty or forty men, each one of whom is laid up in bed.

'Do you like the canary?' he asks.

Wang looks at the small cage to which he is pointing. He grimaces as he remembers the day he first met Rong Meifan.

'One of my colleagues' ideas,' Blyth says. 'Just because we're in a hospital doesn't mean that we have to be miserable all the time. Not that Niu would agree with me, of course. He's got a terrible head wound. Do you want to have a look?'

Wang is not sure that he does but, as refusal isn't an option, he follows Blyth to the bed where the groaning man lies, and stands respectfully by while a dresser carefully peels back the white cloth that covers his head. He tries not to wince when he sees the suppurating wound. The man has lost so much of the left-hand side of his skull that Wang can make out what he imagines to be the red raw inner workings of his brain glistening like the tongue of a banded red snake.

'Now, what do you think caused a wound like that?' Blyth asks quietly as he carries out a quick inspection.

'I am not too familiar with the different types of shell as yet, sir,' Wang replies.

Blyth looks at him inscrutably. 'That wound,' he says, 'that excavation, was caused by a lump of frozen earth, albeit a lump of earth thrown sixty yards by one of the Boche shells. Poor Niu here lost half his skull to a piece of the land he'd come to protect.'

'I don't know what sort of work you were expecting when you signed up,' Blyth says, once he has finished in the ward, 'but I have a special job for you this evening. One of our enthusiastic Americans from the Y is coming to give a lecture to the coolies and he needs an interpreter.'

'I'm sorry, sir,' Wang says, 'but I don't fully understand. You mentioned the "why".'

'The YMCA. Young Men's Christian Association. They dole out tea and prayer and do a damned fine job with both. Can you do it?'

'I will, of course, do whatever is required, sir.'

'Well, that's cleared that up then. Report to the recreation hut in an hour's time.'

Wang salutes as he has been taught and makes his way back to the men he travelled with, hoping that someone has saved him a bed. He is pleasantly surprised by the dormitory; it is certainly cleaner and brighter than the one he was subjected to at Weihaiwei. His bed is basic but comfortable, and though the men with whom he shares the room might not be his first choice of companions, he knows that he is called upon to make sacrifices in time of war. Unpacking his few belongings, he prepares himself for work.

When, an hour later, he arrives at the recreation hut, he finds Captain Blyth's over-enthusiastic American already pacing up and down in a state of some excitement.

'Hey, are you the interpreter?' he shouts as Wang approaches.

Wang confirms that he is.

'Well, let's get this show on the road then, shall we? I gotta hundred men inside and I can't understand a damned word they're saying. But you know what?'

'What, sir?'

'They don't understand a damned word I'm saying either. And that's worse.' He flings out an arm. 'The name's Wallace.'

Wallace shakes one of Wang's hands with both of his while Wang tells him that he would be glad to assist in any way that is within his power.

'Just tell 'em what I'm saying, pal. Just tell 'em that.'

The hut is indeed full. At least a hundred men are crammed into every imaginable space. Some are playing cards. Some are chomping on peanuts. Another is, improbably, cuddling a small puppy. The air is thick with noise, laughter, and cigarette smoke.

'Say, pal, your buddies certainly know how to enjoy themselves.'

'I would say that they do, sir.'

'OK, so let's get some order here.'

He leaps onto a table, causing considerable consternation among a group of card-players, and shouts out in a tremendous voice that he is about to start talking and so could he please have some damned quiet. The hut falls silent so quickly that Wang begins to doubt whether his presence is going to be required.

'OK, so let's start,' Wallace says. 'Tonight I'm going to talk to you about venereal diseases.'

The labourers look up at him. Wallace looks at Wang. 'Are you going to translate, pal, or what?'

'Oh, yes, sorry sir.' He hesitates. 'Today's talk,' he says after another look, 'is about moral laxity.'

'Yep, that's right—sex. We all want it. We can all get it. But we don't all face up to the consequences.'

Wang feels himself starting to sweat. Wallace looks at him again. 'Relationships are very important,' Wang translates.

Wallace narrows his eyes. 'Is that it?'

Wang nods.

'Amazing language, Chinese,' Wallace says before turning back to the hut and raising his voice once more. 'I'm not here to talk to you about your wives. I'm not even here today to talk about the Lord Jesus Christ. I'm here to talk to you about the prophylactic stations.'

The sweat is beginning to stream freely now. For a moment Wang considers walking out, but Wallace's eye is heavy upon him and so he has no choice but to stay. He is new, but he knows as surely as he would have done had he been at Noyelles for six months that there will be uproar if he translates what is actually being said, and so he does what he always does under pressure. He turns to Shakespeare.

'Some of your French crowns have no hair at all,' he intones, 'and then you will play barefaced.'

A few faces turn towards him. Several playing cards are lowered. Dozens of men look at the American in bewilderment.

'Yep, that's right—the prophylactic stations. You've heard about them. You may even have seen them. But do you know what happens there? Do you know what sort of treatment gets dished out?'

Wang gives his imagination free rein and lets the American's words lead him where they will. 'And this same progeny of evils comes from our debate, from our dissension. We are their parents and their originals,' he says.

Most of the labourers resume their card games and their conversations, but a few stare at him and the American as if unsure which one is the more unhinged.

'Well tonight, my friends, I'm going to tell you,' Wallace continues. 'First the medicos whip out your genitals and scrub them all over with soap. Then they coat 'em with bichloride of mercury. Mercury. That's the stuff that they put in thermometers.'

Wang wipes his hands nervously on his trousers and continues with his creative translation. 'Now Mercury indue thee with leasing,' he says, 'for thou speakest well of fools.'

Maxwell looks in his direction to check that he has finished and then, taking a step forward on his table, sends a pack of cards flying.

'And now this is the good bit,' he says. 'They inject a teaspoon of protargol solution into your dick.'

He breaks off and turns to Wang again. 'OK, pal, this is where you earn your corn.'

Wang nods sagely. 'Forgive me, king of shadows, I mistook,' he says, momentarily wishing he were back home in Shanghai.

'And then,' Wallace continues with a mime, the accuracy of which perfectly matches the enthusiasm of his voice, 'you have to hold it inside with your finger and thumb for a good five minutes. I tell you what, my friends, you'll wish the Boche had got to you first if some medico gets to inflict that treatment on you.'

Wang tries to find an adequate quotation but, before he can speak, a roar of approval erupts from the hut. Suddenly his compatriots are getting not a litany of Shakespeare's best lines but a vivid demonstration of American manhood, and there is no doubt which they prefer. Wallace struggles on manfully for another five minutes, but the audience is never so rapt as it was at the start of the talk or as appreciative as it was when he took to acting out his message and so, eventually, he bows to the inevitable and brings his lecture to an end. It is only as they fight their way back out through the crowds that Wang sees Lieutenant Fell again. His eyes are streaming as he pushes his way through.

'A masterly performance, Wang,' he declares, clapping him on the back.

'Is that so?' the American asks.

'It is indeed. You couldn't have had a better translator. I have a feeling Wang is going to fit in here just fine.'

Chapter 11

The next day, as the weather breaks, Blyth takes him to the Eighty-Third General Hospital in Boulogne—'There's trouble with the patients and with some of the bloody doctors, but if you're going to work for us, Wang, you'd better see what we're up against'— and, while they bump along the terrible French roads, he opens up a new front.

'Have you noticed how often the eyes are mentioned in Scripture?' he asks.

Wang feels trapped. He is willing to listen to lectures on venereal diseases, but he is less comfortable with religion.

'I can't say I have, sir. My family had only the loosest of connections with the missionaries.'

'Well, let me tell you,' Blyth says, growing animated. 'It runs through the entire Old Testament and into the New. The God of Moses demands an eye for an eye, Isaiah proclaims sight for the blind, and then Jesus actually heals them—Bartimaeus, the man born without sight, and the beggar who saw men as trees walking. It was one of the ways in which Christ proclaimed the kingdom, one of the most important ways in which he demonstrated that the Old Testament prophecies were being fulfilled. "Tell John what things ye have seen and heard," he said to the Baptist's disciples. And the first miracle he mentioned was "that the blind see". I could go on, but I can see that, despite your admirable Oriental manners, you are growing bored.'

Wang does his best to look interested.

'Not at all, sir.'

Blyth smiles. 'Do you know what happens to the labourers we find to be infected with trachoma?' he asks.

'You send them back to China, sir?' Wang suggests.

'Only if we absolutely have to. Back home in China, who knows what'll happen to them? Begging in the streets if they're lucky. We'd rather get them to work. We can't afford to do otherwise. They have been hired to do coolie work and so coolie work they must do. But it isn't easy digging trenches, unloading ships, building railway lines, or constructing tanks when your vision's half gone. These men live in a country of the blind but know what it is to have seen. They suffer, but, because they are Chinese, no one listens when they speak. It's really no surprise that sometimes they take desperate measures. The suicide rate among Z Company coolies—those with manifest cases of trachoma—is considerably higher than it is among non-trachoma sufferers but, sadly, that's not what bothers us the most.'

'No sir?'

'Maybe you have heard of some of the disturbances involving coolie regiments? Strikes, fights, even the occasional mutiny. It drives the French crazy, to say nothing of our own superior officers. And this is what they most fear—Z Company unrest, mutinies among men blighted with trachoma. Frustration leading to anger leading to desertion and the spread of this eye-eating menace among the good citizens of France and the armies that have come to protect them.'

'Surely that could never happen?'

'It happened to Napoleon in Egypt in 1798. There's no reason why it shouldn't happen again. You have a great deal still to learn, Wang. That's why I'm taking you to Boulogne.'

Wang is confident that he has already come to terms with the horrors of military hospitals, but what he sees and hears in the hospital at Boulogne still shocks him. In a converted hotel dozens of westerners are lying on their backs, their chests inflating as if uncertain whether they will ever rise again. It takes Wang some minutes to realise that the pervasive sound of bottles being slowly filled with water is the wounded soldiers breathing. He watches as a nurse holds a soldier's legs up while another pushes on his chest, then turns away in disgust when a steady gurgle of liquid flows out of the man's mouth and nose, causing him to cough, whimper and clench his fists.

'What happened to him?' he asks quietly.

'Chlorine,' Blyth replies.

At first sight, the Chinese ward into which Blyth leads him is more heartening. None of the patients are in their beds and, with the exception of one man who has a bandage across his left eye, there is no indication that any of his compatriots have the slightest thing wrong with them. Some are lounging about in the doorway. Others are playing desultory games of cards. Until they spot Captain Blyth, one or two are smoking surreptitiously. A strong tang of cigarettes, unwashed bodies and boredom fills the room.

'Stick around, Wang, while I track down Briggs,' Blyth tells him. 'You'll cotton on soon enough.'

He glances at some patient notes that have been stored at the foot of one of the beds, then strides from the room, leaving Wang alone and uncomfortable. Uncertain where to look, he avoids eye contact with the patients by pulling out the medical notes Blyth had flicked through, but they make no sense to him.

'The eyes, is it?'

One of the card-players is looking at him suspiciously.

'What's that?' Wang replies.

'Your eyes,' the man repeats, drawing his fingers across his face. 'Got the worms, eh?'

'Ah, no,' Wang replies. 'I'm here to translate.'

The man spits on the floor. 'There's no need for that here. The doctor knows more Chinese words than I do. What was that one he said this morning, Liu?'

His playing partner looks up. 'Granulated,' he says.

'That's it. Said we had granulated eyelids. I told him to keep it simple for Liu here.'

As Liu responds with a punch, a pale young doctor walks in and announces to no one in particular that it is misting outside.

'Good morning, sir,' Wang replies. 'The weather is definitely inclement.'

The doctor looks at him curiously. 'It's a good job we're in here then.'

He returns to his clipboard.

Wang tries again. 'I am the new interpreter, sir.'

The doctor doesn't look up. 'We've no need of an interpreter here.'

Wang shifts about uncomfortably, but if the doctor feels awkward about Wang's presence he doesn't show it.

'I've come to gain an acquaintance with the labourers, sir, so that I might be of some assistance when they begin their work.'

The doctor looks up again as though surprised to find him still there. 'They'll be unloading boats. I can't imagine a whole lot of talking will be required.'

He begins to walk around the ward while the patients fall back into their expected positions. Slipping on a pair of surgical gloves, he everts a few eyelids and tells several labourers to lie on their backs. They grumble but do as they are told even when, as Wang watches in fascinated horror, the doctor pulls out a knife, nicks the corner of their eyelids and paints them with silver nitrate.

'So what exactly did you say you're doing here?' the doctor asks when he has finished inflicting treatment on his patients.

'I've been sent by Captain Blyth, sir.'

For the first time the doctor seems to consider what Wang is saying. 'Captain Blyth?'

'Yes, sir.'

'Well, he could have told me. What does he want?'

'What he wants, Lieutenant Briggs,' Blyth's voice booms from behind him, 'is to see what you're up to here.'

Lieutenant Briggs breaks into a big smile. 'And there was I thinking he'd just wandered in off the streets.'

The two men clap each other on the back while Wang stands back and waits for the signal to speak.

'So, what's your next step, Briggs?' Blyth asks, once all the back-slapping is over.

'Work is the next step, sir,' Briggs replies. 'I've done my morning round and this little lot are now ready to do what they're paid for.'

Blyth turns to Wang. 'And what about you, Wang? Are you ready to do what you're paid for? Are you prepared to work with this dreaded Z Company, the company that has to be quarantined, segregated, and avoided at all costs?'

'Yes, sir,' Wang stammers, 'but I am uncertain about what exactly it is you want me to do.'

Blyth puts a hand on his shoulder. 'I don't need an interpreter at Noyelles, Wang. We've got enough men who are fluent in your language to get us through the simple translation work we need. I need something more. I need you to spend time with these men. I need you to listen to their complaints and to defuse any tension before it grows serious. I need your help in reintegrating these labourers into the British military machine. Sometimes I'll make use of you at Noyelles, of course I will. But I'll also need to send you out across Northern France to wherever the Chinese Labour Corps has been stationed. I need you to win the labourers' trust, to speak to them on our behalf, to get them to do what is in their and our best interests. I need you to leave the camp and be our go-between. What do you say?'

Remembering what he left behind in China—the years of university study, the family who never understood him, Rong Meifan—Wang tries to give the moment the significance it seems to deserve.

'It would be an honour, sir,' he says.

Blyth claps him hard on the back and leads him to the door, while Briggs bellows at everyone else in the room.

'OK, you lot. Fun's over for the day. Get your stuff and get out of my hospital.'

During the next month Wang scarcely sets foot inside the camp at Noyelles. Though severely hampered by practical difficulties, he is sent out across northern France to visit detachments of the Chinese Labour Corps. Some are building tanks, others are mending railway lines, and many more are unloading the ships that steam in and out of the Channel ports. Enthusiasm for work carries him so far but, for all his determination to get his hands dirty, to bridge the gap that his education has created between him and the labourers, he finds it difficult to communicate in a language that either the British or the Chinese understand. For all its obvious foreignness—its miserable climate, its peculiar food, its impenetrable religion—France is far less of a mystery than the labouring his own countrymen are doing.

Refusing to observe from a distant prospect, Wang plunges into the dirtiest parts of the factories and the most unsanitary areas of the camps, but looking makes him no less distant or different. His problem is words. Words for the tools the trench diggers and railway workers sling across their shoulders. Words for the lathes, pulleys and spindles he is shown in the factories. Words for tank tracks, impossibly large guns, and the bewildering variety of bullets, shells and flares that the labourers, peasants almost to a man, are made to make. He has always thought of translation as an art, a way of sculpting the beauties of one tongue into subtle lines that speakers of another will appreciate, but here in this strange half-world that is neither French nor British nor Chinese, he realises that it is a slog. Tool for tool, machine for machine, word for word, he has to match the hard material realities of the labourers' lives with solid equivalents in his other languages.

In a factory near Calais he stops mid-sentence as he is being taken on a tour of a furiously loud and dirty work shed. Closing his dead eye, he tries to find his bearings among the serrated metal, the dusty workbenches, the furnace and turbines, and pulleys that jerk stiffly from one rusty wheel to another. Three woollen-hatted

129

labourers stare at him suspiciously as he circles slowly on the spot. The paraphernalia of the British military machine spiral in front of him—pistons driving relentless metal into unyielding machines, swirls of dust like incense in some backstreet temple, inadequate lights, confusion. He searches for the words he needs to enable him to carry out the most straightforward of conversations but realises how little of what he sees makes any sense to him. He comes to a standstill and then backs slowly out of the room.

Feeling wholly overwhelmed by the job he has been given to do, he tries to drag himself back into usefulness by thinking about the sheer scale of the operation behind the military campaign. The work the Chinese Labour Corps is doing is on an immense scale. Spread across the whole of northern France and, for all he knows, other parts of the world as well, they are merely one unit among many. In the theatre of war, it is the backstage crew that keeps the illusion going. Working frantically in the dark, under impossible conditions and to improbable deadlines, they are the ones who ensure that the khaki-clad actors can gain all the glory. Wang has only a walk-on part in the grand drama but, even when he feels most overwhelmed, he refuses to believe that his role is any less important for its invisibility.

He goes to Wimereux to placate members of the Nineteenth Regiment who are complaining about the damp, marshy terrain on which they are compelled to camp. He travels to Dunkerque to deal with complaints from munition workers about bullying and inadequate rice rations. He is sent to Étaples to negotiate with dock workers and to Audruicq to assist a labourer who has been arrested after a gambling session turns violent. He is more negotiator than interpreter, but he begins to enjoy this job for which he never applied.

In early summer he is sent to negotiate with striking munitions workers in Rouen. It takes him most of the day to get there, but as soon as he arrives he is bundled into a meeting with the self-appointed leader of the strike, a Sichuanese peasant called Guo Ziqin.

'So you're the yellow white man they've sent to shut us up, are you?' he demands. 'You might as well know right now that we're not interested in what British lackeys have to say.'

'Wang Weijun,' he says. 'Pleased to meet you.'

When Guo spits on the floor, turns his back, and refuses to open negotiations, Wang retreats to the mess where he finds that the British are more than happy to voice their opinions. Guo has scarcely ever been outside the confines of his village, but now he is in France he is a troublemaker of the first order. Neither rank nor weapons nor discipline have any effect on him when he believes he is in the right, and he always believes himself in the right.

'These are my complaints,' he announces, once Wang has eventually managed to persuade him to come to the negotiating table. 'One: we are treated like dogs by our overseers. We came to work for the pale-faced foreigners, not to be their slaves. Two: we are not getting the rice rations we were promised. If those fucking bastards want us to make their shells and bullets then they need to feed us properly. Three: we demand the right to celebrate our festivals. The French take holidays more often than they drink that bloody foul wine of theirs, but they won't let us celebrate Qingming.'

'And you want me to take these grievances to the factory owners?' Wang asks.

'I don't give a damn what you do with them,' Guo replies. 'We're not doing any more work until we get satisfaction.'

Wang does his best to tease out a few concessions, just as he works hard to soften Guo's bargaining position, but there is no moving him. When he tries to bypass him entirely by negotiating directly with the munitions workers, the ploy also proves unsuccessful. Guo is feared and respected in equal measure, and there is nothing Wang can do to undermine him. He writes a report recommending that Guo be reassigned, that an overseer be replaced, and the rice ration increased, and returns to Noyelles. His job is done.

'Ah, Wang,' Lieutenant Fell shouts when he gets back. 'Long time no see! What are you doing tomorrow?'

'I've no idea, sir. I'm still awaiting orders, sir.'

'Then I order you to accompany me on a little trip to the River Somme. If you haven't seen the Baie then you haven't seen France.'

Early the next morning, they hitch a lift on one of the supply trucks that trundle up and down the coast road as regular as Sundays. Wang isn't sure what to expect, but the closer they draw to the great bay that is more sea than river and more mud than sea, a place where land and water merge, the more his bafflement grows. Fell is grinning like a schoolboy. He is animated, open, innocent even. Though all Wang can see is absence and the brown wings of birds, Fell looks out over the mudflats with something verging on religious ecstasy.

'Here's some wonderful Somme mud for you, Wang,' he says wistfully. 'Mud and sand and water. Just look at those lovely flats.'

'The lone and level sands stretch far away, sir.'

'Yes, something like that,' Fell replies. 'Do you know what always amazes me? Here we are blowing each other to smithereens, and the birds keep flying. When I first came over, I was sent to the trenches, and it felt like the end of the world. The sky seemed to explode. Shells screamed like whole companies of men being ripped apart. Explosion followed explosion followed explosion. Then, for a moment before the offensive began, the noise stopped. But there wasn't silence. The larks still sang. We were destroying the earth, and the larks were still singing.'

There is nothing Wang feels he can say in response, so he keeps his mouth shut.

'Then I was sent here to the mouth of the Somme and it was as if war had never been declared. The birds kept coming. Migration didn't stop. The wigeon and shelduck took no notice of borders and treaties. They kept flying. So whenever they let me out of the camp for a day I make my way straight here.'

Wang is used to cities and people, not sky and birds and mud, but he tries to see the Baie with Fell's eyes. 'I can see what you mean, sir,' he says, not wholly truthfully.

'They call it the Baie de Somme and I tell you, Wang, this is the only place for me. Forget the camps and the camaraderie. Forget the forests and the hills. I live for places like these where mud and water rule.'

They settle down into a hollow and watch as the lightest of breezes and hundreds of wading birds wash across from the English Channel. Wang keeps his head low and tries to spot the different species as Fell names them—golden oriole, Kentish plover, little egret, crested lark, marsh warbler, common rosefinch, black-winged stilt. Then, turning onto his back, he waits until the birds fly directly overhead and tries to identify them by their wing markings.

'It's not as easy as you make it sound, sir,' he whispers.

Fell whispers something back but it is lost in the rustle of the breeze and the cry of the birds. Wang closes his eyes and tries to block out the rumble of trucks along the coast road and the occasional boom of a field gun somewhere further down the coast. The French are in training, but the noise and confusion of war is dismantled by the quiet of the salt marshes.

'Do you know what they call these little things?' Fell whispers, handing Wang a bunch of green leaves he has plucked from the bank where they are lying. '*Oreilles de cochon*. Pigs' ears. Go on, try some. They're a bit salty, but after all that bully beef and Maconochie they're something of a luxury.'

Wang chews on a handful but, like irony and sweet tea, *oreilles de cochon* are a western taste he has yet to acquire.

Fell shrugs his shoulders.

'If you don't like them,' he says, 'I'll take them back for my rabbits.'

The rabbits are a surprise. Everything about Fell's demeanour

—his jokes, his casual tone, his broad smile—suggests a man comfortable among men. Wang can't quite work out how he finds time for children's pets.

'Great animals, rabbits,' he says. 'Do you know how often they blink, Wang?'

'I can't say that I do, sir.'

'About ten times an hour.' He drops down again with a sigh of satisfaction and stares through his field glasses, following the progress of a water pipit as it hops across the dune. 'We're trying to find out more about the effects of mustard gas,' he whispers, 'and the little buggers are perfect for the job, not just because they have very human eyes, but also because they breed like, well, like rabbits.'

Wang is unexpectedly appalled by this information, but there is no escape. In between sweeping the shoreline with his glasses and explaining the difference between *crevettes grise* and *coques*, Fell explains in great detail—though always in a whisper— the correct technique for applying mustard oil solution to a rabbit's eyes and the various possible treatments for the terrible injuries thus imparted—merthiolate of mercury, irrigation with sodium bicarbonate and cod-liver oil drops, the intravenous injection of ascorbic acid.

'We're pretty sure that ascorbic acid is the chemical to use,' he confides, 'but we're playing around with the dosages just in case.'

Wang nods. As a child he kept a hare in a hutch in the corner of his back yard and fed it *ye cai* twice a day. One January he found it gone, stolen presumably by a neighbour who wanted a present for his family or a meal for his table. He didn't feel greatly upset. He could always get another. But now, at the mouth of the Somme, he feels differently.

He fingers his own false eye. 'Can you learn anything that would help me, sir?' he asks.

Fell puts his field glasses down. 'Your eye's long gone, Wang,' he says. 'We've got other priorities now.'

Images of Shanghai resurface. The dark back yard in winter. The scowling buildings. The sharp lights. As Wang walks back to barracks, he sees a ghostly reflection of the Bund where the unfocussed edge of sight gives way to the uncertainties of memory. The sounds of the camp elide into the blare of a busy port, sirens replacing engines, Shanghaihua overwhelming English, China displacing France. Wang feels Europe drain from him as China drips slowly back. The emptiness that enveloped him after Rong Meifan abandoned him returns. It isn't that Fell's blunt assessment has come as a shock; what distresses him is that he should have been hanging onto hope without realising it.

'I hear that Fell's been boring you with his birds,' Blyth says when they meet the next day.

'We had a most informative trip to the Baie de Somme, sir,' Wang replies.

'I bet you did,' Blyth says. 'I made the mistake of letting him drag me out there once and it took me months to recover. My boots stink of salt to this day.'

Wang is accompanying him on a ward round and, with labourer after labourer laid low with trachoma, it is a dispiriting business.

'Trachoma's a disgrace in this day and age,' Blyth says. 'By my reckoning, approximately one hundred million of your countrymen have the disease, with five million new cases arising each year, chiefly in children. I estimate that one million Chinese are blind in both eyes and that another three or four million are blind in one. It's a waste. But do you know why it's a disgrace? Because I can treat it. Give me a plentiful supply of copper sulphate and a few good doctors who know what they're looking for, and I can send this terrible disease into headlong flight. If I can get to them in time.'

He thumps the side of the bed, causing a recuperating labourer to jerk upwards in surprise, and then marches off down the ward, leaving Wang to rush after him. By the time he catches up, Blyth is outside, scuffing at the dusty earth with his feet. A long line of cotton-capped labourers looks indolently at him as he peers into the distance. They are waiting for the day's rations which are being scooped out of an array of flour bags and milk cans. Most of the men are standing, but a few are squatting in the dust, resting their legs and shielding their faces from the glare of the sun.

'Do you know what I do when I need a change of scene, Wang?' Blyth asks abruptly

'All I know is that you don't watch birds, sir.'

'That's right, I very much do not,' he says. 'I go to the cinema. There's a chap called Chaplin, and I don't know what it is about him—maybe his walk, maybe his sheer silliness—but it takes me out of myself in a way nothing else really can do. There's a show tonight. You ought to give him a try.'

Wang has already seen several Chaplin films with Rong Meifan in Beijing, but he doesn't want to embarrass Blyth by letting on. He salutes briskly.

'Thank you, sir. I'll be there.'

By half past six, the recreation hut is packed, and the labourers are as boisterous as a Beijing opera crowd. They throw back drinks, wave their cigarettes around in front of the projector, and roar their approval every time the operator sticks his head round the door. Wang, who has bagged a prime seat in the front row, listens to the jokes that swirl around him while the YMCA orderly tries to keep the men queuing outside under control.

'Keep back, keep back!' he shouts. 'You'll get in eventually.'

With a stampede becoming increasingly likely, his voice rises in pitch. 'You won't go home disappointed,' he shouts. 'There will be multiple showings.'

Wang keeps his head down, but the labourers around him continue to spit pumpkin seeds on the ground and shout their demands. One man gets up from his seat, grabs a broom from the corner, and starts to perform an impromptu Chaplin impression. Wang grimaces at its awfulness, but he seems to be alone.

'He does realise how silly he looks, I hope?'

Wang turns in his chair to see Lieutenant Fell standing behind him. He struggles to his feet, but Fell puts a hand on his shoulder and keeps him where he is.

'It's getting a little sticky out there,' Fell continues. 'For some reason I can't fathom, they all want to see this Yankee nonsense. I don't mind the excitement, but I can't allow a riot.'

'Of course, sir,' Wang replies.

'So can you speak to them?'

'Speak to them, sir?'

'Speak to them, Wang. Calm them down. Work the wonders of the Orient on the restive masses.'

Wang considers the request for a moment. 'What would you like me to say, sir?'

'I don't give a damn what you say, Wang. I don't want anyone killed, that's all.'

Wang is shocked by the size of the crowd that has gathered outside the hut. Neither the noise nor past experience has prepared him for the enormous body of men he sees arrayed in front of him. During his tours of Northern France, he has grown used to restive groups of workers, but he is not sure what to do in his own backyard. For want of a better plan, he steps onto an old ammunition box that has been dumped outside the hut, holds up a hand and motions for quiet.

'He's trying to do a Charlie,' one of the crowd shouts.

'He thinks he's the tramp,' another man joins in.

Wang shifts around uncomfortably. This is going to be more difficult than he has imagined, especially now that Fell has disappeared.

'I have something to say,' he shouts, without having the slightest idea what it might be.

'Try speaking proper Chinese then,' the first man calls out.

'I'll start speaking proper Chinese when you start behaving like a proper Chinese,' Wang replies. The man, encouraged by his neighbours, shouts back, and Wang's voice is lost in a welter of sounds, some jocular, some confused, a few apparently angry. Knowing that he has to move fast or lose control completely, he tries to find words for the moment and involuntarily scratches his head.

'It's Stan Laurel,' someone shouts.

'Sitanli, Sitanli, Sitanli, Sitanli!' the shout goes up.

Wang kicks the box and waves his arms in disgust, inwardly cursing Fell for having placed him in an impossible situation.

'It's not Sitanli,' the man with the loud voice shouts, 'it's Charlie Chaplin! Give us the walk, Charlie!'

Wang looks at his tormentor. Feeling his body tense, he begins to walk away—'Not like that, Charlie. Turn your feet out!'—and then, in an instant, he sees not the crowds nor the muddy roads of the camp, but an audience. He stops and, shutting his eye, sees the *Daying Xiguan*, Shanghai's Great British Theatre. He hasn't performed in years, but suddenly the thrill of the stage comes back to him. He thinks *Why not, why not?* and, when he opens his eye again, the audience is still there.

'All right, all right,' he shouts and, grabbing a peaked cap from the head of one of the labourers nearest to him and a cane from the hands of the astonished YMCA orderly, proceeds to waddle in front of the recreation hut.

'It's the walk, it's the walk,' his tormentor yells. 'Charlie's arrived.'

Roared on by a crowd of several hundred enthusiastic labourers, Wang launches into the best impressions he can manage of Charlie Chaplin, Stan Laurel and even, for one improbable minute, Oliver Hardy. When he has exhausted his full routine—a routine gleaned from half-remembered viewings of *Charlie Shanghaied* and *The Vagabond*—he tries to recall the gags that used to keep his schoolfriends entertained. He doesn't have a pack of cards on him so there is a limit to what he can achieve but, despite the lack of resources, he has one great asset at his disposal. He jumps back onto the box, holds up his hands for quiet and brings most of the crowd to order. The heckler is not so easily quietened.

'We want more,' he yells. 'Can you do a Mabel Normand?'

Realising that he is about to lose control again, Wang pulls his enamel eye from its socket, holds it high above his head and shouts, 'Watch it, labourer, I've got my eye on you.'

The crowd roars its approval. A couple of men start pounding the heckler on his back and someone else, to Wang's surprise and delight, starts a new chant.

'Wang Weijun! Wang Weijun!'

He presses on before the moment is lost. Popping the eye in his pocket he waits for a moment, and then pulls it out of the YMCA orderly's ear. As the crowd roars, he closes it in his hand and makes it disappear before popping it back in when his back is turned. Then, putting his hand into his jacket pocket to check that he still has a spare eyeball with him, he lowers his voice to get that devastating silence which all great performers require.

'And now, gentlemen,' he announces, 'before I leave you tonight I have one last trick—one final illusion, the like of which you have never seen before. Hold your breath and cover your eyes for I, your humble interpreter, your Chinese Chaplin and Oriental Olly, am about to be transformed. Gentlemen of the Chinese Labour Corps, I ask you to look deep into my eyes.'

This time not even the heckler speaks. The crowd edges forward in near silent anticipation. The labourers in the front row push up against his box. Wang sweeps an arm out in front of him, waves his hand across his face two or three times, pulls out his false eye, and stares at the crowd from an empty socket.

'Gentlemen,' he shouts, slipping the brown eyeball into his jacket pocket and surreptitiously extracting the other, 'the trick you have all been waiting for. When I return this eyeball to its proper place it will have changed. I who am Chinese will become like one of the foreign devils. I will be half the man I used to be.'

He waves his hand in front of his face two or three more times and, with the effortless grace that comes from practice and necessity, slips his artificial blue eye into place. The labourers at the front of the crowd take a step backwards. Everyone else

139

surges forward to catch a glimpse of this strange hybrid. Gasps are replaced by roars and the chanting resumes.

'Wang Weijun! Wang Weijun!'

He smiles and steps down from the box. Dozens of labourers crowd round, patting him on the pack, thumping him on the shoulder, and poking at his eye. The tension and threats, such as they were, are gone. Wang accepts the adulation and pulls away only when he hears Fell's voice over the chatter of the crowd. The lieutenant fights his way through and clasps him by the hand.

'Well done, old chap,' he says. 'Quite a show you've got there. A damn sight better than that bloody awful Shakespearean nonsense you keep going on about.'

Wang bows and allows himself to be led back into the hut where *The Immigrant* is about to be shown. He collapses onto a front row seat and waits until the lights are turned off and the projector begins to whir. Then, as it drones like a badly made shawm, he closes his blue eye and lets the other stare.

Chapter 12

During his first few months in France, Wang is bothered by his distance from the fighting. Though Fell and Blyth try to persuade him that there is more to the war than unseen men blowing each other to pieces, he feels as though he is cheating somehow.

'Look, Wang, why do you think we went to all the trouble, not to say the expense, of transporting tens of thousands of labourers from the hinterlands of China if we didn't have need of you? We need our men to fight, and we can't rely on the women to build our tanks and unload our ships. If we're going to fight then someone's got to churn out the shells and the bullets.'

'But I'm not doing that either, sir,' Wang complains. 'I'm travelling around France like a tourist.'

'You're keeping the labourers happy. You're focussing their minds on the job at hand. That sounds pretty important to me.'

Wang looks as he feels—unconvinced.

'Well, have it your own way,' Blyth says, 'but just remember—they also serve who only stand and translate.'

Wang does his best to be at least half-convinced by the officers' arguments, but when Fell enlists his help to organise a football match his doubts resurface.

'Football, sir?' he asks incredulously.

'Yes, football, Wang. A match between the officers and the labourers. Eleven-a-side.'

Wang looks down at his feet in some embarrassment.

'Oh, come on, Wang, it'll be great for morale.'

'And what exactly will my role be in this affair, sir?'

Fell frowns. 'I don't like to teach you your job, Wang, but I'm not convinced "affair" is quite the right word. But, be that as it may, your job is to organise a team and then to translate during practice sessions. We've got you a coach.'

'A coach, sir?'

'Yes, Wang. A coach. Second Lieutenant Stevens. He used to play for Wolverhampton Wanderers.'

Despite his impeccable English, Wang has no idea what Fell is talking about. 'Very good, sir,' he says.

'He'll be in the rec hut at ten hundred hours exactly. Get your boys together and then let battle commence.'

Wang doesn't move.

'What's the matter now, Wang?'

'I'm unsure about the principles involved in organising a football team, sir.'

'Oh, for goodness sake, Wang, just find eleven men who have some inkling of the rules and, if you have a choice, choose the best footballers.'

As soon as he is outside, Wang kicks the ground in frustration. He can do without the distraction of little boys' games, but with no choice in the matter he does as he has been ordered and, with the help of some of the other interpreters, gathers eleven labourers who have some knowledge of the game. By ten o'clock the next day, ten men are ready for him at the recreation hut.

'Where's Liu?' he asks, exasperated at the big man's failure to appear.

'Fell off a ladder,' comes the reply.

Wang is about to demand that he be fetched anyway when Second Lieutenant Stevens arrives. The coach is a stocky little man with muscles most of the labourers would have been proud of, but it is his outfit which Wang finds most alarming—long black socks, black shorts and a black and orange-striped shirt, the combined effect of which is to make him look like a mutant bee. Striding up to Wang, he peers at him out of a tiny pair of eyes.

'You must be Wang the interpreter.'

142

'That's right, sir.'

'Know much about football?'

'No, sir.'

'Well, never mind. Just tell them what I tell you and we'll soon have them licked into shape.'

It is becoming increasingly clear to Wang that he needs to learn more colloquial English. 'Yes, sir,' he says.

Stevens turns to the footballers and, widening his stance, stands with his hands behind his back and his chest thrust out like a late-Qing concubine.

'Good morning, team,' he says.

The players all nod and smile.

'I said, "Good morning, team."'

The smiles fade away. Stevens stares at them all for a moment before bellowing again.

'That's not good enough. If we're going to win this match, we're going to have to show commitment. So let's hear a great big good morning from you all!'

Wang translates again. A few of the players look at him quizzically. 'He wants you to repeat the words loudly,' he says.

'Good morning?' one of the labourers asks.

'That's right,' Wang confirms.

'These foreign devils have strange ways of greeting each other.'

'Never mind, never mind,' Stevens interrupts. 'There's no need for a full-blown inquest. Let's do some warm-ups and then we'll sort out team tactics.'

He leads the players in a curious routine which involves running from side to side, stepping over a line of stones, skipping along a line and, finally, running to a post and back. Stevens clutches the football and shouts a lot while the players do their best to follow Wang's hasty translations.

'Don't we have to kick the ball?' one of them asks.

'I suppose so,' Wang replies.

'Then why's he holding onto it?'

Wang has no idea, so he doesn't reply. Unmoved by the labourers' incomprehension, Stevens pounds up and down the field like a dynamo. The further he runs, the louder he shouts, and the more irritated he seems to become.

'Right. Let's sort positions then,' he bawls. 'Has anyone kept goal before?'

When he later reflects on the occasion, Wang isn't entirely convinced that his translation at this point was wholly accurate.

'Right, you then,' Stevens shouts when nobody volunteers. 'You're the tallest. Stick these gloves on.'

Wang is confused. 'Do you mean me, sir?' he asks.

'You're the tallest, aren't you?'

Wang looks around. He does seem to loom over most of the others. 'I am really here in a translating capacity,' he says.

'You can do that too,' Stevens says. 'Now let's get going.'

Wang looks at the gloves Stevens has thrown at him. They seem rather small. Tentatively he pulls them on but, as he tries to work out what he is supposed to do next, he realises that Stevens is already in full flow, so he refocuses and attempts to catch up with his translation.

'Now, we're going to play a two-three-five formation. It's not perfect but it's probably the best one for this sort of pitch. It'll only work if the half backs drop back quickly when the other team's on the attack. Two of the forwards might need to help out the midfield as well as keeping an eye on the wingers, but that will still leave the other half back to become a centre back as necessary. Of course, it's vital that the outside left and the outside right keep to their positions, otherwise we'll lose the width and their wingers will cut us to shreds. Why have you stopped translating?'

'I'm terribly sorry, sir,' Wang replies, 'but I lost you after your advice about starting halfway back.'

Stevens gives him a look such as he has never seen before from a European. Then he lowers his voice in a way Wang finds rather intimidating.

'When I asked you whether you knew much about football ...'

'Yes, sir,' Wang replies.

'And you said, "No, sir".'

'Yes, sir,' Wang says.

'Did you actually mean, "No, sir. Nothing at all, sir"?'

'I have not had the honour of witnessing the eleven-a-side version of this noble game before, sir.'

'Good God above,' Stevens says, raising his eyes to the sky. 'Do any of you know the first thing about football?'

A Beijinger called An Rushan raises his hand, thereby marking him out as a former student at one of the missionary schools.

'Preston North End, very good, sir.'

'I see.'

'Percy Smith, sir. Very good player. My favourite.'

'Well, that's a start I suppose.'

An smiles encouragingly. Stevens clenches his fists. 'OK, let's forget about formations and kick the ball around for a bit, shall we?' he says.

This eminently sensible suggestion brings the team to life and relieves Wang greatly. Before long, An is booting the ball around the field while the others run after him. Stevens continues to shout instructions, but as Wang can neither keep up nor understand more than half of what he says, Stevens soon dispenses with his translating services altogether and sets about demonstrating what he wants by kicking the ball himself. Every now and again, when the ball comes his way, Wang politely returns it to the man who has given it to him. For reasons that he doesn't fully understand, this simple act sometimes sends Stevens into paroxysms of rage and sometimes elicits effusive praise. It is only after he leaves the field that he realises he should perhaps have mentioned his lack of an eye.

A few days later, Guo Ziqin, the striking workers' leader who gave him such a hard time during the negotiations at Rouen, limps into the camp, crippled but immediately recognisable with his triumphant grin. He has sprained an ankle and sustained some unspecified damage to his back, but though he is clearly in pain, and though he is quick to argue about the unequal treatment that is meted out to his fellow countrymen, he doesn't complain about his own health. Wang cannot decide whether he is deeply phlegmatic or merely a wily old campaigner. A coolie with too many injuries is destined for hasty repatriation.

'So, you're still here are you, you little lump of shit?' Guo says when the two of them meet in the reception hut.

'It is a pleasure to see you again, my friend.'

'You sold us out in Rouen.'

'I translated for you in Rouen.'

'I don't know what you told them, but they busted me good and proper when you left.' He squats down on the floor and picks his teeth.

'I am sorry to hear that,' Wang says.

Guo hawks onto the ground. 'I'm sure you are. I'm sure you were when you got back to your comfortable little coop. What have they got you working on now? Washing British arses?'

'I am still doing all I can to assist my countrymen in their disputes with the Europeans.'

Guo levers himself up. 'Do you know where they sent me after you pissed off?' he says. 'To some village just behind the front line where they'd dumped a sackful of Seneghalese bastards. Those coal-faced bags of shit cheated us every day, but because they're soldiers and citizens of the glorious French Empire they got away with it.'

'Look, Guo, I'm a busy man. If there's any help I can provide, please let me know. Otherwise, I've got work to do.'

'Do you Shanghai dogs have your brains in your knees?' Guo replies, thrusting his face into Wang's. 'I don't need you. I don't want you. You so-called interpreters are idiots raised by dogs. Your balls have been eaten by pigs. Just piss off and leave us alone.'

Wang decides that, for his own safety, he will do as he has been asked. 'Maybe we can talk again another day?' he says.

'Maybe the shit in your brains will ooze out all over your face,' Guo replies.

Guo is an irritation but nothing more. Wang is so overloaded with work and so preoccupied by other concerns—learning the rules of football being one of them—that he scarcely gives the man another thought. Labourers come and go, with hundreds passing through the camp at Noyelles each week. Some are registered and checked for the first time, while others return for running repairs. Wang has a better idea than most about the places to which they are dispatched and the tasks to which they are assigned, but even he finds it difficult to keep track of all the different work parties, especially those which are sent eastwards towards the front lines from whose dangers he is protected.

War work and football practice dominate daylight hours, if not his thoughts. He is sent to Desvres to investigate a disturbance and spends a frustrating week standing in for a sick translator at a munitions depot near Montreuil where there have been ongoing tensions between Chinese and French workers. When he returns he is pressed into writing an article for the *Huagong Zazhi*, the Labour Corps' own newspaper, but discovers, when he eventually gets to see the published version, that what he has written has been garbled beyond any labourer's powers of comprehension. He is unsure what annoys him most—the time wasted on the article in the first place, or the fact that he has been made to seem semi-literate by some unseen, incompetent printer.

However, these work frustrations are as nothing in comparison with his annoyance at the time given to football. Do what he may to escape his goalkeeping duties, he cannot wriggle free from Fell's obduracy. He has been given a morale-boosting task to do, and he cannot rest until his duty has been done and his orders obeyed. On an almost daily basis he is compelled to change into an apian boy scout's uniform and dance around a field while a ball is kicked in random patterns around him. If it comes his way, he catches it; if Second Lieutenant Stevens comes his way, he does his best to avoid him. He is not particularly successful in either case. The only benefit that comes from the sorry, sodden business is that it keeps his mind off other irritations, Guo included, so it is something of a rude awakening when, several weeks after their previous encounter, the Sichuanese labourer thumps on his dormitory window long after curfew.

'What do you want?' Wang demands, once he has surfaced enough to work out what is going on.

When Guo mouths incomprehensibly at him through the window, he lies back down and pulls his blanket over his head. Guo bangs on the window again.

'Will you shut that southern bastard up?' a voice calls from his neighbour's bed.

'He's nothing to do with me,' Wang replies.

'Doesn't bloody sound like it.'

Groaning, Wang pulls himself up, takes one look at the labourer's angry expression, and pulls on his boots.

'What do you think you're doing?' he asks once he has got outside and ushered Guo away from the dormitory.

'I've come to find out what you're still doing here.'

'What on earth are you talking about, Guo? I'm still here because I work here. I'm still here because the war hasn't miraculously ended. I'm still here because it's the middle of the night and I was trying to get some sleep.'

Guo stops pacing up and down. 'I want to know what you're fucking up to, working for the foreign devils.'

Wang looks up to the sky. 'I don't know if you've noticed, my friend, but you work for the foreign devils too.'

Guo is having nothing of it. 'I work for myself,' he says.

Wang sighs. 'You're here under contract, Guo.'

With no word of warning, he sees Guo's face, horribly magnified, arrowing towards him and then feels himself falling backwards with the labourer's hands around his throat. So this is what war is like, he thinks, as Guo lands on top of him. This is what it means to come under attack. He tenses himself for the fight but suddenly—and wholly unexpectedly—Guo disappears from view.

When Wang pulls himself up he sees him thrashing around on the ground like a garoupa fresh from the tank, clutching his back and moaning. Wang edges away and waits until the twitching stops.

'Don't ever mention the fucking contract to me again, Wang,' Guo whispers through clenched teeth.

Wang stands up gingerly, backs up to the nearest tree, and leans slowly against it.

'I'm here because I need the money, not because of some European contract.' Guo levers himself up onto one arm. 'Oh my fucking back,' he moans, rubbing himself violently. 'Do you know what the white devils had us doing?'

Wang shakes his head and steadies himself against the tree.

'Digging their trenches. Clearing their dead. Clearing their fucking dead. Do you know the first thing I saw when they sent me to the front line?'

Wang shakes his head again.

'A pair of feet. Feet with no body attached. They still had the bloody puttees on. They sent us to the front line, Wang. The bloody front line. "Oh no," that ghost said when I challenged him at Weihaiwei. "You'll not be sent anywhere near the fighting. You'll be doing coolie work miles behind the lines." I tell you what, Wang. When I shouted and screamed I couldn't hear anything with the noise of all those fucking shells. I might as well have been spitting down a mountain for all the words I could hear.'

He pauses for breath.

'All that was left was his feet.'

Wang waits for a few seconds before replying. 'I'm sorry, Guo,' he says.

'No you're not. You're bloody relieved. You've been hanging around here, licking officer arse and sleeping sound at night, while we were kipping in the shit. Do you know what sleeping in those mudholes does to a man? I saw one of the white devils wading across the trench with bloody great boxes on his feet. I thought he was trying to keep his boots clean, but he wasn't. His feet had swollen up so bad he couldn't get his fucking boots on.

149

He tied some rope to the sides of the boxes and pulled his feet up to get them to move.'

Wang stays silent.

'We dug the bloody trenches for them. Do you know what that means? It means we stuck our spades through rotting heads. It means we had to stand back whenever we found a bloated body in case it exploded all over us. I was so dog tired I'd grab hold of lumps of wood in the ground and, when they came away in my hand, I'd find I was holding a fucking arm.'

Wang tries to cover his ears, but Guo pulls himself up and shouts louder.

'Do you know what happened to Zhang Wanye? He was digging a pit with some Xinjiang fucker and his shovel hit an unexploded shell. The only bit of him they found was the helmet which got stuck in a tree a hundred yards away. Do you know what happened to Zhang Rushi? He found a grenade and, because they hadn't told him what it was, he pulled the fucking pin out.'

He slumps back onto the floor. 'Don't ever tell me I'm under contract again.'

Wang's face is damp despite the cold, but he dares not move to wipe the moisture away.

'What happened to you?' he asks eventually. 'What did you do to your back?'

Guo doesn't answer at first. When he starts speaking again his voice is strained.

'An industrial accident. That's what they called it. A fucking industrial accident. I fell off a train. After we'd finished digging trenches, they set us to work digging up their bloody railway lines. They said that the Germans were about to attack and they didn't want them using them. So they got us up in the middle of the night and took us through the front lines. They took us on the bloody train and then told us to dig up the line. And do you know what the worst thing was about it? We had to pile the rails so high that the bloody trains could hardly move, even with tractors pulling them. They just picked us off like chickens: Zhu Guochao, Zhuang

Yuan, You Shizan. None of them came back. An industrial fucking accident! I fell off the bloody train because the fucking Germans were dropping shells on top of us.'

Unable to bear hearing any more, Wang starts to walk away.

'Can't you see what they're doing to us?' Guo shouts after him. 'Can't you see what they're doing to you? You're a dupe, a one-eyed lackey. They've half-blinded you with praise and cushy jobs behind the lines, while they're slaughtering the rest of us—the ones who don't have your fancy words.'

Stung into a response despite his determination not to answer, Wang shouts back. 'That's not what it's like, Guo. I chose to come here. I chose to do this job. I came into it with my eyes wide open.'

Disconcertingly, Guo starts to smile. 'You poor fool,' he says. 'You dupe. You idiot. You've no idea, have you?'

But Wang doesn't let him finish. 'I know exactly what's going on. Yes, I know that they give us work, that they train us to be doctors, that they give us the opportunity to escape from a country that's gone to the dogs. What's so very wrong with that?'

'What's wrong is that you think it's all sunlight and lilies,' Guo replies, still smiling contemptuously. 'You think it's jobs and freedom. You've lost all perspective, that's what's wrong. Why don't you ask that fancy boy of yours what they do in the barbed wire prison at the top of the hill? That bit of the camp you've never asked about, let alone visited.' He spits on the ground. 'Go and ask that question and then we can have a talk that's more than just words.'

Chapter 13

With no intention of doing anything Guo tells him to do, Wang concentrates on the matter at hand, which, for the time being at least, is Fell's preposterous football match. When the day he has been dreading finally arrives, he joins the rest of his team for a final practice before trudging across the camp towards what is fondly referred to as the pitch, though, as An Rushan has often pointed out, it is merely a muddy patch of grass marked out by four flags. There Stevens announces one of his curious pre-game routines, leaving Wang no choice but to join the rest of the team in running round in circles, stretching his legs at strange angles, and skipping like a girl.

A crowd of curious labourers has already gathered and when the team starts kicking footballs about they go wild. Wang has never heard such a noise, not even at a Saturday evening film show. After a few minutes, Stevens leads the team to what he calls the dressing room, but everyone else calls the recreation hut, throws out a few stray labourers and then turns to the players.

'Right, men,' he says. 'This is it. Wang, translate will you? I'm not going to speak slowly so you've got to bloody keep up. Now then, this is the day when we get the chance to kick a ball in front of a crowd of hundreds. This is the day when we're going to show those bastards how to play.'

Wang shifts uncomfortably in his seat and clears his throat. He translates as best he can.

'I've had enough of Bairstow's jibes, so we're going to stick them up his arse and then kick it round the park. Which means that you've got to do what I say. No running round after the ball like headless Germans. You've got to stick to your positions. Get the ball out wide and pass the bloody thing. Got it?'

Wang translates as idiomatically as he can manage, though he suspects that much of what Stevens says is essentially untranslatable.

'Yes, sir,' the labourers mutter.

'And let's use our firepower up front, all right? Get the ball to An Rushan. They're not going to know what's hit them when he starts firing.'

'Yes, sir,' a couple of players reply once Wang has found a Chinese equivalent.

'And another thing,' Stevens suddenly shouts. 'Let's hear some bloody noise. Talk to each other. Give each other some stick if you need to. I want to hear some passion.'

The labourers all look at Wang. Once he has spoken, they all turn back to Stevens.

'Yes, sir,' An Rushan bellows.

'That's more like it. Now then, let's get into our kit.'

When the team marches out of the hut ten minutes later, resplendent in their new uniform, they are surprised to find a tunnel of labourers all the way from the recreation hut to the football pitch. Someone starts to blow on a shawm, and soon cymbals, trumpets and voices unite as though the war has come to a sudden and victorious end. Wang looks over the heads of his fellow players in disbelief. As the team walks up to the brow of the hill, the labourers cheer, chant and sing.

'What are they saying?' Stevens bawls into Wang's ear.

'Add oil, sir,' Wang replies. Then, in response to Stevens's look of incomprehension, he adds, 'It's an encouragement to play well, sir.'

As they get closer to the pitch the crowd increases in both size and volume. In places the labourers are six deep. Wang feels a sense of national pride surge through him and wishes he had spent longer practising. The British team is already on the pitch when the Chinese arrive. They are kicking the ball about to the accompaniment of jeers and less-than-complimentary, but untranslated, comments.

Stevens leads his team onto the field and waits for the British to form a line next to them. When Captain Bairstow gives a signal, there is a flurry of activity as Major Greenstreet rides onto the field on his magnificent grey horse. He dismounts, shakes the hand of each player, says a few words to the British team, and then gives a short speech to the crowd.

'Even in the most trying times,' he shouts through a megaphone, 'men have been brought together by shared enterprise. Even in the darkest days, the light of common endeavour has united that which has always been parted.'

Captain Blyth has been co-opted into translating but is clearly struggling to turn the major's rhetoric into comprehensible Chinese. He does his best, and the British clap politely.

'So it is with no little pride that I come here to oversee this football match, remembering that what brings us together is not merely this noble game, but the hope of the growth of friendship between nations.'

He pauses in the expectation of more applause. The officers do their best to oblige.

'It is a sign of the progress we have made that those whom we previously knew only as shifty foreigners from far across the seas should have been brought to Europe not only as workers but now as competitors, and one day soon, I dare to suggest, even as friends.'

Wang is glad that he is not translating.

'So let battle commence. I wish both teams the very best of British luck, and may the best team win.'

As Greenstreet finishes with a flourish, Blyth steps back in obvious relief, the British applaud enthusiastically, and the Chinese begin to roar once more. The major holds out his arms for silence, and then a lone trumpeter leads the two teams in a rendition of *God Save the King*.

When they have finished slaughtering the anthem, the game begins.

Second Lieutenant Jameson blows his whistle, Hu kicks the ball back to An Rushan, and the roar of the crowd grows so loud that even the shouted instructions of Lieutenant Stevens are lost. Wang watches him jump up and down but, though his lips move, it is as if he has been struck dumb, for no words seem to emerge.

If he is honest, Wang does not fully understand what is happening in the game. Though he has gradually mastered the sport's essential principles, some of its more technical regulations have passed him by. Men run furiously up and down the field, even when the ball is nowhere near them. Second Lieutenant Jameson blows his whistle for reasons which mystify not only the majority of the spectators but many of the players too, and sometimes, especially when the ball is kicked quickly from one player to another, the British clap politely. There is little for Wang to do and so, despite his best efforts, he loses concentration.

He is brought back into the game by a sudden roar from the crowd. When he looks up, he sees Second Lieutenant Smith and Lieutenant Barker shouting at Second Lieutenant Jameson, while another officer lies on the ground at his feet. Wang thinks for a moment that he has been shot, but the officer eventually clambers to his feet, Second Lieutenant Jameson waves the others away, and the game resumes.

Wang has sometimes been embarrassed by his height but, as the British bang balls into his area, he revels in the ease with which he leaps and catches them above the heads of Second Lieutenants Barker and Smith. Even better than catching is punching the ball away. It is an approach Stevens has recommended in training and he soon puts it to good use, getting to the ball ahead of an onrushing Smith and then clearing it from an inswinging corner as Barker clatters into him. The next time Barker tries the same trick, Wang sends both him and the ball flying. To Barker's dismay, and the crowd's loudly expressed approval, Second Lieutenant Jameson waves all demands for a penalty away.

When the first goal comes it is a perplexing affair. Wang boots the ball upfield and watches as Hu Jieshi passes to Liang Lei, who swings the ball out wide to Wu Penggen. Wu then knocks the ball into An Rushan, who seems to get his legs tangled. Then, as the ball falls behind him, he swivels, hacks, and watches as the ball flies in the opposite direction to the way he is facing.

'Did you see that?' Stevens yells, running round and round in circles with his arms out like the wings of a plane. 'A bicycle kick. A bloody bicycle kick.'

He hugs three or four startled labourers.

'We're going to do this. We're going to bloody well do it.'

When Second Lieutenant Jameson blows his whistle again, he runs onto the field, calling the Chinese team to him as he comes. By the time Wang gets there from his goal-bound position, they are already in a circle and Stevens is clapping An Rushan on the back. The British players, by contrast, are sitting on the ground, staring disconsolately at the grass. In Wang's opinion, they are not setting a very good example for their men.

When the match resumes, the atmosphere is tangibly different. The crowd is louder and the British quieter but more determined. Hu Jieshi and An Rushan are kicked, and Liang Lei has to be helped off the field with a bad gash to his leg. Major Greenstreet climbs grimly onto his horse to watch proceedings, and Wang has to try hard to suppress a grin. The Chinese are on top, and no one can quite believe it.

Wang makes one fine save, tipping a dipping drive from Barker round the post, but when Hu Jieshi slips he finds Barker charging towards him with the ball at his feet. With his one eye, he finds it difficult to judge distance, but he rushes forward anyway and flings himself at the ball. When he arrives, neither Barker nor the ball are there and, looking back, he sees the ball slide gently between the two goalposts. He has been made to look a fool by Barker's sidestep and is tempted to punch him instead of the ball the next time he enters the box.

The game remains at one all for the next quarter of an hour, but Wang plays in something of a daze until Stevens shouts at him to pull himself together.

The Chinese are becoming ill-disciplined now, and even though they are at least as fit as the British they have less footballing experience. When Smith punts the ball into the corner, Hu Jieshi tries to keep the ball in play but succeeds only in giving it back to the opposition. Wang is forced to make three quick saves in succession and wishes that An Rushan would make another of his surging runs to take the pressure off his creaking defence. When Stevens starts shouting again, this time demanding that Second Lieutenant Jameson stop the match, he knows that he doesn't have to hang on for much longer.

'It's ninety-six minutes!' Stevens yells. 'You've played six minutes of added time. Where the bloody hell did that come from?'

With Stevens growing increasingly agitated, and Barker bursting into the area with the ball at his feet, Wang is delighted when Jameson finally gives into Stevens's pleading and blows his whistle. He turns away in relief and is about to call out to Shi Fengren, one of the other interpreters who has come to watch, when he hears Stevens explode behind him.

'No, no, no, no, no! That was never a penalty! He was outside the area! You can't do this to me!'

As soon as the crowd realise what has happened, they begin to scream insults at Jameson. Wang is relieved to hear that most of them throw abuse in their local dialects, but, even so, he fears he will be called away from his goalkeeping duties to translate for yet more court martials.

When a couple of labourers invade the pitch and are hauled off by camp guards, Stevens turns bright red and uses language Wang has never heard before. But Jameson simply blows on his whistle again and points at the ground in front of him. After a while he marches over to Stevens and shouts in his face.

'Stevens, I'm warning you. If you don't keep your bloody trap shut I shall have you on a charge.'

'I don't care,' Stevens yells back. 'You can't do this to us. That was never a penalty and you know it.'

'Who's the ref, Stevens?'

Stevens throws his cap to the ground and turns his back on his fellow officer. Wang cannot quite believe he is seeing such naked indiscipline and considers consoling Stevens, but when Second Lieutenant Jameson blows his whistle again, the coach strides off towards the far side of the field. Lieutenant Barker picks up the ball and places it on the penalty spot, Jameson waves the other players away, and Wang suddenly realises that he still has a chance to save face and save the game. He wipes his gloves on his shirt and tries to decide which way to dive.

With the crowd bellowing contradictory advice, and his teammates screaming unhelpful instructions, he concentrates on blocking out all sound as he skips from side to side on the goal-line. When Barker begins his run up, Wang thinks about flinging himself to the left, then changes his mind at the last second and stays rooted to the spot as Barker fires the ball in off the post. Major Greenstreet gives a loud hurrah, the rest of the British officers start running round like madmen, and the Chinese players sink to the ground as though caught by the blast of an unseen explosion. Wang covers his face in horror and walks from the pitch alone.

Chapter 14

If Guo is at the football match, Wang doesn't see him. But, even though he seems to have shaken off Guo himself, he can't escape the memory of his patronising smile and his jibes about the fenced-off parts of the camp he hasn't had chance to visit. So, to his own surprise, he finds himself asking Captain Blyth the next time he sees him about the isolated building Guo mentioned.

'Ah, yes,' Blyth says. 'That wasn't on the tour, was it?'

'Should it have been, sir?'

'Well, it's not the sort of place that visiting dignitaries usually get shown.'

'I wasn't aware that I was a visiting dignitary, sir.'

Blyth laughs. 'You're not. So let's do something useful instead, shall we?'

Maybe it's the way Blyth puts him off. Maybe it's the sense of humiliation that clings to his performance in the football match. Whatever the reason, Wang digs his heels in and refuses to be brushed off. When a raft of complaints come in about coolies causing trouble in the regions, he sees an opportunity to badger Blyth again.

'I would be delighted to do what I can to quiet the restive masses, sir,' he says when Blyth presents him with the list of problem areas. 'Then perhaps I could complete my tour of the camp when I get back?'

Blyth removes his cap and runs his hands through his hair.

'You've settled in, Wang, and no mistake.'

'I certainly hope that I have been of some assistance, sir.'

'And you're bloody persistent, I'll give you that.'

'I am determined to do a good job, sir.'

Blyth flicks through his pile of papers. 'All right then. Maybe we can make an exception for you, though I've no idea why you're so keen to see the place. Most people steer well clear.'

Since Wang isn't sure either, he keeps quiet.

'Give us a shout when you get back and I'll see what I can arrange.'

Such is the scale of the labourers' unrest that Wang is away for almost three weeks. After spending two days in a sawmill in Eawy Forest, he hitches a lift to a military grain depot in the heart of the Picardie countryside where there is a dispute about the use of a conveyor belt. The labourers are being ordered to carry what seem to Wang unbearably large sacks of oats from one store to another, while a serviceable conveyor belt stands idle. When, after hours of patient negotiation, that dispute is resolved, he travels by truck to a powder plant where three men have been killed and several others injured in an explosion. There too he is kept away from the worst of the aftermath, though there is no hiding the anger of the labourers. By the time he gets back to Noyelles, he is strangely excited by the prospect of a confrontation with Blyth, but there is no need—the captain is ready for him when he enters the camp.

'What's the name of the book that scoundrel Freud wrote?' he asks as he leads Wang uphill.

'*The Interpretation of Dreams*, sir?' Wang suggests.

'No, the other one.'

Wang shakes his head. He has not taken much interest in the new science.

'*Totem and Taboo*, that's it,' Blyth answers himself. 'I haven't read it, but I find the title intriguing. This little settlement is our taboo area.'

Wang looks sideways at him. 'What is it exactly, sir?'

As Blyth unlocks a gate and salutes a sour-faced private, he

160

explains. 'It's where we keep the lunatics and the lepers. It's not the soldiers' favourite posting.'

Leading him towards a standpipe, Blyth encourages him to wash his hands thoroughly.

'But there's no expense spared here,' he continues. 'The lunatics see the same doctors, wear the same clothes, and eat the same food as the rest of the men. The only difference is that we don't use those hot-water-jacketed trays to bring the grub from the kitchens. A fellow called Gu got hold of one a few weeks ago and ended up with first degree burns to his hands and face.'

He unlocks another door and beckons Wang through.

'Come on, let's meet a madman or two.'

Wang hesitates but, as Blyth locks the door behind them, he realises the time for choice has gone.

'Righto, sir,' he replies more jauntily than he feels.

The camp at Noyelles is always awash with noise. If the labourers aren't talking or singing, they are shouting or complaining, though it is the animals that seem to make the most sound. There is a thriving black market in dogs, and many of the labourers befriend the feral cats that roam the camp. A few men even managed to tend a couple of chickens, until a tour of the dormitory's storeroom by a senior officer put paid to their avian ambitions. None of these animals—and few of the men—are ever silent, but the madmen are, and their silence disturbs Wang more than any of the camp's noises. If Blyth notices the contrast, he doesn't comment.

'We try to keep them entertained, of course,' he explains. 'Quite a number of them do basket weaving, though you'd be amazed at the damage they can cause with just a few yards of twine. They get their magazines and puzzles too, just like the rest of the men, but we have to make sure they can't get their hands on anything too sharp because they can be sly devils. In fact, they're so ingenious I sometimes think we ought to put them in charge of military planning.'

Wang retains a quasi-instinctive respect for authority

161

and never enjoys hearing the British banter about incompetent generals or ignorant politicians. Nevertheless, he tries to force a smile. It fades as soon as they enter the asylum.

There are few patients, but Wang has never met men so pitiful. In the first room, a fetid place perhaps one third the size of the wards, five men are sitting in easy chairs. One of them, a tall, gaunt figure, is rocking back and forth while picking at the scabs on his hands. Another is pulling at threads in the armrest and moaning as though he has just been shot. The others are completely immobile. Two are staring at the floor and the other is looking intently at a blank wall. The guard sniffs dismissively.

Blyth shepherds them into another room, where a young man is being restrained by two Chinese nurses. He kicks and spits with all the venom of a snake, but they soon tip him onto his back before forcing his arms behind him.

'Tried to attack Pan Shuhan again, sir,' they explain.

Blyth nods and keeps walking.

'You ought to see their recreation hut,' he says in a vain effort to lift the tone of the visit. 'It's got everything the main rec has but with far fewer customers. We even show films here. It keeps them entertained and stops them thinking about themselves for an evening.'

Wang inclines his head. There is nothing to lift the spirits that he can see. There is no sign of the magazines and puzzles, let alone the crafts and movies Blyth mentioned. When Blyth suggests that they move onto the leper ward, Wang jumps at the opportunity.

'Do they do basket weaving too?' he asks, in an attempt to revive the flagging conversation.

'We tried,' Blyth admits, 'but the poor buggers' fingers blistered so badly we had to drop it.'

Never having met a leper before, Wang struggles to understand how it is in France of all places that he is about to meet one for the first time. When they meet the first patient, he fails to control his disgust.

'Zhuang Guancai,' the man says, holding out his hand in greeting.

Wang steps back instinctively.

'It's all right,' the man says. 'It'll not come off.'

'I'm sorry,' Wang splutters. 'That's not what I meant.'

'Of course it is. It always is, the first time. You'll soon get used to it. If you come back, that is.'

Blyth steers him away and tries to crack a joke, but the leper ward is not a place in which to be frivolous. It is a place where men sit on the edge of their beds picking at their red skin. It is a nether region where labourers are force-fed, where arms are bandaged after unspecified incidents, where even Captain Blyth is not wholly safe.

When a one-armed labourer attacks him as he walks into a dormitory, Wang asks if they can leave.

'Can't you get me any poison?' the labourer shouts after them. 'This is no good. I can't live like this. Look at my fucking fingers. Just look at them!'

Wang jumps, but Captain Blyth and the sullen guard have already stepped in.

'Now, calm down, Chu,' Captain Blyth shouts. 'You know you can't go around confronting the visitors. If you'd only follow the course of treatment you've been given—'

'Get back, you little shit,' the guard interrupts, 'or I'll blow the rest of your bloody fingers off.'

As soon as they get through the three or four gates between them and the main camp, Wang tries to rush away, but Blyth lays a restraining hand on his arm.

'These poor devils need help, Wang. You know that, don't you?'

Wang turns away. Blyth sighs and tries again.

'These are Chinese men with Chinese illnesses. This has nothing to do with the horrors of trench warfare. This is what China has brought to us—there's no leprosy in Europe—so we could just ignore it and hope it will go away. But, do you know what? If treating the Chinese is what the Good Lord wanted me to do when he called me to Peking, then I reckon it's what he wants me to do here as well. I could have been festering in some putrid war zone, but I'm here instead, in the largest Chinese hospital in the world, doing what I was trained to do, bringing relief to a people I love.'

Wang looks down.

'Do you know why I let you come here today? I'm not supposed to take anyone into the leprosy wards, but I thought I'd bend that little rule because I wanted you to see just how much there still is to do.'

Still Wang says nothing.

'That's why I need people like you, Wang—educated Chinamen who love their country and love their work. I need you because there's still so much work to do.'

When, a few days later, he is summoned to the camp prison, a bare Nissen hut guarded by five bored privates, Wang is not wholly surprised to find Guo squatting on the ground of a bare cell.

'So you've escaped from that Blood Pond Hell have you?' Guo demands.

Wang chooses not to rise to the comment.

'You're nothing if not predictable, Guo,' he says.

'What did you see? Ox-headed men and white devils with faces like horses? Water dissolving into streams of pus, and food becoming fire in the mouth? Were the white devils nailing us onto platforms with forty-nine spikes?'

'Do you want to hear the charges they've laid against you, Guo?'

'No, I do not. I want to know what you saw in that hell house none of the rest of us are allowed near unless we're locked up there. Chests cut open and hearts exposed? Faces with the skin peeled off? Blood pouring out of ears and noses? Of course

164

you didn't, because you didn't want to. With your one eye you've swaggered around, but you haven't seen anything. You've looked with that fucking glass eye of yours, and you think you've seen it all.'

Wang feels his hands clench into fists, but Guo simply laughs at him.

'What? Are we going to see Wang the man at last? Are you strong enough to take on a coolie with a bad back?'

Wang slowly unclenches his fists.

'Listen, Wang, and I'll tell you what you've missed for all your one-eyed looking. You've not seen women pushing their children behind them when we march down the street. You've not seen the way they pull at the corners of their eyes when we approach. If you'd spent more than just a few hours in the factories and workshops, you'd have seen the way they thrash us, cut our pay, and spit in our food, just because they can't stand having to rely on yellow men to help them win their white war. If you'd actually bothered to look, you'd have seen that they speak to us like we're women and fence us in like prisoners. And then they tear their own contracts up and send us to the fucking front line. You'd think we'd get a bloody medal for all that, but instead they lock us up here in this pit with shitholes like you.'

'Do you want to hear the charges?' Wang repeats.

'Do you really think that I care about what charges they've cooked up?'

'One. That on the evening of the third of March 1918, Labourer 40505 was discovered in the vicinity of the village estaminet without the requisite pass.'

Guo levers himself up but Wang holds his ground.

'Do you think that it makes the slightest difference if I hear them or not?'

'Two. That he did resist arrest. Three—'

'But you've got a choice.'

'Three—'

'If you're a British bastard in a Chinese body you'll do exactly what they ask you to do, but if there's any remnant of Chinese left in you, you'll help me get out.'

Wang takes a step forward and tries to hit him, but Guo easily deflects his flailing right arm.

'What do you mean if there's any Chinese left in me?' Wang shouts. 'While you've been organising strikes and sit-ins, it's I who have been helping our countrymen make themselves understood.'

Guo smiles derisively. 'You don't really believe that, do you?' he says. 'All that shit about helping the coolies get understood? You've just done what the bloody British told you to do. You've helped keep us in order. You haven't the faintest idea what life is like outside the camp.'

'I've seen more of Northern France than you have, Guo.'

'And for all your looking you've seen fucking nothing.'

He hears that Guo has been sentenced to a week's imprisonment, three days of which are to be spent in solitary confinement, but Wang has no chance to see him because he is almost immediately sent to Fécamp to deal with a small group of Chinese dockers who are complaining about their overseer. After questioning the ringleader—a Guangzhou textile worker with an accent he can barely decipher—and meeting the overseer at the centre of the dispute, he realises that there is little he can do. The overseer is arrogant, and the labourers have had enough. He lets the dockers vent their frustration at him, recommends a transfer for the overseer, and rushes off to visit the house where Guy de Maupassant once lived.

Despite working almost exclusively in English, he has not thought about England itself for some time, but as he stands on the seafront, looking across the Channel to where he imagines Hastings might be, he yearns once more for the place he dreamt about in Shanghai, a nation that straddles the world confidence and charm, a chivalrous country where battles are fought with bravery and valour.

It is a cold winter, and the sea breeze is strong enough to

push him onto the coastal rail, but he stays put and tries to make sense of what he has seen in the leprosy and lunacy wards. Not so much the suffering and the misery as Captain Blyth's attempts to explain that suffering away. He cannot accept Guo's intemperate disparagement of men he has come to admire, but he cannot reconcile what he saw and heard with what he has always believed either. Gripping the rail more firmly, he makes a strenuous effort to regrasp the glory that he imagined while reading himself into a love of England back in China. But however hard he tries, he cannot do it—the past is past, and the future seems delayed.

Returning to Noyelles, he calls in on members of the Chinese Labour Corps in Rouen, Amiens and Abbeville, so that he can prepare a report that will probably never be read. He is used to these journeys now and has become resigned to intense negotiations followed by tedious hours waiting at windswept stations.

He doesn't approach his trips away from Noyelles as a tourist any more, but instead begins to measure the progress of the war by the activity he sees while moving from place to place. When he first arrived, some of his compatriots seemed to do very little. Labourers in the tank factories trundled slowly through their tasks while their overseers disappeared for the day; dock workers waited around for the next shipment of men or munitions to arrive; railway gangs lounged about in provincial sidings until an order came. Those days are now past. The Chinese, like the British and the French, are given no rest. Dockers, railway workers and labourers are forced to work harder, as the armies of both sides grow hungrier for munitions.

It seems as though change is coming, but there is no fundamental change as yet. The war drags on. Men kill and are killed. Most Chinese labourers hope that the Allies will triumph. It is the munitions workers that Wang feels most sorry for—the war may be in a state of stasis, but it is one that is maintained by enormous firepower, and they are always overworked.

Wang recalls his trips to the birdwatching grounds of the

Baie de Somme. Like the tide, the war seeps up and over the muddy flats of France and then retreats imperceptibly, leaving nothing behind but food for the migratory birds, only to advance once more when it has apparently gone for good. It has become as natural as the half-hearted European seasons, and he sees no reason why it should ever come to an end.

Since most of the labourers are getting more money than they have ever been used to before, they show little interest in the war itself. While they are away from the front, and while they are being paid, they don't greatly care whether Cambrai has been taken or the Ludendorff Offensive will be successful. Most of the translators and some of the better-educated labourers follow the war news in the *Huagong Zhoubao*, but even they are pretty philosophical about what they read.

'They will grind themselves down to a flour,' Shu Junrong, a former teacher turned labourer, tells him one day, 'and then we will see what sort of bread will be baked for the future.'

Fell's take, when Wang dares to ask him directly what he thinks about the war, is subtly different. 'Men died last year,' he says. 'Men are dying this year and, the way things are going, more men will die next year.'

Wang is not satisfied with this answer. 'But surely there must be some progress,' he insists.

Fell shrugs. 'That's what you'd think,' he says. 'All I know is that I've got work to do so, if you'll excuse me, I'll get on and do it.'

The one man who can be relied upon to give a straight and detailed answer to Wang's questions is the one man Wang cannot speak to. Almost as soon as his sentence is over, Guo attempts to break out of the camp and, almost immediately, he is caught. In lieu of a lawyer, Wang is summoned to help him but, after an argument about why he didn't at least wait a few days before starting to cause trouble again, Guo kicks him out, claiming he would rather deal with the white devils than a Chinese turned white. Predictably, he is found guilty but, unpredictably, he is not sent back to China. Some of the British seem to be impressed by a coolie who can break out of camp with a bad back. They sentence him to fourteen days' imprisonment followed by burial fatigues.

'Fourteen days is fourteen days,' Guo tells Wang triumphantly, 'but burial duty means I get out of this fucking prison camp.'

'You can't risk another offence,' Wang tells him.

'You said that last time.'

'You're not one of the immortals. You can't get away with it forever.'

'I've got away with it so far. I do as I want, not as some white-faced devil tells me.'

There is nothing Wang can do to convince Guo to behave differently. He believes that he has grown closer to the common labouring masses during his time in France, but between Guo and him there is still an immeasurable gap. Even so, he finds the man intriguing. There is something about his certainty, something—he hates to admit it—about the directness of his grievances that compels attention, so when Guo's fortnight in prison is over Wang asks Captain Blyth if he can join the next burial party.

'I would have thought there were more pleasant outings in the vicinity,' Blyth says, 'but if that's what you want to do, I can arrange it. One of the lunatics fell off the water tower this morning—God only knows what he was doing up there—so we'll have to get him six feet under pretty soon. I'll speak to the padre about you joining him.'

When Wang arrives at the main gate the next morning, Guo is lying on the grass. He doesn't seem to be the worse for wear after his period of incarceration. Ignoring him, Wang speaks to the padre, a former Baptist missionary from Nanchang, who is more obviously prepared for the burial.

'I don't really need any help, you know,' the padre says. 'My Chinese is really pretty good.'

'I have come to pay my respects, sir,' Wang replies, 'not to translate.'

The padre is not listening. 'We always held our funeral services in English when I was in Kiangsi,' he says. 'We didn't use this service, of course, so that'll explain why I might stumble a bit.'

'I am sure your grasp of the language is excellent, sir.'

'I didn't have the same advantages as the chaps who were based in Peking.'

'Nanchang is a noble city too, sir.'

'Well, just as long as you understand. Now, where are those men?'

He paces about, drumming his fingers on the service book as he walks, while the burial party lounges around at the base of the pagoda. Guo sticks a piece of grass between his teeth and only stops grinning when he rolls over to spit. Eventually the coffin bearers arrive, carrying a Union Jack-draped casket on their shoulders. There are six of them, but one is considerably taller than the rest, so the coffin dips and bucks alarmingly as they make their way up the road.

'Where the devil have you been?' the padre shouts. 'We're twenty minutes late already.'

Still drumming nervously on his service book, he leads the way, while the coffin bearers follow jerkily behind. The orderly medical officer and Wang walk respectfully behind the coffin and try not to be distracted by the dead man's final fluctuating journey or the padre's increasingly anxious over-the-shoulder glances. Guo and the other labourers trundle close behind, looking more serious than Wang expected. An elderly couple who are standing outside the village church stop talking as the procession passes by, the man removing his cap and the woman bowing her head. Outsiders in their own country, they are cut off from the Chinese by more than death, though that separates them too. As the burial party skirts around the village cemetery, Wang tries not to dwell on the fact that segregation continues into the afterlife.

The procession climbs slowly across the gently sloping Somme countryside until it arrives at a well-tended plot in which the graves of former members of the labour corps are marked by two or three hundred white crosses. The coffin-bearers lay their load on the ground, to the obvious relief of the padre who orders Guo and his fellow workers to finish digging the hole that other labourers have previously started. The going is extremely slow, but eventually they satisfy the padre, and the service, such as it is, begins. The whole party stands around the grave while a few prayers are read in halting Chinese. Then the coffin bearers lower the casket into the ground with two ropes.

'Ashes to ashes. Dust to dust,' the padre says, but the words have a strange ring to them in the cold, foreign land.

As a trusted ganger presides over Guo and the others, Wang, the orderly medical officer, and the padre walk back to the camp. The noise of the hard black soil falling onto the coffin lid merges with the sound of their footsteps as they leave the dead man behind.

'So how was your first burial, Wang?' Major Blyth asks the next day.

'It was a moving occasion, sir, though quite different from what I am used to back in China.' The memory of his mother's funeral with its *sheng guan* music, its white hemp, and its burning of the cart comes back to him with sudden force.

'Your lot chose the site of the cemetery,' Blyth says. 'Did you know that?'

'I did not, sir.'

'Good Feng Shui, I heard. Up on a hill overlooking a stream. Not sure it's quite as simple as that, but you get the general drift.'

'It was a generous gesture, sir.'

'It was the least we could do in the circumstances. If you're going to come all this way to help us in our war, we can at least ensure that you get a decent send-off.'

'I suppose so, sir.'

'Well, if you ever want to go again, just say the word, do you hear?'

Wang has no desire to attend another funeral. He loses himself in work instead and pushes Guo and all thoughts of mortality to the back of his mind.

Work is hard but bearable. What he finds trickier are evenings in the camp. Sharing a dormitory with a hundred illiterate labourers from rural Shandong, while the British sleep in their own comfortable billets, is something of a trial. There is rarely enough light for reading and never enough quiet for rest—men cough and spit, gamble and argue, or carry on rambling, one-sided conversations in their sleep. He has grown used to shutting himself off in his own little bunk, but he cannot wholly escape the attentions of his compatriots.

Sometimes he is manhandled by labourers wanting help with a letter home. On other occasions he is confronted with some indignity they have suffered during the day. Occasionally he is taken to task for his supposed complicity with the enemy, the enemy being the British rather than the Germans. He remembers what Guo said about his one-eyed looking but thrusts such thoughts away for fear of what damage they might do. But he can only thrust them so far.

A couple of weeks after the burial party he hears Guo banging on the window above his bed again.

'What do you want?' he whispers fiercely, but Guo simply gestures to him to come outside. It's raining and it's cold, but he has little choice. He pulls on his jacket and trousers and scrabbles under his bed for his boots.

'What do you want?' he repeats when he gets outside.

'I want to get out,' Guo replies.

Wang bangs his head with his fist. 'When will you ever learn, you Sichuanese idiot?' he says.

Guo ignores the question and starts walking away from the dormitory hut towards the limited shelter of the trees.

'I need you to get me out of here, Wang.'

'It can't be done,' Wang replies, hurrying to keep up.

'Of course it can be done. And if there's any Chinese left in you, you'll help me do it.'

'And what if I do?' Wang demands. 'What are you going to do then? Swim back to China?'

Guo grabs hold of his collar and pulls him into the shadows of the trees. 'I don't want to go back to China, you tortoise egg. I just want to get into the village.'

'Look, Guo,' Wang says, pulling himself free, 'I've been to the village. There's not much there. It's not the sort of place that's worth getting arrested for.'

Guo tries to grab him again. 'No, you look, you arrogant bastard. I've been to the village too, and I know exactly what's there.'

'What are you talking about, Guo.'

'I've been seeing a woman,' he says, and for the first time Wang detects a note of hesitation in his voice.

'A woman?' Wang repeats incredulously.

'Yes. At the estaminet.'

'A Frenchwoman?'

'Don't sound so surprised. You'd do the same if you had a chance.'

The rain is falling hard now, so he moves further under the tree cover.

'The village is out of bounds,' Wang points out as he follows him.

'Oh, come on, Wang. You know as well as I do that there are ways of getting in and out.'

Wang does indeed know this, though he has never thought about what might be involved in practice. 'How long has this been going on?' he asks.

'A month or so.'

'A month or so?'

Guo stops and faces him. 'You've been an interpreter for these foreign devils for too long, Wang. All you do is parrot words. Don't you have any of your own?'

173

'But if they catch you—'

'If they catch me they'll stick me in prison.'

Wang bangs his head with his hand again. 'Haven't you had enough spells in prison already?' he asks.

'I've had far too many. Which is why I've come to you. Now, will you help me or not?'

Wang runs his hand through his hair. 'I still don't understand what it is you want me to do.'

'Isn't it obvious, Wang? The woman likes me. They sent me to the front, but now I'm here and I don't know how long they'll let me stay.'

He is striding up and down in great agitation. Every now and again he winces and puts his hand to his buttocks, but then the striding resumes.

'Wait a minute, Guo. Let me be clear about this,' Wang says, trying to wipe the rain from his face and wishing he had brought along a coat. 'You want me to translate for you?'

Guo stops suddenly. He takes a step towards Wang and looks at him with such intensity that he forgets the rain. 'Yes. I want you to translate. And do you know why? Because I know about as much French as you know what's going on over here.'

Wang takes a step back. 'How much do you know?'

'The usual. *S'il vous plaît. Thé. Vin rouge. Vin blanc. Merci. Bang bang.*'

Despite the ridiculousness of the situation, despite the cold and the rain and Guo's clearly aching buttocks, Wang cannot stop himself from smiling.

'*Unlearn'd, he knew no schoolman's subtle art, No language, but the language of the heart,*' he says.

Guo clenches his fists in sudden anger. 'Are you insulting me?' he demands. 'Because if you ever fucking insult me I'll throttle you.'

Wang stops smiling and puts on a serious face. 'I promise I'm not insulting you,' he says.

Guo grunts disbelievingly and kicks at a tree root.

'What's her name?' Wang asks.

Guo looks up suspiciously. 'What's her name got to do with it?'

'Just tell me, Guo.'

'It's Katell.'

'Katell?'

'It's like Catherine. She's from Brittany. They speak funny there.'

Wang is amazed to see Guo look a little sheepish. An unexpected image flashes into his mind of his father's study in Shanghai. Recalling his book-lined shelves, he remembers reading *Henry V* for the first time.

'Catherine,' he says nostalgically. 'Katell. Well, you could always start by calling her *la plus belle Katell du monde*.'

'You are insulting me!' Guo shouts.

Wang puts up his hand to ward off the blow, but the blow never comes. When he withdraws his hand he sees Guo half striding and half limping back towards the huts.

'Guo, come back!'

'You're not the only interpreter in this camp. I'll find someone else,' Guo shouts back without turning to face him.

Wang runs after him and pulls on his arm. Guo swings round in anger.

'I can't speak the fucking language, Wang. I have no idea what she's saying to me. I've come half way round the world, and I can't understand a fucking word she says. Wang, I haven't got any time. I could be in some fucking trench again next week. Life is short in this shitty country, so I can't wait until the words come. If I'm going to have this woman I've got to have her now.'

There is nothing Wang can say. He looks into Guo's rain-drenched face and remembers Rong Meifan, her qipao, her elegance, her beautiful legs. There is nothing he can do to undo what was done in Beijing, but as Guo stares at him he tries to sweep the swirl of impressions and experiences that have been forced upon him in France into some sort of order. He sees men queuing to wash their hair in rusty iron buckets in a quarry yard, dozens of bare-chested northerners breaking stones by the side of a road, hundreds of munition workers squatting on the floor of their factory as a British officer and a half-educated peasant slug it out over rights and contracts and rations. He stuffs them back into the crammed pack of his mind, but the only sight he cannot force away is the one-armed leper who thrust his red-raw fingers in his face.

'All right, Guo,' he says. 'This time only. You get me out of the camp and I'll translate.'

Chapter 15

Wang resents being led but has no choice. As Guo steers him away from the dormitory huts towards the workshops on the other side of the camp, he stumbles. Guo puts out his arm to prevent him from falling, but when he stumbles again Guo takes him by the arm and, muttering and cursing, leads him as though he were completely blind.

'Keep your eyes on your feet,' he urges. 'I'll take you where we're going.'

Wang does as he is told but, being used to taking control, is unsure how much he can trust this man. As they skirt around the leper ward and the lunatic asylum, he hangs back.

'Where are we going?'

'Shut up and follow me,' Guo replies, heading away from the main gate and towards the work huts. When they reach them the rain is falling harder and there is little indication of an escape route, so Wang holds back. But Guo is insistent.

'Up here. Just do what I say.'

Grabbing hold of Wang's foot, he heaves him onto a window ledge. 'Grab hold of the fucking brick,' he says. Steadying himself, Wang finds the brick jutting out just above his head. 'Now pull yourself up. Quick.'

'I'm not a monkey, Guo. How do you expect me to get up there?'

'Just hold on and keep out of my way.'

He springs up onto the ledge and, before Wang can see exactly how he has managed it, hauls himself up onto the brick and from there onto the hut roof. Wang does his best to scramble after him.

'I thought you were going to stick your boot through the fucking window,' Guo huffs, once he has pulled him up the last few feet.

As he bends over, trying to catch his breath, Wang considers turning straight back round and returning to the security of his bunk, because what they are doing is madness. If Guo is caught again he will surely be sent back home, and Wang cannot bear the thought of being caught himself. He is not a common labourer. He is an interpreter, a link between workers and officers. The loss of pay would be bearable, but he would never be able to stand the humiliation.

'Let's get going,' Guo whispers fiercely.

'Where?'

'Just shut up and follow me.'

They scurry to the far side of the hut.

'How far can you jump?' Guo demands when they get to the building's edge.

'Jump?'

'As far as a man with a crooked back?'

And then he is gone, flinging himself across the darkness onto what it takes Wang a good minute to make out is the overhanging branch of a sycamore tree. After several more minutes and a great many more insults he jumps too and is steadied by Guo before he falls.

'Please tell me we're not going back that way.'

Guo grins. 'Depends how good a job you do.'

As they rush into the village, a dog barks, the rain turns to drizzle, and Guo grows less and less communicative. He is nervous, but the extent of his nervousness isn't clear until he grabs Wang just outside the estaminet.

'I swear I will kill you if you mess up this evening, Wang. If you make me look a fool in front of Katell. If you squeal when we're back in camp. I have not been shot at and had my back twisted like a corkscrew for you to fuck up now. This is it, Wang. This is my chance. This is the woman—she's got enormous tits and her own business. You'll fucking speak for me, and so help you if you say one word out of place.'

Wang pushes Guo's hand away and shoves open the estaminet door. It is as if he has stumbled upon France for the first time. The shelves behind the bar are stacked high with glasses. The counter is laden with bowls of sugar, racks of cutlery, and blue and white plates. There are old pictures on the wall—a faded imitation of a Monet garden, a village church, a child's bright splashes on a torn piece of paper.

As Guo disappears into the kitchen where all the sounds suggest Katell is preparing a meal, Wang explores the room. He runs his fingers across the back of the mismatched chairs and tables and peers at the blackboard which must once have advertised the day's special option, but which is now adorned with a British soldier's obscene graffiti. He follows the line of cigarette burns in the tablecloths and tries to make sense of the ship's barometer on the wall above the door. He looks longingly at the battered piano, which has a brass candle holder attached to its front, and allows his fingers to play gently on the surface of the keys. It seems another era when he played *Für Elise* and the *Moonlight Sonata* in Shanghai. Candles flicker dimly around an immaculately laid table in the centre of the room. The windows are blacked out and the doors all closed.

'Wang, come here,' Guo orders from the kitchen door. 'Come and meet Katell.'

Wang puts the piano lid down and nervously crosses the room, though it is Guo who is the more nervous when Katell appears in the doorway.

'This,' Guo tells him unnecessarily, 'is Katell.'

Wang is surprised. He has been expecting someone smaller, someone malleable, a woman Guo could dominate. But now, as she stands with a wooden spoon in one hand and her other on his shoulder, he seems diminished beside her. Not just her height

179

but her self-possession demands attention. As she appraises him, Wang notices Guo shifting uncomfortably, as though waiting for a court judgment. Wang is no longer diffident among women but, even so, he finds the directness of Katell's stare unnerving. Unable to hold her gaze, he sees enough to get an impression of brisk efficiency and poverty postponed. Her dress, which has been obtrusively patched below the level of her cooking apron, is green and floral, and her dark bulky hair is crammed ineffectively under ill-positioned clips. Stepping forward, she kisses him on both cheeks.

'I hate it when you do that,' Guo mutters.

'*Bonjour, monsieur*,' she says quietly, ignoring Guo's complaint.

'*Bonjour, madame. Je suis ravie de vous rencontrer.*'

'What did you say?' Guo demands.

'I said hello. Don't worry—I know my role in this evening's entertainment.'

'Well, just as long as you do.'

'I promise you that from now on the only words I shall speak will be yours and Katell's and, if you will permit me, I will explain as much to her too.'

Guo nods his assent.

'*Madame, ce soir, les seuls mots qui sortiront de ma bouche ne seront que les votres et ceux de Guo Ziqin.*'

'*Merci, monsieur.*'

Wang has been imagining a French version of Rong Meifan, but Katell is different. It is true that she has been cooking in a hot kitchen, which cannot have done a great deal for her sense of composure, but, even so, he cannot imagine that she would ever look beguiling in a qipao. Appraising her as he speaks, he finds that he is troubled by her looks. There is something compelling about her, but looking at her hands as she wipes them on her apron, which seems to be strewn with dog hairs, he sees no sign of voluptuousness. He tries to imagine her body in Guo's arms but cannot picture the two of them embracing. He thinks about what Guo told him outside the estaminet, but what strikes him are neither the breasts nor the business, but the wisps of hair that keep falling across her reddened face. Whenever she pushes them out of her alluring western eyes they fall straight back, and it is all he can do to stop himself from taking one of her hairclips and using it where it would do some good.

'*Voudriez-vous un verre de vin, monsieur?*'

'She is asking whether I would like a glass of wine, Guo.'

He grunts again.

'*Non merci, madame. Seulement un verre d'eau, s'il vous plait.* And I am refusing. I am on duty this evening and so shall drink only water.'

As Katell busies herself with the pots and pans, Guo sits at one unlit table with a glass of beer, while Wang sits at another with a glass of water. Every now and again, Guo gets up from his seat and attempts to infiltrate the kitchen, but he is always despatched with unseemly haste. Wang translates from the doorway the first couple of times but then opts for discretion. Katell and Guo understand each other perfectly well without him, and his interventions are doing little to improve the temper of the evening.

Not knowing where to put himself when Katell comes in with the first course, he pulls his chair back and stands awkwardly while she places a salad on the table. A small dog follows her in and sniffs around the table leg until Guo gives it a kick.

'It's tomato and mozzarella,' Katell says, glancing over her shoulder at the aggrieved animal.

'Is that some sort of *doufu*?' Guo asks once Wang has translated.

She laughs. 'No, silly, it's cheese.'

Guo looks suspicious. 'Are you sure?'

She laughs again. 'Do you want it or not?'

'It's food. Of course I want it.'

He picks up his fork and skewers the nearest piece of mozzarella like a fish. Wang sits back and back and stares, not at

Katell but at the food she has prepared. It had been a long time since he has seen such loving attention to detail. In the camp, the Chinese eat food to keep them well, to help them recover, or to give them the energy to work. They eat vast quantities of rice, salted fish, and meat when they can get it, and what passes for vegetables in the sickly French war zone. This meal is different. Or, at least, it is meant to be different. He watches in embarrassment as Guo plunges his fork into a mound of tomatoes.

'Where did you get these things?' he asks with his mouth full.

'I've been keeping them for you.'

'But where did they come from?'

'I've been growing them. You're not the only one who can keep a secret.'

Guo wipes his plate with his bread and belches expansively. 'It's good,' he says.

As Katell prepares the next course, Guo rolls and then smokes a cigarette, while Wang sits awkwardly in the corner of the room.

'What is she doing?' Guo mutters.

The two men listen to the sound of distant saucepans.

'I know you're not here,' he continues, 'but you can talk when I ask you a question.'

'I'm sorry, Guo. I thought you were speaking rhetorically.'

'I thought I was speaking Chinese. Maybe you've lost the knack.'

'I heard what you said, my friend. And my answer, if you want an answer, is that she is almost certainly preparing a meal you will never forget.'

'That's not what I came here for. It's not grub I want to remember.'

He lights another cigarette. When Katell walks in a few minutes later with a pot of *coq au vin*, he is sitting at the piano, silently dabbing at the keys as though he has spilled his wine and doesn't want Katell to notice. Proudly she beckons him over. As Guo sits down, Wang pulls up his own chair and waits respectfully until it is his turn to speak.

'*Bon appetit*,' Katell says and then waits with her fork poised as Guo turns to Wang for a translation.

They eat in silence for a few minutes while Wang continues to sit in the shadows, feeling awkward.

'Look, this is no good,' Guo bursts out, seizing Katell's hand across the table. 'We've got to talk before those bastards send me away.'

Wang edges forward and starts to translate. The dog wanders in again, finds some dropped food, and licks it up.

'It's what I've wanted all this time,' she replies.

'Look,' he repeats, glancing over his shoulder at Wang, 'we've just got to take our chance while we can.'

Katell nods as Wang translates.

'They've got it in for me. They're accusing me of all sorts—nicking food, starting fights, disappearing from camp without leave.'

She tries to reassure him, but he talks over her.

'They're going to send me away, I just know it. They'll find an excuse to send me back to the front line. They want me dead.'

Katell puts her fork down and closes her mouth.

'There's nothing I can do,' he says.

'You mustn't say that.'

'It's true. There's nothing I can do. But you can help me.'

'What can I do? I'm just a shopkeeper. I can cook and I can serve drinks, but I can't buy you your freedom.'

'Look, Katell.' He reaches over some more until his shirt covers his meal entirely. 'How long have we been seeing each other?'

'A month and fourteen days.'

The precision of her reply stops even Guo in his tracks, though only temporarily.

'And you have feelings for me?'

Maybe there is something wrong with Wang's translation because Katell smiles. 'Of course I have feelings. Sometimes I feel frustrated and sometimes I feel exasperated.'

Wang hesitates. Guo turns round and stares at him before Katell cuts in.

'It's a simple French joke. Of course I have feelings for you. You don't need another man's words to tell you that.'

This time Wang doesn't hesitate to translate.

'Look,' Guo starts—and Wang can tell, even from behind, that he is nervous—'I'm a labourer. A Chinese labourer. There's nothing much to me. I haven't had schooling. I've not had a chance to develop fancy manners. I'm a poor plain man. I've never had to speak like this before.'

'I don't care if you're poor. I don't care if you're plain. I don't give a damn about education, and I certainly don't care that you're Chinese. But I do want to hear you speak. That is, I love hearing you speak, and now I want to understand what it is you're saying. So don't stop now. Don't stop because you think you haven't got the words. Just tell me, Ziqin, and tell me now.'

She doesn't pronounce his name correctly, but Wang is sure that Guo understands even before he translates.

'I like you, Katell. I like you and want to be with you. But they're going to send me away. I know it as surely as I know that I'm sitting here. And only you can stop them. If we were married—'

She doesn't let him finish. As Wang is still translating, she seizes Guo by the collar, pulls him across the table, sending both plates and most of the *coq au vin* to the floor, and kisses him full on the mouth. Wang edges backwards.

When eventually she lets him go, Guo straightens his collar, smoothes his sodden shirt and slides back across the table. Then without looking back he says, 'You can go now, Wang.'

When he gets to the door, Wang glances back. Katell is wiping Guo's shirtfront with the hem of her dress and Guo is grinning with the exuberance of an over-excited schoolboy. It suddenly occurs to Wang that he is going to have to find his way back and break into the camp alone.

Chapter 16

It takes Wang almost a week to get over his annoyance at being abandoned by Guo, but when he does it occurs to him that, like Guo, he need not keep the curfew either. Though freer than any of the labourers, he realises that he has not made much use of his freedom. He hasn't stolen into Abbeville by night or had a drink in Noyelles once the British officers have returned to barracks, but now that he has breached the camp wall he is surprised to find that he wants to do it again, even if it leads to the indignity of clambering over a wall to get back into the camp once more. Leaving the camp surreptitiously has released something unexpected in him—a sense of freedom, a longing for another kind of existence, an anger with the British that he did not know he had.

Reluctantly, he also acknowledges that he wants to see Katell again. Though she is as different from Rong Meifan as a woman can be, there is something about her that reminds him of his former lover. He tries to hold both women in his mind, but it is impossible to keep both images together. One always hives off from the other, leaving him unsatisfied and uneasy. Even so, when the next moonless night gives him cover, he climbs over an isolated wall in a dark corner of the camp. Since arriving in France he has had all his excitement vicariously—now he is determined to seize it for himself.

'What are you doing here?' Katell whispers when he bangs on her door. She pulls him roughly inside. 'Next time come round the back like everyone else.'

'I'm sorry,' Wang says.

Katell brushes him down. 'And you've got leaves and mess all over. What did you do? Hide up a tree?'

Wang tells her about the bush he fell into and tries to be offended when she laughs.

'Well, there's only one cure for falling into bushes that I know of, and it comes in red, white or rosé.'

Disappearing behind the bar, she emerges with what she calls a carafe and a small glass.

'Now, tell me all about Ziqin,' she says. 'It's not every day I get the chance to listen to someone who speaks my language.'

Words are his life now. The ability to sort and shape letters into mounds of sentences which he can plunder and redistribute whenever the quartermaster general of his mind requires them has become so familiar, so embedded, that he rarely thinks about the mechanics of the language. But sitting with Katell, he feels as though he has been given a verbal demotion. Despite the freedom he has to travel, he is not used to speaking French with a French woman, least of all a woman as bold and confident as Katell, a woman he cannot file away in safe, sharply-defined categories.

As the gears grind slowly in whatever part of the engine it is that connects his brain to his vocal cords, Katell chats away, telling him about the first time she met Guo—'he was wearing pale blue pyjamas and a Stetson'—the lengths he'd gone to visit her—'he disguised himself as a British soldier but you can't hide the Chinese eyes of course'—and the presents he'd brought— 'my favourite's an engraved shell case. For a big man he's got surprisingly delicate fingers.'

Wang nods and smiles and drinks his wine rather too quickly.

'But what I really want to know is what you know?' she says, settling back in her chair and giving him a steady look. 'You must be great friends to come and translate for him like that.'

'Well ... it's difficult to put something like friendship into words.'

'Oh come on, Wiejing. I can call you Wiejing, can't I?'

'It's Weijun actually.'

'That's what I said. How did you meet? What's he like in the camp? Who are his other friends?'

Acutely embarrassed by the situation in which he has placed himself, Wang buys time by stroking the dog who has wandered in and flopped down by his feet.

'That's Dingo,' Katell tells him, clapping her hands enthusiastically. 'He's got his mother's ears.'

Unsure of the etiquette around dogs' ears, Wang starts talking about Guo. 'Yes, Guo. Ziqin as you call him. A fine fellow and an honest worker. What can I possibly tell you that you don't know already? We met in Rouen. Have you ever been to Rouen?'

Katell shakes her head.

'It's an amazing place. A deep river that reminds me of home, and a giant cathedral. Umm, and some fine buildings. But we were working on the outskirts of the city.'

'Tell me about the work. I want to know exactly what he was doing. I want to picture it just as it was.'

'Well, I was translating and Guo ... Guo was helping set up a sort of charitable enterprise for Chinese workers.'

'Oh, that sounds just like him! What sort of charitable enterprise?'

'It was medical, well semi-medical. He was arranging care for the men who needed it, and extra food and breaks when the work became too onerous. He saw a need and, rather than wait for anyone else to meet that need, he pushed himself forward and did what needed to be done.'

Dingo looks up as Wang's stroking becomes faster.

'Ah, I'm sorry, dog. Yes, he saw the need and organised a sort of collective. Always thinking of others, you know.'

'Oh, I do know! What else has he done?'

'Well, he ... he damaged his back, as you know, doing the work of two men, but he refused to rest. He insisted on being part of the burial party. "When the day comes that I can't dig a grave for one of my fellow workers, then I might as well not be here," he said. "If he's come all this way to help the Europeans then the least I can do is give him an honourable burial." '

Katell puts her hand in front of her mouth to stop her smile escaping. A couple of brown cats slink out the shadows, sidle up to the long-eared dog, and then slink away again.

'I've never met anyone quite like him,' Wang continues, 'so when he asked me if I'd translate for him, there was only one answer I could possibly give.'

'Oh, thank you, Weijing. We do so appreciate it. Let me get you some more wine.'

As she bobs down behind the bar, Wang expels a relieved breath. He has had precious few opportunities to act in recent years, but the power of performance has not left him. When she re-emerges, Katell tells him about her surreptitious meetings with Guo, about the ruses they adopt to throw the British off their scent, and the meals she has cooked him. She explains what it's like to be courted by a man who communicates in quickfire Chinese, exasperated hand gestures and mime. She wishes she knew what moved him.

Wang thinks about what really moves him—all-Chinese food queues, being forced to join the sanitary gangs that empty the oil drums underneath the latrine seats, having to parade in clean work boots at dawn.

'I just wish I could get him to appreciate Dingo a bit more,' Katell adds wistfully.

Wang looks down at the dog lying prone at his feet. 'He may be more of an animal lover than you think. There's a British officer in the camp who keeps rabbits, and Guo regularly helps him clean out the hutches.'

He leans down to give Dingo's ears another stroke and tries not to think about what Fell actually told him about 'your lot' being partial to rabbit meat and clearing out the first batch of rabbits in a matter of hours.

Katell claps enthusiastically. 'I knew it was all a front. We'll have Dingo eating out of his hand before the month's up. Just you wait and see.'

Wang keeps stroking Dingo to avoid having to look her in the eye.

'Come on,' she bursts out enthusiastically. 'Since you and Dingo are getting on so well, I'll show you one of my greenhouses. You're specially privileged. Not even Ziqin's been there yet. Just mind the path. There's cabbage and carrots planted all over and I don't want them damaged.'

Following her out of the back door, Wang doubts whether he will ever get to grips with western customs. Quite why Katell wants to show him the contents of her greenhouse is entirely beyond him.

'Well, here it is,' she says after a short meander.

Wang tries to match the sorry-looking glasshouse she is standing beside with the excitement in her voice. He tries to convince himself that war has rebalanced the world, that the everyday is now extraordinary, but, in truth, it is a very ordinary greenhouse. Where it lurches to the left, a branch has been lodged to keep it upright. Where the branch is ineffective, a few bricks have taken up the task. Wang is tempted to take a step backwards, thinking that any sudden movement on his part might bring the flimsy edifice down.

'This is my darlings' little home,' she says. 'A second home for me too, if truth be told.'

Katell's unexpected and clearly unbalanced enthusiasm for the horticultural makes Wang doubt his wisdom in accompanying her into the back yard in the dark, but there is no quenching her.

'Come on, you're going to love my little ones, I just know it.'

He thinks about fleeing to the safety and relative sanity of the camp, but Katell has already got her hand on the door.

'We have to be quick, or they'll escape,' she adds.

Wang edges forward, unsure whether he really wants to be trapped inside a tiny greenhouse with a lunatic Frenchwoman, but his education has not prepared him for a situation like this and so, reluctantly but maladroitly, he edges along the path to where she is standing. Katell takes her hand off the door and places it on the small of his back.

'You'd better go first,' she says. 'They're much less likely to bolt for freedom if you confuse them.'

She shoves him inside before he has a chance to object and then pushes herself through behind him. Wang turns to protest but, before he can open his mouth, two unchallengeable facts shoulder their way through the closed door of understanding. The first is a rich, offensive, and pungent smell, a smell no plant ever had call to make. And the second is the sight of dozens of tiny grey mice swirling around the greenhouse like bathwater vainly attempting to escape the lure of the plughole.

'Mice?'

'Yes, mice. Lovely mice. Didn't I say?'

'No, you didn't, Katell. I thought you were going to show me your secret supply of vegetables.'

Katell laughed.

'That comes another time, if you're really, really good.'

Chapter 17

As the war ebbs and flows, Wang keeps his head down and works. Roumania is threatened, the Americans argue about whether they should be forced to join French and British companies, St George's Day is celebrated limply, but Wang is kept busy translating for Captain Blyth, when he is not restoring morale in Boulogne or visiting mutinous workers in Amiens. He also increasingly finds himself summoned to the Château de Fransu to work for Major Greenstreet. It is mind-numbing work, but the major's occasional outbursts sometimes enliven otherwise dull days.

'Oh, for Christ's sake!' the major shouts one morning in early April, as he scans the piece of paper he has been handed.

'What is it, sir?' asks Captain Bairstow.

'One of the local farmer's fields has been raided.'

'Is that all, sir?' Bairstow says.

'Some bugger's dug up his turnips, cut off the tops, and replanted them. Wang, get here! I need to speak to the bloody Chinks again.'

When he next sees Guo in the estaminet, Wang mentions both the turnips and Katell's mice, but Guo doesn't care about either. He has received orders to report to the work camp in Crécy Forest and is determined to drink himself through the few days he has left in the estaminet. While he slumps in the corner by the piano, Wang talks to the other labourers who have dared break out of the camp—Pang Wei, a teacher from Suzhou; Zhu Qinan, a cheeky giant who bangs his head on the door frame every time he comes in; and Ma Gaoteng, who is so hopelessly in love with

Katell that he cannot see that she can hardly bear to look at his horribly pock-ridden face. Every time he visits he brings her a present, usually shell casings engraved with Chinese flowers, and waits patiently for some sign of affection.

Katell mothers them all, even Ma whom she pities. She feeds them and tries to teach them a few phrases in French, sometimes calling on Wang to help, but more often working on her own. When she can no longer tolerate their mangling of her language, she reaches into the past and pulls out the chants her Breton mother taught her. Guo chunters about the bloody nonsense she's singing, but Wang is fascinated by this language whose existence he has never suspected.

'*Kousk, ma mabig,*' she sings, '*kousk aze, Dindan askell ael Doue, Kloz da zaoulagad seder, Kousk aze ma bugel kaer.*'

The labourers take to it like toddlers. Zhu Qinan, a man who was so silent at first that they all thought him deaf and dumb, develops a particular fondness for the childish rhymes. After a drink or two, he leaps onto one of the tables and, assuming they are love songs, bellows them at the top of his voice.

When Guo's movement order to Crécy comes through, Wang feels an unexpectedly keen sense of disappointment. With Guo dispatched to another neck of the woods, he cannot see how he can spend any more time in the estaminet, but when he says his goodbyes to Katell she begs him not to go.

'They're sending him away again, Weijun. I'm not sure I can stand it any more.'

'It's only Crécy. It's just round the corner. He'll be back again before you've had chance to miss him.'

'It doesn't matter how far away he is. He's gone! And it isn't just round the corner. It's Crécy. How can you not understand that? I've only just got him back and they're sending him off again.'

'Don't be unreasonable, Katell. He's here to work.'

Katell thumps a pan down onto the table with enough force to make dust fly.

'Don't tell me to be reasonable! They come, they go, they die.

That's what they do with our men. That's what's unreasonable. They take them from us and serve them up again in coffins. I can't stand it any more, Weijun, I really can't. I dared to hope things might be different this time, because he's not a soldier. What harm could possibly come to a simple labourer? I'm asking you, Weijun, what harm?'

'Well—'

'I'll tell you what harm,' she interrupts, banging the table with her fist this time. 'All the harm in the world. They've already sent him to the front and twisted his back until it's worse than a gnarled apple tree. And why should they stop there? They'll keep using him until he's worthless and they can throw him away. They don't care about us French, Weijun, why should they care about you Chinese?'

'Actually, I've always thought they treat us rather well,' Wang begins.

'By all the saints, why are you defending them, Weijun? Why are you talking such nonsense? He's gone, and I might not get him back again.'

As Dingo anxiously rubs his muzzle against Katell's leg, Wang revolves his cap in his hand. 'Then I'd better go too. It's not right that I should be here when he's not.'

'No, don't go. Not yet,' Katell pleads, catching hold of his hand, and stumbling over Dingo in the process. 'I need someone here with me, and I don't mean Ma Gaoteng. I can't just—'

Her legs buckle as she breaks off but, as Wang rushes to catch her, she steadies herself and falls back onto the chair. When Dingo whines his distress, she ruffles his ears with affection bordering on the violent. Wang watches until it becomes apparent that, whatever she says, she is done with human company, and leaves her to the ministrations of her dog.

Whenever he can get away from the Château de Fransu over the next few weeks, Wang finds a way to join Katell in the estaminet. Her animals take some getting used to, but her food and drink are a constant consolation. The camp chefs do what they can to rehash the meagre rations into something approaching fine Chinese food, but there is only so much that can be done with salted fish and sorghum, or kaffir corn as the British call it. They make sporadic attempts to capture the wigeon and shelduck Lieutenant Fell is so fond of, but whatever their skill with bait, the camp is avoided by the wary birds. Wang assumes that Katell, by contrast, is a highly adept gardener, growing early-season tomatoes and vegetables in some greenhouse, but when they are disturbed by a muffled knocking late one evening and a whispered conversation is ended with a hurried exchange of money and hefty cardboard boxes, he realises that she has access to supplies that are never to be spoken of.

When he is not eating, drinking, or talking, Wang sits at the piano, coaxing his fingers back into patterns they have little memory of, while Katell cleans and talks about Guo, the war, coffee, and British table manners. He doesn't much care for the sheet music she keeps in her piano stool—*Quand Madelon*, *The Aba Daba Honeymoon*, *Home on the Range*—but, making do with fractured music, he reassembles what he can from the sonatas he played as a child. It is frustrating not being able to recall complete pieces, but Katell is content with the incomplete.

'Play that part again,' she says. 'It reminds me of a sea at night.' Or, even more obscurely, 'I like that bit. It sounds like stars that twinkle and shoot.'

The dog, a couple of cats, and even, once, a rabbit,who seems quite at home indoors, wander in and out as he plays, the cats jumping onto the keyboard or rubbing themselves against his legs as he tries to concentrate. Unsure whether this is a demand for food or a sign of affection, Wang lets them express themselves until either Katell intervenes or they become too much of a distraction. When he spots a tortoise clambering across the bar, he decides that he finally has the right to comment.

'You've got a lot of pets,' he says.

'There's a few you haven't seen yet—I'm not sure you're

ready for my polecat—and I used to have a lot more. My goat disappeared near the start of the war, and then they requisitioned my horse. I hope it's all right; it used to bolt if it heard loud noises.'

'I imagine that could be a problem on the battlefield.'

'Oh no,' she replies, laying her accounts to one side for a moment, 'it used to bolt very sensibly.'

Sensible or not, Wang cannot imagine that it has escaped the carnage. Thinking about the horse makes him reflect on the fighting, which is no longer a distant rumour. Ever since the Germans launched their Spring Offensive, the impact of the war has been increasingly felt at Noyelles. With the railway network targeted by enemy planes, labourers are distributed widely across what is increasingly being referred to as the war zone. As the camp leaches labourers, the British also cut back on the number of guards. An unexpected benefit of the perilous war situation is that it becomes increasingly straightforward to slip out of the camp in the evening and to enter the estaminet by the back door.

As he sits in a small back room where he is hidden from the street, Wang tries to escape the worry of war by bathing in Katell's cosy domesticity. Gnawing over his concerns by day, he loses himself in the company of whoever is in the estaminet in the late evenings. As Katell watches or cleans the dishes, Shu Junrong, Pang Wei, Zhu Qinan and Wang play mahjong or cards—though Wang has become so adept at separating them from their money that they are never as keen to play as he is—and, as they play, they talk.

Without ever explicitly agreeing to do so, they keep to the same safe topics. Not the war, or the CLC, or even their various pasts in China, but their increasingly implausible plans for the future. None of them mentions Guo, though his shadow lies heavy in the room.

Katell watches them as they talk, humouring them when their ideas become obviously outlandish and plying them with drinks however they are feeling. Believing that his time with Rong Meifan has freed him from physical inhibition, Wang is surprised to find that he is completely unsettled by Katell's tendency to lay a hand on his arm or to give his hair a quick stroke as she passes by. He tries not to pull away when she touches him and avoids catching her eye.

The evenings pass slowly, but Katell's visitors are always reluctant to leave. They wait until their conversations lurch into silence before draining their wine glasses, bringing their games to an end, and shuffling one by one through the back door into the dark Picardie night.

One night, as they are playing mahjong, they hear the sound of Gotha engines for the first time. Throwing himself to the floor, Wang crawls under one of the tables, where he is convulsed by uncontrollable fear. As he shuts his eyes and blocks his ears against the sound of the terrible engines, his body rebels against him. Realising with great shame that he can no longer control his bladder, he lies still and feels the warm damp come.

He flees to the safety of the camp as soon as he can, but the raid so unnerves him that he finds that even the sound of men coughing in the night is enough to wake him, though he has always prided himself on being able to sleep through the most ferocious of Asian storms. And, when daylight drags him away from night fears, he discovers that new troubles await him—he is ordered to dig trenches outside the dormitory huts along with the rest of the corps, for now that the war has drawn near there are no special privileges for translators.

Filling bags with sand, he props them against windows and doors. He checks gas masks, practises raid drill, and anxiously checks the skies. For the first time he feels truly part of the corps. For the first time he feels sure that he is going to die.

At least once a week he takes part in a raid drill. It is a shambolic business, especially for the patients in the hospital. When the siren sounds, hundreds of casualties help each other out of their beds and into the dubious protection of a hole in the ground just a few yards away. Many of them are in no fit state to be moved, but they move anyway and help their compatriots too. Some forget their crutches in the confusion and hang desperately onto men scarcely less disabled than themselves. The blind and half-blind form queues that shuffle pitiably along the long corridors and out into the other dark. The lunatics and the lepers, as far as Wang can tell, are left to fend for themselves. Lying in a hole outside a hospital ward, Wang finds himself thinking of that day when Zhou Lianke's arrow sped inexorably towards him and feels as helpless.

As the war stumbles towards some kind of conclusion, he is sent back out across Northern France to translate for his increasingly desperate compatriots. The journeys now seem interminable. Maps are inadequate, cars are called away at the last minute, trains run to no timetable ever understood by man— all these frustrations build up until he longs once more for home. Having constructed an image of the West that sustained him through the darkness of his last days in Beijing, he finds it difficult to place what he now sees onto the great canvas he unrolled in China. Soldiers lounge exhausted by the side of the road, farmers flog ancient horses, cows graze behind barbed wire. In his dreams he tries to restitch the fraying picture, rediscovering an impossible England in his sleep—Stratford-upon-Avon bordered by rows of poplar trees, Chatham populated by bare-footed chimney sweeps, the Tower of London guarded by labourers holding pikes.

As he thinks about England, he comes to realise how little he knows of the French. He travels with the English, negotiates with the English, takes orders from the English. Unless he is speaking to Katell, almost his only exposure to the French language comes from the signs he sees as he passes through the countryside: *tabac*, *gare*, *maison medicale*, *mairie*, and even, impossibly optimistically, *terrains à vendre*. With the exception of Katell, who assumes an almost mythic force in his imagination, he knows next to nothing about the lives and opinions of the people he has come to protect. As villagers troop into their churches on Sunday mornings to enact their strange rituals, as children play by the side of the road, as farmers trudge behind their ploughs with heads down, he tries to imagine himself into this country

197

he is living in and yet strangely distanced from. Looking at the strangely impassive faces of the Frenchmen he meets in the factories, he becomes aware for the first time of how foreign his CLC uniform must appear. Then he makes his way back to Noyelles and becomes English again.

When Katell eventually lets Wang into the kitchen, she makes it extremely clear that she will be enforcing her regulations.

'I've only just got this place set up how I want it after those Australians got in,' she says, 'and I'm not going to have you messing it about.'

A chicken sticks its scrawny head round the door until one of the cats, which has been lying by the window, spots it and, with a flick of its tail, jumps to the floor, upsetting a porcelain bowl in the process.

'I just want to watch,' Wang says.

'What do you want to do that for? It's only cooking.'

'It's not only cooking to me. Where I come from we don't boil and bake and use those heavy pans you do. For me it's not so much cookery as anthropology.'

'You do speak funny,' she says. 'I never know whether you're joking.'

Wang smiles disarmingly and leans on the door frame. He wants to reassure her that his presence is not a threat, that all he wants to do is observe. He doesn't tell her that he has become as fascinated by the cook as by the cooking. The lilt and tilt of her voice as it shifts between Breton and French reminds him of his mother reading him bedside stories as a child. The simple inflections, the elision of guttural Ks and Qs into soft Cs and Ss, the rolling of the language into one hybrid whole, reminds him of nothing less than *fin de siècle* Shanghai, a Shanghai that has become a blur of decaying images, a series of photographs fading in a drawer at the back of his mind.

As he watches her bustle from stove to shelf, from shelf to table, and back to the stove again, he slips into a slow, trance-like state and recalls stolen mornings in the kitchen of his parental home where he first grappled with the notion of his mother's essential separateness. He remembers watching as she fired the new stove into action and threw choi sum, garlic, ginger, black fungus, and shredded pork into the wok. He stares at the tall Frenchwoman as she leans backwards and stretches her shoulders, as a glimmer of leg escapes the green floral dress and the steam swirls through the gloom and his memories of Shanghai. He sits back in his chair as Rong Meifan steps elegantly back into his head and smiles. He has traded the allure of the traditional Chinese beauty—her shapely legs, the hint of mystery the qipao provides—for a wet corner of France, a hot kitchen, and an animal-loving Breton. But, as he closes his eyes and tries to fix the scene in his memory, he understands what it is that brings the two together.

For years now his existence has been shaped by words, by intangible objects that have an existence only beyond themselves. Ever since the arrow pierced his eyeball, he has been happiest alone. Lost in the glamour of language, he has escaped the expectations of others older and more far-sighted than himself. Immersed in the grandeur of literature, he has found places he could never have visited under his own steam. But words were never enough for Rong Meifan, nor are they now for Katell. What brings the two together across five thousand miles is their love of things—animals for one, clothes for the other, food and men for both. The material world in all its insistent physicality.

'Are you laughing at me?' Katell demands.

Wang opens his eye to see her with her hands on her hips and a frown on her face.

'I was thinking of home,' he says.

The sirens sound almost every day now, but Wang cannot get used to their unearthly wail however often he hears them, and nor can many of the labourers. They dutifully obey when an air raid drill is performed but, when they see real planes, they plunge into witless terror. Ma Gaoteng is killed when, running round in

199

a panic, he falls into the river and drowns. Twenty men desert during another raid, some of them running to Abbeville, others trying to make their way to the port. All of them are rounded up within a few hours.

The camp itself isn't targeted, but there are a few near misses. An ammunition dump on the outskirts of the village takes a direct hit from a stray bomb, creating a fireworks display that would have graced any New Year's celebration in Shanghai. Several off-duty officers are killed while they are seeking consolation in the brothels of Abbeville. The buildings either side of the Number Eighty-Three General Hospital in Boulogne are completely destroyed in separate raids. Wang keeps his head down and shuts off that part of his mind which demands answers. He does his best to wheedle hard information about the progress of the war from Captain Blyth but, almost immediately, wishes that he hadn't.

'I am a doctor, Wang, not a strategist. While there are men to treat, I will treat them. While there's a war to fight, I will do my bit.'

'But you must talk among yourselves,' Wang insists. 'You know how to sift truth from rumour.'

'We talk—of course we do—but we are as prone to error and gossip as you are. The Germans are on the march—that's all I know. I suspect we will drive them back, and then maybe this war will finally come to an end, but I know no more than you do.'

Wang is experimenting with brandy for the first time, swirling it experimentally at arm's length, when Katell asks him if he knows how she first met Guo. Wang shakes his head, not trusting himself to speak.

'He was walking past the cemetery wearing his pants over his trousers and his flannel body-belt on top of his pants. And what was worse was he was wearing a feathery fascinator perched on a top hat. The way he swaggered and tipped that hat to me, he obviously thought he looked quite the man, but I had no time for fools and jokers. It wasn't long after my fiancé had been killed.'

She stops washing up and puts her hand on the stone sink. Wang tries to figure out where to look.

'I haven't told you about Jean, have I?' she says eventually. 'He was my childhood sweetheart. He signed up at the start of the war but the first gas attack of 1915 did for him. He lingered on for nine months while I nursed him but then ...'

Wang looks away in embarrassment as she bangs glass after dripping glass onto the side of the sink.

'All the young men from our village went to war, and the first one to come back was mine. I thought about leaving, but then the British came and built this camp so I had to stay. I had some English, you see, and I needed the money so I could pay all the bills I'd racked up. And then the Chinese came. You came, I mean. At first I thought you were all soldiers, and I was terrified. Like all the villagers, I thought the Chinese weren't to be trusted, that you were thieves and murderers and opium addicts. But the businesswoman in me won through. I did all right for myself. It wasn't long before this place was full of British officers entering by the front door and Chinese labourers entering by the back.'

'It must have been a strange time,' Wang says, for want of anything more coherent to offer.

Katell turns away and gives another glass a vigorous wash.

'I couldn't tell any of you apart at first. You all dressed the same, you all had the same haircuts, and none of you spoke any French. But gradually I came to know my regular visitors. *Med ac'han di a zo pell bras, O ma Doue! pa soñjan, Evit mont gant an aelez, War-zu bro gaer ar Werc'hez.* Come on, sing with me, Weijun.'

Taking his hand, she tries to cajole him into action, but Wang pulls his hand away, rather more abruptly than he intended, and offers his excuses.

'I'm not much of a singer, Katell,' he says, staring into the bottom of his brandy glass and swilling the warm drink round.

Katell sighs, but she can't stop now.

'They were always getting into trouble, those boys of mine.

201

If they weren't stealing pairs of glasses they were trying to distract poor Marie at the milliner's. Do you know, in the early days, when they were still allowed out of the camp, they actually used to queue up so that they could try her hats on one by one. It didn't matter what she had in stock—women's straw hats, children's sailor caps, men's trilbies—they tried them all. The British stopped them coming in the end, they caused so much trouble, but they couldn't stop Ziqin. It was early evening, there were still British officers around, and he was coming out of Marie's. He had a hat and a fascinator on, and he looked so pleased with himself.'

Wang can believe it. Guo is not given to embarrassment or self-doubt.

Katell pulls up a chair and, sitting beside him, takes his hand again.

'I tried, Weijun, I really did. I'd lost my fiancé. I couldn't bear to lose anyone else. But then this cocksure joker came along and I found I couldn't keep him out of my mind. He was so handsome—he is so handsome—and I couldn't keep my eyes off him. If you'd asked me at the start of the war whether I'd ever find a Chinaman good-looking I'd have laughed in your face. Oh, I'm sorry, there I go again. I've spent so long with the Chinese now and your French is so good, Weijun, that I completely forget you're a foreigner.'

Wang inclines his head politely and tries to pull his hand away again, though this time more gently.

'Do you know what I thought, Weijun? I thought that I'd never met anyone with as much life in him as he had and, since most of the eligible young men from round here have had their life blasted out of them, even a little life goes a long way.'

She is crying now, and yet Wang cannot bring himself to comfort her.

'I thought we'd be all right because he had a job which kept him away from the trenches,' she says, her voice breaking and the tears running down her cheeks like rain overflowing a gutter. 'And then they took that away from me too. But they can't take him away completely. Not while he's alive. Not while he stills loves me. This time, I'm not going to let them do it, do you understand?'

Wang looks down at his drink but finds the glass empty. He searches each of his languages for words but, for once, neither French nor English nor Chinese have the vocabulary he needs. He keeps quiet, pulls her close, and hopes that words will quickly return.

Chapter 18

In June, the Germans launch another offensive, advancing along the Matz River. Wilder rumours reach the camp—that Calais has been captured, that the Germans have built a new tank which is as fast as a car, that the French are preparing for surrender. Wang realises that most of what he hears is untrue, but he also knows that the outlook is bleak. The casualty figures are worse than ever, and the British are more disheartened than he has ever known them. As he travels across Northern France, he begins to consider the idea that Noyelles might one day be overrun by the Germans.

On his way to Etaples he sees his first refugees, several dozen villagers who have been forced to flee the fighting and who are pulling a cartload of bags along the road from Hesdin to Montreuil. He sees them again on the way back. Their cart is stuck in a roadside ditch, apparently forced off the carriageway by one of the Allied lorries that plies the road. The lorry driver and some of the refugees are arguing fiercely, but the rest of them scarcely even bother to look up as the car in which Wang has hitched a lift passes. Wang stares at an old woman dressed in a ragged black shawl who is perched in the back of the cart, and she stares blankly back. As he looks back over his shoulder, she slowly fades away.

When he gets back to Noyelles, he is exhausted and depressed. He has seen nothing but dusty roads, dirty labourers, and disheartened men, and he has had enough. Shu Junrong greets him at the gate, but he can't even summon the strength to hold a conversation with him. He slips off to see Katell instead, telling her that he has seen Guo, passing on a non-existent message, and feeling only the slightest trace of guilt as Katell wipes her tears away with the collar of her dress and then gives him a suffocating embrace.

It is, in fact, another week before he sees Guo again, when he limps back into the camp, his right foot having suffered some sort of stress fracture. Dr Wong, one of the hospital's few Chinese doctors and a foot specialist, bandages him up and orders three weeks' rest.

'But I can't just sit about,' Guo complains.

'If you don't, it'll break worse and then they'll send you home,' Dr Wong replies.

'This is all I need,' he moans, when Wang visits him in his hospital bed. 'It's just what they've been looking for, an excuse to get me sent back to China. As long as I'm repairing their fucking roads they don't mind keeping me here, but as soon as I'm laid up in bed they'll chuck me out like a corpse in a trench.'

'It's three weeks, Guo, that's all,' Wang tells him. 'You need to recuperate for three weeks, and then you can get back to work.'

'You've read a lot of books, Wang, but you're still a bloody fool,' Guo says. 'They've been watching me, do you know that? They've been keeping me under observation. I shouted at a bastard in my work gang the other day and one of the ghosts beat me until I collapsed. This is it, Wang. I've had it.'

Wang is surprised to find himself growing angry. He is tired, so he is less tolerant than usual, but it's more than that. He is fed up with the defeatism that surrounds him, and he's not going to take it from Guo as well.

'What would Katell say if she could hear you now?' he demands. 'What would she think of her fiancé? She'd be disgusted. She'd kick you out of the estaminet. She'd start looking for someone else. Come on, Guo, where's your fire gone? So they're after you. What difference has that ever made to you?'

Guo slumps back into his bed. 'Fuck off, Wang, I've heard enough.'

'No, I'm not going to fuck off,' Wang shouts, to the great surprise of everyone else in the ward. 'I've had to take your nonsense for too long to stand by while you whimper and whine just because your bloody foot's hurting. I've asked you a question, so you can bloody well answer. What would Katell say if she could hear you now?'

It's not been his finest speech, but the raised volume and the passionate intensity with which he delivers it takes even Guo aback.

'She'd understand,' he says eventually. 'She wouldn't get a bloody word I'm saying, but somehow she'd understand.'

Feeling an obscure impulse to protect Guo now that he has become morose, Wang tries to see him every couple of days. Guo ignores him at first, but after a few days' siege he sits up when Wang comes into the ward.

'You've got to take her a message,' he says peremptorily.

Wang looks around the ward. Four or five men are sitting on the edge of their beds listening to what the two men are saying.

'Why don't you go yourself?' he asks, lowering his voice in a vain attempt to shut the rest of the labourers out of the conversation.

Guo pulls the cover off his bed and waves his foot about. 'That's why,' he says.

But it isn't his foot that's keeping him from seeing Katell, Wang knows that. If he can leap from roof to tree with a crippled back, then a foot injury's not going to stop him breaking out of an unguarded hospital ward.

'Don't be ridiculous,' he says. 'An injury's never stopped you before.'

'They haven't been watching me before,' Guo replies.

'So because you think you're being watched you're going to ignore your fiancée?'

'I'm not ignoring her,' Guo says, 'I'm sending you with a message.'

Wang feels his fists clenching. 'I'm not your go-between,' he says evenly.

Guo lifts his head, and a hint of the old grin returns to his face. 'That's precisely what you are,' he says.

To his own surprise, Wang swings hard at Guo, who jerks his head back but only succeeds in banging it against the frame of the bed. Lurching forward, he throws a fist at Wang who bobs out of the way, only to find that his opponent is on the floor screaming with pain.

'Bloody hell, Wang, you'll pay for that,' he says, clutching his injured foot.

'I'll be in my dorm,' Wang says, walking out. 'If you can make it as far as that I'll get you the rest of the way. If you want to give Katell a message you're going to have to give it to her yourself.'

Guo winces with pain as he attempts to pull himself up the wall by the fence, so Wang reaches down to pull him onto the roof beside him. He might be able to bribe his way out of the main gate, but he knows that Guo has no chance.

'Who'd have thought it'd be the *shudaizi*, the white devils' lackey, who'd be pulling me along as I break out of this shitty camp?' Guo says, hauling himself up and limping towards the edge of the building. 'This is going to be fucking difficult.'

As Wang peers into the darkness, he can't help but agree. Getting Guo this far has been harder than he anticipated, but he's damned if he's going to stop now.

'If I can do it, then so can you,' he says, before throwing himself across the gap that separates them from freedom and Katell. Guo curses audibly and then, after several more minutes' indecision and some well-aimed taunts from Wang, leaps across as well. He jars his foot on landing and is almost in tears as Wang pulls him down from the tree. He leans on the translator all the way to the estaminet and falls theatrically through the unlocked back door. As Wang translates his broken explanations, and as Katell envelops him in a voluminous embrace, Guo sobs with

207

shame and pain. But Katell doesn't care. She has her man back, and that is enough. She rushes off to heat water for a bath to help ease his aching foot and leaves the two men together.

'Don't come too close,' Guo warns Wang, 'or I might just kill you.'

When Katell returns, she asks a few more questions and looks anxiously at Wang as he translates, before hurrying Guo off for private treatment. Wang is unsure whether to hang around on the off-chance that further translations might be required or to leave on the basis that he has kept his promise to get Guo to Katell and is now clearly intruding on increasingly private moments. He stays until the noises emanating from the back rooms change in nature and then, carefully checking to see that there are no soldiers on the streets, returns the way he has come.

A few hours later he is shaken from sleep. From the light that is filtering in through the window he guesses that it is early morning.

'Wang, Wang, get off that lazy arse of yours!'

He feels a rough hand on his shoulder. 'What is it?' he mumbles.

Looking up, he finds himself surrounded by half a dozen angry men. 'They've taken Guo.'

'Taken him where?' Wang stammers

'We don't know. Perhaps to prison. Perhaps to the parade ground.'

'To the parade ground? At this time of the morning?'

'Their mothers are dogs. They don't care what time of day it is.'

'What do you expect me to do about it?'

'You've got to find him.'

'I can't go wandering around the camp before reveille. You know that.'

'You're the only one they'll listen to.'

'Not in the middle of the night they won't.'

'It's Guo, Wang. You can't just let them beat him.'

Wang hesitates, partly because he feels a sense of responsibility for the man—though he doubts whether there is anything he can do for him if he has been caught—but partly too because he is no longer sure whose side he's on. A few months earlier, he would have argued that the British had the right to cane anyone who'd broken the rules but, now that he regularly breaks the rules himself, his own position is ambiguous at best.

The labourers in his dormitory do not give him the opportunity to hesitate for long. One of them pulls him to his feet and, standing uncomfortably close, hands him his uniform. As he is manhandled towards the door, the trumpet sounds for reveille and then again for parade. It is at least an hour early, but none of the labourers complains.

When he reaches the parade ground, the first person Wang sees is Guo. His arms and feet have been tied to a wooden cross, and his head is lolling down despite the calls of several labourers. His back and legs are covered with lacerations. Turning away in horror, Wang sees one of the men who has just roused him staring reproachfully. As Wang tries to justify himself, the labourer spits into the ground at his feet.

'The British army has been in France for almost four years now,' Major Greenstreet announces, once a roll call has been taken. A captain Wang doesn't recognise translates. 'For four years we have lived among the people of this country, fought for the people of this country, and kept strong military discipline for this country.'

Several hundred men stand to attention and listen. If the major has any idea how sullenly his words are being received he gives no sign of it.

'But we do not fight for the French alone. Our own country—every country in Europe—is threatened by the German menace. They have not hidden their imperial ambitions, nor have they been slow to ally themselves with whoever would aid them in their expansionist ideals.'

The captain begins to stumble over his translation. Despite his discomfort, Wang feels a little sorry for him. It is never easy finding words to match the major's rhetoric.

'There is no one who is safe from the Hun and his animalistic greed,' Greenstreet continues. 'His reach stretches far across the world. From Europe to Africa to the furthest reaches of Asia, the German has already stretched out his martial hand. And having stretched, he has clenched it into a fist.'

The captain is increasingly paraphrasing rather than translating. Thinking that he might be able to help, Wang involuntarily takes a step forward. Then, realising the farcical nature of his situation, he steps back into line.

'You yourselves have seen what destruction the Hun can wreak. He has bled your own country dry. It was only because of the brave efforts of our forces, together with those of our Japanese allies, that we managed to loosen his grasp on the Far East.'

Wang looks round nervously. The labourers' anger is now being expressed in the shifting of feet. The major is impervious.

'But do not be deceived—this war is not yet won. And until it is, no place is safe. Not Belgium, not France, not Britain, not China. That is why you are here, an army without arms, a company of labouring men whom history will remember as saviours of their people. Do not be deceived—you are fighting in this war as much as those men who hold a gun. With your spades and your picks you may strike such a blow as will wipe the German menace from this earth. That is why we must have absolute military discipline in this camp. That is why we will not tolerate absence without leave. That is why we will punish wrongdoing immediately and harshly.'

He waits for his translator to catch up. When he is satisfied that enough has been said, he gestures towards Guo for the first time.

'You have all seen this man,' he says. 'You all know why he must be punished. Now you all know that we will not hold back should we need to punish once more.'

He turns on his heel and leaves, without pausing for effect or to see what impact his words have had. The translator trails off. Not one of the labourers moves. Only when Guo starts to spit blood is the order given to dismiss. Wang looks helplessly on but is ushered away before he has chance to speak. As he leaves the parade ground, Guo is dragged off. The next day he is sent away. It is a long time before Wang dares look any of his countrymen in the eye again.

Chapter 19

Katell is inconsolable, but Wang does his best to console her anyway. There are days when she refuses to see him, and days when she will hardly let him go, embracing him and crying until his hair is wet with her tears. Her sadness and anger drive the rest of the Chinese away, even as the Allies' fortunes begin to turn. As the summer drags on, there are no more late-night gatherings of card-playing, wine-swigging, guard-evading labourers. The estaminet no longer draws the rebellious, the bored and the angry. Katell will only see Wang, and Wang, burdened by a terrible sense of guilt, is the only one who dares to break out of the camp to see her.

He still travels across Northern France but, when the Allies begin their counter-offensive, he is required more often at Noyelles. Le Hamel is recaptured. Château-Thierry is taken. The French drive the Germans back across the River Marne. Everyone he meets is noticeably more carefree. The British walk around the camp chanting a strange litany of victories, and the labourers, to whom these names are little more than half-heard mythical regions, scramble to keep up. Men still work, suffer and die, but Wang knows now that the end is in sight. A British officer even ruffles his hair. He knows that it cannot last.

Only Katell, it seems, is distraught, though Wang knows she cannot be alone in mourning the loss of a loved one. There must be hundreds of thousands of women like her, wives who have lost husbands, mothers who have lost sons, fiancées who will never marry or who have seen their men come back damaged beyond repair. He lets Lieutenant Fell drag him off to watch the birds on the Baie de Somme one final time but can no longer dredge up even a pretence of enthusiasm. Fell looks at him sadly and tells him to bugger off back to the camp, though there is little for him to do when he gets back. It is Liu's day to translate for the Major and nobody else requires his assistance. For a while he trails around after Captain Blyth, but the Captain is so cheery he doesn't notice Wang's despondency.

'What's the matter with you?' Shu Junrong asks when he finds him in the recreation hut.

'Everyone's talking about going back to China,' Wang replies, 'and I don't know that I want to anymore.'

'It's got to be better than this mound of shit,' Shu says. 'If nothing else, the women have got something these French pigs don't come close to.'

Wang slips out of the camp even before the sun has gone down, no longer able to bear being alone in a camp full of men. He hopes that Katell will cook for him and hopes too that their individual miseries will cancel each other's out. Ignoring a convalescing labourer who is having a cigarette by the fence, he takes his usual route, the route Guo first taught him. He no longer cares if he is seen. But Katell is in no fit state to see him, let alone cook for him.

She lets him in after a short argument but then slumps onto her bed and refuses to talk any more. Wang kicks one of the chairs and almost walks out in disgust. Then he catches sight of himself in the mirror and sees not Noyelles but Beijing, and not Katell but Rong Meifan. He picks up the chair and walks back into the bedroom.

'Go away,' Katell says.

He sits on the edge of her bed.

'Go away, I said!'

He is about to tell her that he doesn't feel good either, that he has suffered indignities and snubs, but the sight of her curled up on her bed like a baby with no one to comfort her stops him. He edges a little closer.

'I have something that might make you feel a little better.'

She turns over and looks at him through her red, swollen eyes. She can't quite see what he is pulling out of his pocket.

'Pick a card.'

'Oh, for God's sake, Weijun,' she shouts, kicking out at him. 'Get out and get out now!'

Putting the pack of cards back into his pocket, he clumps out of the room, pours himself a glass of brandy, settles down in the most comfortable of the many uncomfortable chairs by the bar, and waits for Katell to come out and see him. He is prepared for a long wait, but when it becomes apparent that she isn't moving, and that he has only Dingo and one of the disdainful cats for company, he starts pacing about.

Eventually he walks into the kitchen. It feels wrong to be there, as wrong as disturbing a woman in her own bedroom. He pulls a few drawers open to see what he can find and then starts to work his way methodically through every cupboard. There is less there than he expected. He pulls out a loaf of bread and cuts a hunk from it. When he has finished that, he cuts another and eats it with a few slices of cheese. It is not what he would have chosen, but there seem few other options.

When he opens the vegetable cupboard, his hunger pangs become too insistent to ignore. Taking a string of garlic, he chops some into fine fragments and then attacks a hand grenade of an onion until his eye fills with tears. Unable to find a wok, he takes a large, flat saucepan and, finding the experience strangely cathartic, pours a generous dose of oil into it.

He has rarely had to cook, though he has often seen it done. Growing up in Shanghai, he always relied on his mother or a servant, in Beijing he ate at the student refectory, in the Labour Corps he eats whatever the CLC cooks are able to concoct from the meagre provisions they are granted.

After hunting around for some matches, he gets to grips

214

with the stove—a huge, blackened, unwieldy affair—fiddling with its controls and trying to make sense of its unfamiliar workings but, however hard he tries, he can't get it to fire. He aims a kick at its solid metal base and immediately regrets his impetuosity.

'What on earth are you doing?' Katell asks from behind him.

Wang turns in embarrassment to find her leaning against the door, her clothes unkempt and her hair bedraggled.

'I'm trying to cook you a meal,' he says, 'but there seems to be a problem with the fire.'

Katell looks first at him, then at the mangled vegetables, then back to him again before slowly beginning to shake. It takes Wang a good few seconds to realise that she is laughing.

'Oh, you poor Chinese baby,' she says, her shoulders leading the rest of her upper body in a strange, rippling dance. 'You poor, lost, little thing.'

Wang doesn't know what to say. He feels naked under her look.

'Come on,' she says. 'We'll rescue the cooking later.'

She leads him back into the bedroom, to disheveled sheets and crumpled pillows. She leads him back to a place that reminds him of Beijing and home. He closes his eye and tries not to remember.

Even though the Allied counter-offensive has been going better than anyone dared expect, it is only in September that the British start to talk openly about the war being over before the end of the year. Remembering the political chaos he left behind in Beijing, Wang attends YMCA lectures on national regeneration and searches the *Huagong Zhoubao* for any information about the return of those parts of Shandong which have been so shamefully ceded to Japan. Blyth keeps him busy at the camp and Katell is strangely reluctant to see him at the estaminet, so he keeps away and hopes that she will come round in time. With Guo gone and the military situation changing on a daily basis, he has to keep his wits about him in Noyelles. The certainties of war break down under the pressure of an enormous future, but Wang is unsure whether it is one he can ever embrace. The fighting may be almost over but, despite learning that his old hero Lu Zhengxiang is likely to lead the Chinese delegation to any future peace conference, he is unconvinced that his countrymen will stand strong when peace treaties are signed and the shape of the post-war world is decided.

Despite Fell's best efforts to explain the ins and outs of European political affairs, Wang never wholly understands how the shooting of an archduke can have led to this four-year slog. How, after four years of stalemate, the end can have come so quickly is also a mystery to him. The last weeks of the war arrive with an almost indecent haste, though even now Wang is too busy to follow the onrushing tide of apparently inevitable victories. As he moves between Noyelles and Wimereux, and a dozen places in between, he becomes even more acutely aware that the war itself has continued without him.

He is in Boulogne when the Armistice is announced, translating for a new doctor in the general hospital. As if ordered by some unseen general, people flow out onto the streets, the bells of Saint Nicolas toll, sirens blare from the port, and a cannon is fired from the ramparts of the old city walls. As the people cheer, dance and sing, more bells take up the rhythm being beaten out by the unknown ringers in the centre of town, until eventually the Cathedral of Notre Dame adds its weight to the symphony. Wang has always thought Boulogne a curious city, dominated by grand old French buildings and yet overwhelmed by foreigners. But it is the French who flood onto the streets and into the squares on Armistice Day. They sing, they drink and they move, as though pulled by an irresistible force, towards *le Quai Gambetta*. And there they burst into song again.

Wang goes with them. He has no choice. A young woman sweeps him across the road and into a drunken waltz before he has time to compose himself or to step out of the way. An old man insists that he join him in guzzling a bottle of red wine. Two French sailors try to teach him a jig and almost get run over by a passing ambulance for their pains. As songs and jokes swirl round him, he is pulled into the centre of the stream and forgets for an instant who he is, imagining himself as a proud citizen of France, a conqueror of the imperialists, and a winner of battles. But when he arrives at the quay he remembers that he does not belong. The people of Boulogne become one in their song of victory but, abruptly and dispiritingly, he realises how alien he is. He doesn't know the tune. He can't join in the chorus. With the crowds singing in some local dialect, he can't even understand the words. *Allaïe, allaïe, Guillaume il est noyaïe quand on l'a ramassaille, il étoit tout mouillaile*, they sing, and as they sing, they laugh. And, as they laugh, Wang begins to cry, for relief at the end of the war, and for sorrow at the poverty of his French. He is an outsider, a translator, someone who will never belong.

He stays in Boulogne that night—the trains are going nowhere—and as he walks through the drizzle he sees the city anew. Gone is the darkness of an industrial port at war; in its place comes a great torchlit procession that threads its way through the streets from the old town to the new, and onto the Théâtre Municipal, where the people sing hymns in French, English, and what Wang's exuberant neighbour tells him with great confidence is Belgian.

He eats bread and cake from the *cartes de pain*, he drinks wine from glasses and bottles and, he later faintly remembers, a bucket in the yard of a most insistent *boulanger*. He dances in the arms of more girls than he ever dreamed possible and, finally, sleeps in one of the shelters that have been dug beneath the old town's great ramparts. The sound of bells, cannons and sirens does not let up all night but, though he has no blanket or pillow, he sleeps as soundly as he ever did in his own bed in Shanghai. The war is over. He is drunk. The future is about to begin.

When he gets back to Noyelles the next day, he bypasses the camp and goes straight to Katell's estaminet.

'It's over!' he shouts as he barges through the front door. A dozen British soldiers look up at him. He is surprised to see that Captain Blyth is among them.

'Thank you, Wang,' Blyth says calmly. 'We'd worked that out for ourselves. Now, if you'd kindly report back to the camp, we'll overlook the fact that you seem to be in a prohibited zone.'

Wang looks at Katell, who keeps her back turned to him as she fills a glass behind the bar. He salutes Blyth in some confusion and backs slowly out of the door. When he returns to the estaminet three days later—it is late in the evening and the camp guards are all drunk—he struggles to get Katell to sit down and look at him.

'Don't you see what this means?' he says, feeling simultaneously guilty and proud. 'It means he'll be coming back. They won't need him any more. You'll be able to get married.'

Katell closes her eyes and clenches her fists.

'You poor, Chinese fool,' she says, once she has unclenched them. 'You don't really believe that, do you? There'll be more work than ever. They've got him on a contract—and you too—and they're going to make sure they get their money's worth.'

'But—'

'No buts. You're going to be mending the roads and railways and pulling down buildings the Germans didn't quite finish off. You're going to be "building a nation our children can be proud of." '

Wang is taken back by the bitterness of her tone.

'And even if they did decide that he was surplus to requirements,' she continues, 'do you think they'd send him back here? They're not going to waste good food on some Chinese coolie. He'll be back on a boat to China as soon as they can find one that won't sink when it leaves Boulogne.'

'You'll be able to see him,' Wang insists. 'They'll give him leave or let you visit.'

'They wouldn't even tell me where they'd sent him,' she says. 'Do you think they're going to help me now?'

He tries to move closer, but she simply gets up and walks away.

'I think you'd better go now,' she says. 'They're going to need you back at the camp.'

'But Katell,' he pleads, 'what will you do?'

She opens the door and waits until he gets up. 'I'll do what I've always done,' she says. 'I'll stay here and wait for the future to come.'

The camp at Noyelles is clearly no longer needed but, even so, Wang is surprised at the speed with which it is closed down around him, though not as surprised as when, in early December, Blyth summons him to his office.

'I'm sorry, Wang, but it seems you're needed elsewhere,' he tells him, without any attempt to beat around the bush. 'We've done our damnedest to put your case, but the powers that be just won't have it. They say that you're part of the Chinese Labour Corps, not the Royal Army Medical Corps, and if the labourers are going to labour then their interpreters have to be with them.'

'Sir?'

'The Eleventh Regiment is leaving today and you're to go with them,' Blyth says. He takes a step forward and claps his hand on Wang's shoulder. 'You've been a fine interpreter, Wang, and more than an interpreter. You ought to consider a career in the diplomatic service now that all this nonsense is over. We'll have you back here before too long, just you wait and see.'

Wang feels his eye mist over. Blyth's words thrust deep into his understanding but, no matter how hard he tries to reshape the sound, the message stays the same. He cannot believe that he is going; he cannot understand how the end can be so perfunctory.

'What will happen to the camp, sir?' he asks.

'The sick will be sent home. The able-bodied will work. The officers will be transferred or demobbed. A few of us will stay on for a while, but after that the only ones who'll be left will be the dead.'

Wang thinks of Katell in the estaminet, of Shu Junrong and his other drinking companions. He thinks of Guo and feels his stomach tighten.

'Will you be staying, sir?' he asks.

Blyth shakes his head.

'I've got my marching orders already. It's back to Blighty for me and then, I hope, back to China. Maybe I'll see you there.'

Wang waits for him to say something more, to pull some stronger message of transnational friendship out of the post-armistice bathos, but there is nothing more to be said. He stands smartly to attention and salutes.

'I hope so, sir,' he says and walks out.

As he gathers his few meagre belongings together, the camp is also gathered up. Lamenting the impermanence of the seemingly permanent, he gives his boots a final polish and checks that he still has his copy of *Henry V*, before marching towards the parade ground for the last time, where he sees car after car, truck after truck, drive along the cold earth and out of the main entrance. Walking past the recreation hut, the work huts, the hospital wards, the lunatic asylum, and the already ragged leper wing, he feels terribly alone. It is the end, but there is no sense of a conclusion. The war has been won, but work goes on. Everywhere he looks, the British are chatting, joking, and smoking, but the Chinese Labour Corps continues as it always has.

When the inspection is over, he picks up his pack, joins a line of labourers and is marched to the station. The men he finds himself amongst tell each other that there is nothing to fear, but they are afraid. They know that they are destined for Belgium—though no one has told them—and they do not want to go where so many hundreds of thousands of men have died. They tell each other that the Germans are now either dead or imprisoned in camps that the British control. They tell themselves what they want to hear, but none of them quite believes what is being said. The British call it 'Plucky Little Belgium', but to the Chinese it is a far country full of mud pits, unexploded shells, and flesh-ripping ghosts. For months Wang has watched labourers sitting in the yard tying bundles of wood together to make fascines. When he asks why they have to spend so many hours doing such apparently pointless work, the only answer he ever receives is that Belgium needs them. Now he is about to find out whether it really does.

It is a bright, cold day, and they are marching straight into the sun. The light is blinding but Wang no longer cares. He is so overwhelmed by thoughts that what he sees around him seems of little consequence. As he marches through the town, he passes the estaminet, but the shutters are down and there are no signs of life inside. He tries to spot Katell in the crowds, but he can't see her and soon stops looking. He concentrates instead on keeping in step and lets his own troubles carry him away. The villagers, their expressions unreadable, stand silently by the side of the road and watch as their temporary lodgers march past. The Chinese have helped to bring them victory, but they will be enjoying it alone.

They have reached Major Greenstreet's headquarters when Wang hears the sound of shrieking. He can't make out the words, but he knows instantly that it is Katell. She is beside herself with grief or anguish or some other emotion he cannot name, and she is, he knows, looking for him. He turns back and sees her stumble along the path, pushing baffled villagers out of her way as she passes.

'Keep marching!' a voice shouts, but he doesn't. He stops and waits for her to catch up.

'You there! Get in line.'

He tries to resist the tide, but the shouting and the mass of bodies grow too great to confront, and he is forced back into position.

'Weijun, Weijun!' Katell shouts as she runs. 'I need to speak to you, Weijun!'

She stumbles, and her voice falls with her. Wang tries to look back, but he can see nothing now but men. He keeps marching and hopes that she will not give up.

'Weijun, please,' she yells.

They cross the railway line and turn sharply left towards the station. The square is full of men waiting, and the sight of those sullen, silent rows gives her strength. Wang hears her voice fill out once more. The departing labourers surge into the square, and her voice surges after. Then, as they come to a halt, she is beside him. He cannot bear to look at her.

'Weijun, Weijun, you've got to take a message.'

She is almost incoherent in her anxiety. One of her legs is bleeding, and her voice is shaking violently.

'You've got to tell him that I'm still here. You've got to tell him that I won't be going, that he must come back. And if he can't, he must send a message. You'll do that for us, won't you Weijun?'

She is pleading now, and the shame of it is impossible to bear.

'I don't know where they have sent him,' Wang replies.

'He's gone to Belgium.'

'Belgium is a big place.'

'No, it's not. Belgium is a wart on the face of Europe. You'll find him. Promise you'll find him. And when you do, send me a message. He can't write. He can't speak French. You know that. But I've got to know he's still alive. And he's ... he's got to know that I'm still here, that I'll wait for him, that I'll not give up.'

She is interrupted by two of the camp guards. 'Come on, Madame, we can't have you here.'

'I'm doing no harm. Leave me alone.'

'This is no place for you, Madame.'

They each take an arm and start to pull her from the square.

'Tell him, Weijun. Tell him that I've not forgotten. Tell him that my house is his. Promise me.'

'I promise,' he says, but she cannot have heard him. A space has opened between them that words can never fill.

No Man's Land, 1919

Chapter 20

They hear the train before they see it, expelling steam as if it were some avenging Yazi dragon fighting the French winter. And when they see it their hearts sink still further. The British have not sent a passenger train to ferry the labourers to Belgium, but a goods train, the like of which Wang has not seen since he first arrived in Noyelles from Boulogne two years ago. *4 HORSES, 16 MEN*, it says on the side of the truck. Twenty-four men are ordered inside.

'There's more room now that they've taken out the benches,' explains the soldier who bundles them into the truck.

Wang has never experienced a comfortable railway journey in Europe. The trains are always overcrowded, unheated and filthy. But this journey is the worst he has experienced, not because of the carriage's condition, but because it is taking him away from a finite war to an indefinite future. He joins the others in sitting with his back to another man's to give himself some measure of protection, but it is dark and fetid, like being buried in a sack of rotting potatoes. However they position their bodies, they are buffeted and soon give up trying to find a comfortable position. In the darkness, Wang loses any sense of time. His French past and the Belgian present merge into something vague, uncomfortable, and indeterminate.

Whenever the train stops, they climb to their feet and attempt to peer out between the cracks in the doorway, but, as often as not, they find that they have come to rest in the middle of a field. They wait for hours, and then the train clanks on. If there is a reason for these pauses, Wang never discovers them. Sometimes the doors are thrown open and a sack of food or canisters of water are pushed in, but not often enough. At first they fight over the supplies, but before long they realise that they have no choice but to work together. They take it in turns to distribute the food and water, while the rest of them stand on the side of the cart and piss over the rich French countryside. The sight of five hundred or so men pissing out of those great grey cattle wagons is one of the few images Wang never manages to shake from his memory.

They try to work out where they are, but the landmarks are so few and the distances so difficult to judge that they have little chance of success and soon give up trying. They will arrive when they arrive, and there is nothing they can do to hasten the process. In the train's gloom, Wang has time to think about Guo and Katell, though he tries to fight them off when they appear. He even lets his mind slip back to China, where his father and Rong Meifan are now as nebulous as the ghosts of the men who have gone before him on the troop trains of northern Europe.

There is little dignity to be had in a cattle truck. At first Wang keeps his head down, but, as time stretches, he starts to talk to the labourers who travel with him—Dai Jiyun, who yammers incessantly about his parents, Yan Ziming, who spits on the floor whenever anyone says something he disagrees with, Duan Shifu, who has shoulders broad enough for two men, Cheng Feiyi, who scowls at Wang every time he tries to join in the conversation, Old Chen, who, at forty, is regarded as the source of all wisdom, and Hu Minghai, who bursts into tears whenever the train stops. Wang gives little away about where he has come from or what he has done in France. It seems safer that way.

Eventually, some three or four days later, they arrive at their destination—the small Belgian town of Poperinghe—and walk to a featureless little village called Reningelst. Almost immediately, they lose any sense of the exultation that comes from being released from their goods wagons. What little they see of Poperinghe is in ruins, and the landscape they pass through on their way to camp reminds Wang of the places his mother used to tell him about when she read him to sleep, places inhabited by demons and fox spirits. He thinks about Taizong visiting the Mountain of Perpetual Shade in the Region of Darkness. For the first time in months, he thinks longingly of home.

There are no cars, no horses, and few people. In one field he sees a cow harnessed with a bridle and collar, ploughing the broken land. It is bitterly cold, and so he stamps his feet as he marches to restore the circulation, but it is not his fingers or his toes that bother him most. He is alone in a company of men he does not know, and he fears that he will not be able to endure working as one of them for long, so used is he to the translators' comforts, so familiar is he with British company. When he tries to engage an officer in conversation, he is bawled at for his pains.

They arrive at the camp of the 101st Chinese Labour Corps a few hours later and are appalled by what they see as they trudge up a rough wooden path and through a tottering Chinese arch to the main gate. The camp is damaged, dirty, and neglected. There are very few British officers around, and those who remain seem tired or bored. The officer who shouted at him disappears as soon as they step inside the camp, and the men who replace him—Lieutenants Hutton, Morris and Hamilton—keep themselves to themselves. They dole out a few basic rations—slices of bread, hard Belgian cheese, and mugs of hot water—before hurrying the labourers towards the dormitory huts and leaving them to make the best of what they find there. As they attempt to plug the holes in the wall of one of the damp, dark buildings, a rat runs across the floor and stops to watch proceedings. When Bai Weiqi throws stones at it, it simply stands and watches.

The men sit listlessly, waiting for orders. When it becomes apparent that no orders will be forthcoming, they grab what space they can and settle down for the night. The most basic of camp beds are laid out on rough wooden slats, but there is nowhere to keep their few possessions; most of the labourers use their packs as pillows and sleep under their coats. When they wake up the next morning, their beds have slumped so much that the slats have been pushed to the sides and many of the labourers are lying on the bare ground.

'Up, up, up, you lot,' a voice calls from outside the window. The unseen officer starts banging on the glass to reinforce his point. 'It's time to get moving. If you're quick, you'll get breakfast. If you're not, that's your lookout.'

Wang starts to translate, but the rest of his hut have already worked out the gist of the message. Within a couple of minutes the room is empty. It doesn't take Wang long to discover, if he didn't know it already, that his days as a privileged man of words are over. He can no longer travel the countryside in search of Europe's literary and political heritage. He no longer has free intercourse with the educated officer elite. Instead, he is expected to join in with what Lieutenant Hamilton calls battlefield clearance, an innocuous name for what Wang soon discovers to be a deadly task. Once he has finished breakfast, he is handed a shovel and ordered to work with everyone else. He half-heartedly protests, but now that the war is over no one wants to listen to a disgruntled Chinese translator.

Whenever anyone at Noyelles mentioned far eastern places like Belgium, they talked about the noise—guns, shells, and explosions. What Wang finds eerie when he sets off for the clearance zones on his first day of work is the silence. There are birds, a few of them, and there is the sound of boots on the road, but, other than that, there is nothing. No one is whistling; no one is singing; there is no sound of lives being rebuilt. The Belgians hardly seem to exist. He marches next to Li Shuping, and together they stare at the stone-cold countryside through which they are led and discuss how they will do the job they have been assigned.

'There'll be no getting through this ground until the sun comes out,' Li tells him.

'I can't imagine that's going to wash with the British,' Wang replies.

'Give them a shovel and let them try then.'

They walk with a kind of dulled insensitivity, until finally the weight of nothingness bears down upon them too heavily and someone in the line starts to sing. It is a simple song, but the very simplicity of its words is what they need.

'One, two, three, four, five,' he sings.

'One, two, three, four, five,' they all repeat.

'Five times five is twenty-five.

How heavy is the task.

How long the way to dinner.'

They chant it several times before another voice takes over. Then they move through raucous versions of 'How wet the world appears' and 'The wild duck scatter' before attempting mournful renditions of 'Last night I heard the voice of demons'. By the time they reach their destination, a featureless field in the middle of a featureless plain, they have worked their way through all the popular songs Wang ever learnt in China, and a dozen more besides.

They are singing the last line of 'The garment and flesh of the winter world are torn', when an explosion resounds across the plain. Most of the labourers rush forward, though a few run away across the Belgian fields, screaming as they go. Wang drops his shovel and joins Li Shuping in a dash towards the front of the line. When he sees blood running from the faces of men coming in the opposite direction, he slows down, but Li Shuping grabs him by the arm and drags him forward.

'Come on, we've got a job to do,' he says.

Wang lets himself be dragged for a few yards and then gives in to the inevitable. Running alongside Li, he only stops when he spots the crater by the side of the road. There is nothing to be done for the dead man, but those who were marching nearest to him are in a terrible state. Yan Ziming is running up and down the lane, with three or four others in pursuit. His face, like a painting left in the rain, is pouring blood, and it has taken him a moment to realise that the blood is not his. The dead man has exploded all over him, and Yan is now running not from the noise and the explosion but from the horror. Eventually Old Chen wrestles him into a ditch and slaps him until he stops screaming. It only occurs to Wang that he might still be able to help when he sees Li Shuping pull his coat off and thread the arm through a pickaxe handle.

'Come on,' he shouts at Wang. 'Get another one over here and help me carry these poor bastards away.'

He gestures to a man Wang does not recognise—a man whose right arm has been severed at the elbow—grabs hold of his legs, helps manoeuvre him onto Wang's coat, and shoves a spade handle through the loose sleeve. Then, grabbing hold of the front of the makeshift stretcher almost before Wang has got hold of the back, he starts to jog trot across a field towards the nearest farmhouse. The wounded man whimpers and moans with every jolt, and it is all they can do to keep him from falling off. Wang keeps his eyes on the ground in front of him but, when Li stops to shift position, he glances back and is surprised to find that they are at the head of a queue of some ten to twelve other stretcher bearers. When they get to the farm, they leave the injured man with the pale Belgian woman who meets them at the entrance and let the British organise transport to the nearest medical station.

Wang never discovers what becomes of either Yan Ziming or the man he has helped carry, and he never asks. The sheer arbitrariness of the moment has unsettled him. He knows intellectually what war is like, but it is not until he sees men he knows being ripped apart that the force of the machine for which he has been working comes home to him. As he trudges back across the field with Li Shuping, he asks the British overseer whether this area has already been cleared, but neither he nor anyone else seems to know. There is no more singing. The labourers march in silence to their clearance area, speaking only when they have to and digging when they arrive, as though to make up for the loss of their companions. The ground may be frozen, but there is a ferocity in their despair that is able to break through even the hardest ground.

When eventually daylight fails, they trudge back to the camp at Reningelst without a sound. Back in the dormitory, laid out on a low makeshift bed, one of the men raises his voice in song once again. Slowly, a few others join in. By the time he gets to the end virtually the whole hut is singing. They repeat the refrain together, and Wang's voice, more used to the level tones of English, merges with those of his people.

And so the days pass. Each morning they rise at five, breakfast at a quarter past, and set off to their destination by six. Each day for months they clear Belgian fields of barbed wire, dead bodies, and the detritus of war. They are given wire cutters, shovels, and stakes to mark the positions of the bodies they find, cresol to soak them with, rubber gloves to lift them with, and canvas and ropes to wrap them with.

Sometimes they are lucky—the ground they are ordered to clear has been marked already. A helmet hanging from a wooden stake, or a piece of wood with the letter E burnt into it, signals the site of a grave. The Germans, for all the stories that the British tell about them, did at least bury the dead and mark their graves. But, more often than not, the stakes have been blown away by explosion after explosion. They waste many hours digging where no body has ever been and, no doubt, sometimes miss places where others still are.

Before long, they grow wise to the true signs of death—rat holes and tiny traces of discarded bones, small pieces of uniform protruding from the ground, blue-green grass and green-black water—the lingering colours of death, the inevitable signs of decay. These are the sites they mark with their flags—blue for larger burial grounds and yellow for the smaller. Only when they have marked the ground are they allowed to start removing the corpses.

At first they try to do their work as quickly as possible, but as one shovel after another plunges through the soft flesh of the dead, as one labourer after another vomits on the remains he has revealed, they begin to slow down. They work, if not with the skill of the archaeologist, then at least with his speed. Painstakingly

231

they dig around the resting place of the dead soldiers, ensuring that nothing is missed, before laying out the canvas, soaking it with cresol, and carefully digging down and under the remains. As they lift the body parts onto the sheet, they detach any personal items—identification tags, letters, photographs—and pass them onto the exhumation officer who always accompanies them. The British watch like eagles in case they steal watches or money, but little is ever taken. There are few who want anything to do with the possessions of the dead.

Each labour company—and there are companies from all over the British Empire—is assigned a different area to work in. The British, whose paths they sometimes cross, are given an area some five hundred yards square. They work from the outside in, clearing barbed wire, filling in trenches, and removing unexploded ordnance. The Chinese, by contrast, are given an area eight hundred yards wide and are sometimes ordered to work from the inside out, which means that they have to march across battlefields of unexploded shells, tangled barbed wire, and decomposing bodies to get to their work site.

As the weeks pass, the ground softens, but their job grows harder. Hasty battlefield burials become more difficult to identify, and so they change their way of working. Grass and nettles now cover much of what were the battlefields, and the labourers have to trust to luck and intuition. A line of darker grass or a flush of nettles might denote the site of a shallow grave, but, equally, it might not. They dig anyway and hope they won't find anything that will blow them sky-high. But, however careful they are, they soon have dead men of their own.

Tang Qianyue and Bai Weiqi are blown up by a bomb they spot too late. Li Xinmin gets into a fight with some of the Egyptian Labour Corps, is stabbed in the leg and bleeds to death. Dai Jiyun drowns in an old shell hole while drunk. Hong Ganren and Duan Shifu break into a village store, are challenged, and so strike out and kill a man. Hong is executed and Duan is taken away to prison. They never hear any more about him. Xin Ruokun pulls the pin from a grenade—they never know why—and blows his head off. You Enlai, Yan Fanbao, and Li Shuping light a fire on a cold morning but are unlucky enough to pick the site of an old German ammunition dump for their improvised breakfast. All that is left of them is Yan's hand still holding out his mug for tea. Shao Zeping disappears. Bai Xiaojing runs off with a Belgian woman. Zeng Zengyou is shot by one of their own sentries when he goes outside one night to relieve himself. Wu Kaiyang loses his leg in an explosion, seems to recover, but then contracts gangrene. He dies three weeks later. Han Binshi dies of an unidentified illness. Rui Boda and Wei Xuanyao are wiped out by the flu. Wang wakes up each morning surprised to find himself still alive.

Wang's dream of seeing Europe founders in the Belgian mudholes. He never sees any of the great medieval cities. Ghent, Ypres, Bruges—all these places were more real to him in Shanghai than they are in Belgium itself. As he walks to the clearance zones each morning, he recalls the pictures he pored over in China—the great squares, the noble churches, the chocolate shops crenellated like castles. He walks automatically while, in his mind's eye, he peers into every cranny of those cities he has never seen. It is only in his imagination that he can pace the cobbled streets and examine the glories of the Belgian past.

Chapter 21

It is easy to forget about the past in Belgium—the routine is unchanging and fatalism seems as natural as the greyness of the surroundings—but every now and again Wang makes half-hearted enquiries about Guo, impelled by stubborn memories of Katell and deep-rooted feelings of guilt or duty he cannot understand or contain. A morose Australian officer suggests that he make enquiries at the military prison at Brandhoek, but he cannot get away from his work party and doubts whether the prison authorities would tell him anything even if he did manage to negotiate a day's absence. He scans the casualty lists, though the Chinese rarely figure on them even when they are dying in droves, and asks each newcomer to the camp whether they have seen the Sichuanese labourer, but all to no avail. Catching a glimpse of someone who looks like Guo, he even races after a group of labourers from another company, but when he catches them up it is someone else entirely. He tries not to dwell on Katell, knowing that there is little he can do to bring her fiancé back, and concentrates instead on staying alive.

It is easy not to think, and the cold makes it easier. He develops a routine instead, a routine designed to keep him from the past, a routine designed to stave off death. Even so, he cannot help but pity the pale, broken Belgian men who stand and watch while Wang and his countrymen work—men who have come to reclaim their land and are left waiting hopelessly as their fields are dredged like a polluted river. It is a pitiful thing to see a starving European, to see men whose families have coaxed crops

234

from the land for generations, resorting to a beggar's tricks. It is a terrible thing to see women standing on the edge of endless fields as Egyptians, Indians, Canadians, and Chinese scrape the dead out of trenches. There is nothing so haunting as the sound of children howling with hunger because the rich earth that could save them has been sown with dynamite and iron. He throws them occasional crusts of bread but knows that he needs all the sustenance he can get to see him through another year of hard labour until he reaches the end of his contract.

Sometimes the CLC works alongside other colonial groups, but the British are too canny to bring different groups together for long. There are fights. There are disputes. Too many men are killed in murky arguments to make it worth their while. The Chinese keep—and are kept—to themselves, which means that Wang constantly meets men from other parts of his country, even other men whom he recognises from Noyelles or Boulogne or Etaples, but never Guo. He keeps asking, but no one is interested in yet another hard man from Sichuan. It is every man for himself now. Eyes are kept to the ground. Contracts are seen out. Money is earned. If Guo were to come within fifty miles of where Wang is stationed, he wouldn't know it.

Belgium seems to be a country of cemeteries, but these cemeteries are not like any Wang has seen before. The cemeteries he knows best are the ones he used to visit dutifully as a child in Shanghai at the time of the mid-autumn festival, the places where his ancestors were buried. They were great pilgrimage sites where hundreds of families gathered to offer roasted piglets, to burn incense, and to chant prayers. Places of memory and belonging, where entire families gathered to share, to recall and to feast. They were places of great beauty, built into the sides of bold hills, overlooking the sea.

Nor are these Belgian cemeteries like the graveyards he has seen in France, full of crosses and crucifixes, of black granite, fresh flowers and fading photographs. They are not attached to towering village churches, whose doors open to reveal a strange red light burning at the holy end, the end Wang has never dared approach. They are not attended by old women, their heads covered with black shawls and their hands full of rosary beads. These are not places that have been looked after. They are not part of any community and have not yet been caught up in any collective memory. The cemeteries that clutter the fields of Belgium are insignificant affairs that merge with the flatness of the land and belong to it. They are places where bodies fell in a desperate attack on some pathetic ridge. They are small squares of remembrance that are fenced off by rope strung from four metal poles, if they are fenced off at all. Wang bares his head every time he passes one of these terrible patches of ground and gives thanks that none of the pitiable wooden crosses that mark the places where bodies are supposed to lie belongs to him. He doesn't want to die on a foreign plain, and he certainly doesn't want to be commemorated by a handwritten tablet stuck to a wooden stick.

Order has returned to Europe, and the age of great rebuilding has begun. This is what Wang reads, but he knows differently. Beneath the serried rows of graves is a clutter of body parts. Confusion has been covered by two or three feet of soil. He is sick of these European memorial grounds and, with every week that he passes in Belgium, he grows more resentful of the cost to his compatriots. If this is the age of rebuilding, then it is the Chinese—and, he is prepared to admit if pressed, the Egyptians, the Indians, the New Zealanders, and even a few of the British, French and Belgians—who are doing the hard labour. If order has returned, then it is order created by a group of ragtag coolies whom the natives despise.

Digging with men who have been digging all their life, and dismantling trenches with men who have built and rebuilt rice fields on the side of Sichuanese mountains since they were old enough to grasp a mattock, pushes Wang far beyond what he ever thought he was capable of doing. With his future stretching ahead of him like the monotonous Belgian landscape, he gives himself to the flat earth as an old man does to death.

Discovering a rhythm in settled despair, Wang orders his days even when they aren't ordered for him. Grabbing what food he can after reveille, he washes at the standpipe only when he has eaten what he can get his hands on, knowing that he won't be given enough during the day to sustain him. Even though supplies are supposed to be more plentiful now that hostilities have ceased, the organisation he was used to at Noyelles has broken down—the teams of Chinese cooks, the supply lines from the east coast, the black marketeers who could always supplement the meagre official rations.

Here in Belgium he eats western food, but rough bread, canned soup, and thin bean stew are never enough to sustain him. As he marches to and from the clearance sites, he tries to recall the smell of Shanghai cuisine, the anticipation of celebratory meals, the lingering aftertaste of *xunyu* and *takecai*, of *niangao* and *tangtuan*. Finding safety in anonymity, he blends into the bland surroundings, never pushing himself forwards, never volunteering for work, always hanging back when they reach the deadly fields they have to clear. Only sullen memories of Guo and Katell's last desperate pleas are capable of compelling initiative.

He sets about mapping Belgium in his head, drawing details from his own limited expeditions and filling in the many gaps from the lacunae-riddled descriptions that other labourers give him. Onto this desperate mental topography he traces all that he knows of the movements of the Chinese Labour Corps—the 101st at Reningelst, the company based at the Canada Huts at Sint-Hubertushoek, and a ragtag group of northerners who were sent to Dikkebus. As methodically as he can, given the lack of information and his own miserable state, he makes enquiries and compiles mental check lists, but there is no sign of Guo. Refusing to give up, but tied to his own base camp, he changes tactics, begging favours of labourers who are being transferred to other companies or sent to other parts of the low, grey country. Supplying them with a name and a description, he waits without expectation and works without hope.

The company is clearing the remains of a restaurant in what had once been the prosperous Belgian village of Westouter when Li Fangbi breaks through the bleakness of their collective existence by digging up a wooden box with unexpected contents.

'Wine! Wine!' he calls out in great excitement.

The rest of the labourers gather round to see the bottle he is grasping and, almost immediately, realise the implications of his discovery. They set to work with renewed vigour and, before another half hour has passed, excavate twenty more bottles of red wine, three bottles of port, and two bottles of gin. There are few evenings during Wang's time in Europe which pass with such singing and merrymaking as that evening does. Nor is there ever more enthusiasm for work than is seen the next morning when Lieutenant Byers calls for volunteers to clear more of the damaged buildings in Westouter.

For the first time in weeks, the labourers sing as they march and joke as they sing. They are a company with a mission, a band of brothers united by a single purpose, and that purpose is drink. For winter, it is a warm day, and so blue cotton uniforms are shed in favour of the labourer's traditional bare back as the men divide themselves across the village and begin to dig with a frenzy. Every now and again a cry of triumph and a breaking of ranks is swiftly followed by groans of dismay, but, for the most part, all that can be heard in the flat, broken landscape is the sound of shovels and picks, the crash of flung stones, and the occasional sharp oath.

Wang is paired with Zhang Xiaohui, a Hunanese giant who was a river boatman before signing up for the European adventure. He has arms like howitzers and soon puts Wang to shame with the speed and ferocity of his digging. Wang attempts to make up for his lack of strength with cunning and guile but, however hard he tries to bypass the remains of outer walls and make straight for what they all think must be cellar after lucrative cellar, he is neither cunning nor strong enough to make any sort of significant impression on the ruins around him. When he breaks for a hurried lunch of bread and cheese, Zhang studiously ignores him.

Ten or so minutes after he resumes, Wang strikes gold. He is thrusting his shovel into the remains of an old house with new strength when he feels something give. He tries again and hears the change of sound he has been listening for all morning. Dropping to his knees, he scrabbles in the Belgian dust until he can make out the edges of a large box, like the one Li Fangbi discovered the day before. He thinks about calling Zhang Xiaohui over to give him a helping hand, but he is out of sight and Wang has no desire to share his spoils. Clearing some rubble with his hands, he begins to lever the lid off with his spade. Eventually it gives and, as it does so, it explodes in his face.

He has no coherent memory of the explosion. All he remembers is the intensity of the light, the rush of the wind, and the force of the blast. His rational mind tells him that he must have been flung away from the box of shells, but his memory insists that he was pulled inwards. As a dozen hands grip him and drag him off, he tries to look up at the pale Belgian sky but sees nothing. The sharp flash of the explosion has scraped his skull clean. Sounds and sights seem to merge into a single sense that overwhelms every other aspect of his being. As he questions why he is not yet dead, pain—intense, all-encompassing pain—hits him with its iron fist. Gouged by a deep agony he cannot comprehend, he fancies that he is being dragged through the streets of Bruges on a cart. He sees Rong Meifan wiping his wounds as his father extracts splinter after murderous splinter from his face. He hears his mother chiding him for playing with a bow and arrow. He tries to look but can see nothing. He tries to open his eyes, but all he can see is darkness. Pummelled by shock and terror, he lets his grip loosen on the thin edge of consciousness and falls into a place of nightmares. When eventually he wakes, the groans and screams tell him that he must be in a field hospital. He adds his voice to the hellish wail until an angry doctor thrusts a needle into his arm.

He wakes and sleeps and wakes again; he is dropped from

a stretcher; he is flung onto a sagging camp bed; he finds himself on a long, broken train journey. In the fractured world of memory and mind, where thoughts, emotions and experiences collide, he sees the explosion that has destroyed him. With juddering regularity, he pulls the lid from the buried box of shells and is thrown backwards by the noise and light and unadulterated force. Sometimes he sees the shell that he has unearthed, sometimes he is overwhelmed by the fullness of light, and sometimes he sees himself from outside, an insignificant figure in a monotonous landscape, flung into hell by a combination of bad luck, ill-will and stupidity.

In a rare lucid moment he remembers Mr Davis telling him that Time is a great healer but, if he thinks anything at all, he thinks that is a terrible lie. If, after unmeasurable suffering, there is any progress, any healing of the mind, any lessening of the pain, it comes not from the passing of time but from sheer habit, from the desire for life that Wang has cultivated for twenty-seven years and cannot now easily abandon. Slowly, snatches of conversation coalesce into meaning, shards of sound re-form as meaningful noise, the far-flung reaches of his mind reconnect and effect some kind of recovery. Gradually, the pain eases, and this is when the true horror begins. His shattered mind catches fragments from an earlier time, from the days after Zhou Lianke's arrow started the job the Belgian countryside has now completed. This searing horror that is pulling his face apart is the source of all pain, the end of all disasters. He has to have his hands tied behind his back to prevent him from clawing at the agony that assaults him. He is harangued and slapped and, if lucky, injected into unconsciousness as he is hauled across an unknown country, a country he can no longer see.

As he begins to function as a human once more, he comprehends what has happened to him. He is told that the left side of his face took the impact, exposing his skull and blowing his one good eye clean away, that he was peppered with shrapnel, and that his left leg is an unimaginable mess. He howls at the unfairness of it and tries to deny what has happened, but his inner darkness will not be diminished, however much he experiments with different ways of opening the eye that is no longer there. He gives way to despair, but his body fights on. However hard he tries to die, his heart still beats, his lungs still breathe, and his brain still digs in around its own Verdun. He smashes his head against the frame of his hospital bed; he pulls at his hair until blood runs down the unwashed skin of his face; he pounds himself back into life.

Another doctor puts him to sleep, and this time he continues sleeping as his body is carted back to France. As the train reruns the journey he took in the darkness of a cattle truck six months earlier, Wang sees and knows nothing. Either the drugs do their work, or his body responds to deep trauma by carrying him senseless through the first post-war spring. If anyone tells him that he is being taken back to Noyelles for treatment, his conscious mind does not register it. If anyone tells him that he is back, he does not understand.

There is no single moment of waking, but a series of impressions that darkly impose themselves upon him. He hears a noise that is not the sound of the storm that has pounded his head for as long as he can remember. He feels a sensation on his fingertips that is not rough canvas or cold metal. He smells the salt in the wind once more, and slowly, bitterly, the brain makes sense of what his remaining senses experience. When eventually he struggles into consciousness, it is the smell that tells him where he is.

'You're a bloody lucky man, Wang,' a voice says.

Wang groans and tries to turn over.

'Don't you dare move!' the voice orders. 'Or I'll have you thrown out.'

It is Lieutenant Fell, and Wang doesn't know whether he is relieved or appalled. Without realising what he is doing, he starts moaning again.

'Oh, will you stop it, Wang!' Fell says sharply. 'You're bloody lucky, you know.'

'What?' Wang croaks. It is so long since he last spoke that he has all but lost the use of his voice.

'A mangled leg, lots of shrapnel wounds, and one hell of a burned face, but if you'd been in any other hospital but ours you'd be dead by now. If you'd got here a day or two later you'd have been dead by now. Your face was so badly infected we almost amputated your whole head.'

Wang tries to pull himself up on his pillow. 'Thank you,' he rasps.

'And another thing,' Fell adds. 'At least it's cured the squint.'

Chapter 22

During the next few weeks, Wang's mind enters a cycle of disintegration and partial restoration that he cannot break. In his lucid moments he discovers that Blyth has returned to China, that Carruthers, Underhill and Bairstow have been demobbed, and that the camp is already a tenth of the size it was when he left. He struggles to keep his mind clear but, even when it is not, he cannot forget what he has seen in Belgium—Wang Ziming, his face daubed with all that remained of his closest friend; Yan Fanbao's severed hand still holding his cup of tea; Dai Jiyun's bloated body bouncing against the side of the flooded shell crater. Ever since the arrow severed his childhood, he has had a tendency towards introversion, but now that his sight has gone completely he has nothing but himself to fall back on. He searches the deep places for some sense of consolation, but all he finds is rage—rage and a profound feeling of having been betrayed by those who brought him across the globe with the false promises of modernity. Attacking the darkness, he tries to recollect the simple comfort that came from moulding foreign words into new forms and patterns. He tries to remember what it felt like to look men in the face.

Fell and the remaining nurses try to bring him back to himself by telling him tales of success at the British Exhibition of Agriculture at Abbeville, by wheeling him up and down the ward, or even by joining him for games of whispered mah-jong, but he would rather they didn't. They tell him that, being blind, he needs to learn new skills, that there is no obstacle a blind man cannot overcome, least of all a man who has been one-eyed for so long. He listens but doesn't want to be brought out of himself. When Fell suggests that he start learning braille, he shouts him out of the room.

'OK, I'll go,' Fell tells him, 'but I'm not leaving you alone.'

Wang attempts to reply but words are no longer wholly under his control. He buries himself under his blanket instead.

'Katell came to see you soon after you returned, but I had to send her away. You were too damaged to speak. I can let her know you're ready for her now.'

At the mention of her name, Wang feels his throat tighten, but he cannot wrench his sense of hopeful anticipation into words worthy of the emotion.

'I don't want to see her,' Wang says. 'Tell her not to come.'

She comes anyway. He recognises the sound of her walk before anyone tells him who it is.

'Weijun?' she says hesitantly. 'Weijun, I came before but they sent me away.'

He pretends to be asleep. It shouldn't be difficult, he thinks bitterly to himself.

'They said you were delirious. They said you'd probably die.'

He hears her choke on her words and feels his own throat constrict.

'I should have stayed with you. I should have insisted, but they forced me out. They said I was getting in the way, but I wasn't. You needed me, Weijun. Weijun, can you hear me? You needed me and I left you. Is that why you won't speak to me now?'

Wang feels the tears coming but cannot wipe them away. He senses rather than hears Katell come closer. One side of his head is covered with bandages, but she cannot escape the horror of the other bare socket and the tears that run from it. She gets out a handkerchief and wipes them from his mutilated face. Wang stiffens and then, realising that he has been holding his breath, begins to sob. He doesn't pull away when Katell cradles his head in her arms.

'What have they done to you, Wang?' she asks. 'What have they done to you?'

The next day she returns with a pot of soup and, taking Wang's head in her arms, slowly feeds it to him with a teaspoon. He keeps quiet, but she speaks to him anyway. She tells him the stories her mother told her as a child and then, when she runs out of stories to tell, when she is unable to bear the silence any longer, she searches her memory for something else with which to fill the darkness. As Wang starts to shift about uncomfortably in his bed, she pulls out the nursery rhymes she taught the labourers when they were still whole and hopeful and strong.

'*Kousk, ma mabig, kousk aze, dindan askell ael Doue, kloz da zaoulagad seder, kousk aze ma bugel kaer,*' she sings.

There is no response, so she lies down next to him and rests one arm on his unmoving body. She puts her mouth to his ear and sings again.

'*Med ac'han di a zo pell bras, O ma Doue! pa soñjan, evit mont gant an aelez, War-zu bro gaer ar Werc'hez.*'

She comes again the next day, and the day after that, until eventually he starts to speak to her. He can't tell her about Belgium, but slowly, haltingly, he starts to tell her what he remembers of Shanghai—the house by the sea, Hall and Holtz's department store, the tutor who first taught him French.

Once he has exhausted what he can bear to recall of his childhood, he lapses into a silence that Katell feels she has to fill. She tells him about the garden she has started to tend, about Dingo and the cats, about the aggravating behaviour of Monsieur Giroud the shopkeeper, about how difficult it is to buy decent quality meat from the shiftless village butcher. She talks about the soldiers who have returned and about those who have not, about grieving relatives and the sons they can no longer hold. She speaks about her own parents, about an aunt who lives in Rouen, and a cousin who married a Dutchman. She complains about the mayor, several farmers, and the old man who has replaced Major Greenstreet. As Wang attempts to hang onto the clip and lilt of her Bretonised French, it occurs to him that the only person she hasn't mentioned is Guo. But then she breaks off suddenly, leans in close to his face and speaks with a sudden urgency.

'Did you see him?' she says.

Wang listens as her breathing almost imperceptibly quickens. He is tempted to lie but knows that nothing but the truth will now do.

'I didn't,' he says. 'I looked but—'

He breaks off.

'And now I never will.'

Katell falls silent. He can hear the heave and fall of her chest. 'You looked?' she repeats. 'You really looked?'

Wang pulls himself up. He is finding it difficult to speak.

'It was hard,' he says. 'We were digging. We—'

He cannot explain and realises that it would be pointless even to try.

'I tried to go myself,' Katell says eventually, 'but they stopped me. There's no war on, but they stopped me. They said it was still a military zone.'

Wang thinks about reaching out a consoling hand but cannot bring himself to move. He is the victim now, and it seems inconceivable that he could offer anything other than hollow gestures.

'How can a whole country be a military zone?' she asks.

Before Wang can reply, another voice intervenes.

'Get that big nose out of here. I'm trying to get some sleep.'

'Don't shout at me, old man,' Katell barks back, before adding a string of expletives in Chinese that she can only have picked up from Guo himself. The old man subsides into silence.

'He can't write,' she says, almost without pausing. 'He doesn't trust words on a page and he's proud. He won't even get someone else to write for him. Weijun, why are you Chinese so stubborn? Answer me that.'

Wang has never thought that they are. 'Maybe he'll come back,' he says eventually.

'They'll never let him,' Katell bursts out. 'He was trouble while he was here, and he'll be trouble where he's gone. They'll either send him home or they'll get him killed.'

'He'll be safe where he is.'

'By all the saints, Weijun, what are you talking about? He'll not be safe wherever he is.'

He knows she is right, but he cannot admit it. His throat hurts. His face hurts. He wishes that Katell would go.

'Just look at you, Weijun,' she says bitterly. 'You were a good-looking man once, and now you only have half a face. The war's over, and they're sending you out to die like soldiers. The generals are safe at home with their families, and they're still taking our men away to be killed. It's not right, Weijun, it's not right!'

She catches her breath again and fights for control.

'Do you know what I do each Sunday?' she says. 'I force Fell to walk with me up to that cemetery of yours and get him to translate the names on the crosses. I spend my weekends looking at graves. It was a tiny patch in an enormous field when they signed the Armistice. Now they're having to cut into the next field so they can dig more holes. The war's over, and they're still cramming Chinese bodies into the dead earth, so don't you dare tell me he's safe.'

Wang turns his head away. 'I'm sorry, Katell,' he says. 'I really am.'

'You're sorry now. But when you go home, you'll forget.'

'I won't forget,' he promises.

'What was the name of that madman you helped bury last summer?'

'The madman?' he repeats. 'I don't see how—'

'What was his name?'

Even though he is dimly aware that Katell is asking more than any injured man should ever have to recall, he cannot prevent himself from speaking.

'It was ... I don't remember.'

'What about that northerner who bred dogs on the sly?'

Wang knows the man she is referring to. He used to sell them as food when the rations grew thin and, as often as not, saw them tucked up under bunks as pets when he returned to the barracks at night.

'I can't remember that either.'

'The man who taught national awareness in the YMCA hut each week? Or the one who taught hygiene and French? What were the names of the officers you worked for? For God's sake, Wang, can you even remember Guo's other names?'

Wang hesitates and, as he does so, he feels her get up. She strides across the room before pausing at the door.

'His name was Guo Ziqin,' she says so quietly he can hardly hear. 'Guo Ziqin, and he was mine.'

The next time Wang hears her voice she is talking to Fell by the foot of his bed.

'Have we lost him?' she asks.

'No, we've not lost him. A shell went off in his face, but that doesn't mean it's just his face that's suffered. At least some of his hearing must have gone, and as for his mind'—he shrugs—'I guess we're only just beginning to see what's happened to that.'

'But he's talking,' Katell says. 'Talking and remembering words.'

'The mind's not like the eye,' Fell replies. 'It's not a question of it working or not. It's more like our bloody generators—a bit hit and miss. Sometimes he'll make sense and sometimes he won't. Just like Shakespeare.'

Drifting back into a confused sleep, he only comes to when he hears raised voices. Katell is arguing with Fell, who is a lot more irritable than Wang can ever remember him being before. Little things set him off these days—patients spilling their medicine, nurses getting in his way, the rain pounding on the ward roof—so his running into Katell on the rampage has inevitably caused an

248

argument. Despite Fell's rank, there is no doubt in Wang's mind about who is going to triumph. As Katell walks into the ward and calls his name, Wang notices that there is something different about her tread. He pulls himself up and listens as she drags a chair across from the other side of the ward. The smallest of whimpers tells him why she hasn't sat on the bed next to him.

'I've brought him with me, Weijun,' she says. 'I couldn't keep him away any longer.'

Wang searches through the darkness for the tiniest flicker of understanding. He reaches out for knowledge, but wherever he gropes he finds nothing but shadow.

'I don't—'

'My baby, Weijun. I've brought my baby.'

What was dark before seems suddenly to become darker still.

'But how—'

'Oh Weijun. You poor, lost little fool. How can you be so simple? How could you not know? He came like all babies came. What were you expecting?'

A strange buzzing fills Wang's ears. He cannot understand how this woman who has lost her fiancé can now have a baby. He cannot imagine how someone who was throwing herself at his feet in despair when he left Noyelles can now have a child in her arms.

'But does Guo know?' he stammers.

Katell falls silent and the baby continues to whimper. Wang feels her shift position in her chair and listens as the baby cries.

'How could he have known,' she says, 'when they took him away last June?'

A slow blur of understanding crosses the dark, and in the stillness Wang hears the sound of his own anxious breaths.

'Surely you don't—'

'May the fourth. He was born on May the fourth.'

Wang tries to turn himself over, to bury his head under his pillow, but there is no refuge now that all is dark. He listens as

Katell comforts the child, as another patient offers an opinion on the new arrival, as fear seeps out through the cracks of memory and desire.

'He's called François. I wanted to call him—I couldn't bring myself to call him—'

She breaks off.

Wang's head starts to pound and a sharp pain drives through his mind. It feels as though a shovel is being plunged into his skull. Through the confusion he hears Katell stand up.

'We should go now,' she says.

'No!' Wang is surprised to hear himself shout so hoarsely. 'You can't leave me now. You can't leave me here.'

'What else can I do?' Katell says.

Wang reaches out until she comes to meet him, until their fingers interlink, and then the baby starts to cry again. In a confusion of tears and soothing words, Katell extricates herself and walks out. When she reaches the door she stops and turns back towards Wang.

'I shouldn't have brought him,' she says. 'I won't bring him again.'

Fragments of memory break through the second darkness in which Wang tries to enfold himself. He screws up his face as if to force his dead eyes tighter shut, but however dark his outer darkness is, he cannot close his mind entirely to the light of the past. Fragments of memory rip him open once more, splintering him with such sharp intensity that he cannot help cowering in his bed. His mother opens her mouth in a silent scream as Zhou Lianke pushes him into the house with the arrow's shaft still protruding from his socket. His father hurls the quack doctor into his precious glass cabinets. Rong Meifan looks pitifully up at him. Unable to shut out any of these sights, he puts his hands over his ears to block out the implacable roar that breaks through every vision—the sound of the sky being pulled apart, of eardrums being burst, of words being slapped into one convulsive blast. But he can no more rid himself of those terrible noises than he can escape the sound of the child Katell has presented him with.

He buries his face in the bed, but new sights drive out the old—the estaminet kitchen, Katell's incredulous gasp as she stumbles in, bleary-eyed and distraught, crumpled sheets and the shock of dawn smashing through her window. He wails and wishes that he had not been brought back.

'Oh, for God's sake, man, shut up!' Fell shouts. 'Pull yourself tobloodygether.'

Shocked by the outburst, Wang whimpers quietly to himself. But Fell hasn't finished.

'She brought him to see you, didn't she? She could have kept him at home. She could have kept you in the dark about him altogether. Count yourself lucky for a change and stop that bloody whimpering.'

Wang sticks his fist in his mouth but cannot entirely suppress the noises he is making. He can't stop Fell either.

'Look, Wang, you're alive, for the love of God. There are plenty dead out there. Dead or worse. Children dead, fiancés dead, sons and husbands dead or gone. But you've got something to live for. No, you've got someone—some two—to live for. But all I've heard from you is wailing and gnashing of teeth, so please, please, please shut up—'

He breaks off, appalled at what he has said.

'Oh Wang, I'm sorry—'

But it is Wang who is sorry. Trying to convince himself that he feels nothing for the unseen bundle, the bag of whimpers and bawled cries that Katell brought with her, he blocks his mind against the demands that the baby's unexpected presence has imposed upon him. But as image after horrific image explodes around him, he discovers that he cannot sandbag his mind. Fighting for breath, struggling against the rebukes the doctor has hurled at him, he realises, with an awful sense of shock, that Fell is right.

He tries to pull himself tobloodygether, but this second

shock compounds the first. Or rather, it reveals the hideousness of what has already torn him apart. He has a son. He is blind. Neither stands within the prospect of belief, but together they are monstrous beyond imagining. Even when one-eyed and helpless in the native doctor's primitive surgery, even when his affair with Rong Meifan was at its most intense, he never imagined that he could be blind, wholly blind, nor that he might become a father. Fatherhood was an occupation for another generation, an activity, an attitude even, that was not to be entered into until more of life had been lived, until China had been changed and the old order swept away. It feels as though he has been tricked, mugged and left to die.

He hasn't thought about the *Empress of Russia* for months, but the constriction he used to feel below decks surges up to meet him once more. It is almost as if he can smell the place again— the salt, the sharp tang of oil, the stench of bodies. Struggling for breath, he tries to escape the choking oppression, but he is no longer sure how he can find the freedom that he used to seek on deck. He cannot see. He can scarcely move. All sense of hope has drained away.

He reaches out for the little that is still under his control— his memories and the images that go with them. Picturing himself in his bunk, with his lifebelt tucked under his head as a pillow, he feels the dip and hurl of the sea again and senses its greyness all around him. He knows he must get up, which means finding the ladder at the other end of the hold. Reaching out his hands, he clambers from bunk to bunk, feeling his passage, trusting the instincts of a body that has never known anything but land, until he stumbles up against the ladder which stretches up with its dim promise of air and spray and freedom. Hand after unsteady hand, he climbs upwards, listening to the roar of the sea as its dull bass grinds on the edge of hearing, forcing himself to concentrate on anything but the sickness in his throat.

When he emerges eventually into the half-light of the Pacific, the boat's drabness is only partially subsumed by the sea's, but he hauls himself to the rail anyway and, holding it like a frightened child grabs hold of his mother, looks over. The sea swirls, grey and unforgiving. Wave is indistinguishable from blank wave. The ocean stretches dark into the distance. He senses rather than hears a presence at his side and, turning, realises that he cannot make out the figure beside him. He turns further, expecting the silhouette to gain focus and precision as he sorts out the light, but focus never comes. It is then that true fear arrives. Something bordering on terror. A sense that there will never be anything other than blackness.

'Weijun?'

He peers into the gloom and wonders how Katell could have got herself onboard.

'Weijun? Are you awake? Are you all right?'

Faceless, he tries to grasp the blank figure beside him, but all Katell sees are his tears and his arms waving helplessly above the blanket. He seems to be mouthing words, but she has to lean in close to catch them.

'My son, my son,' he says. 'I've got to see my son.'

Chapter 23

His mind has been drifting, but the realisation that he can no longer remember what Katell's face looks like jolts him out of aimlessness. If he can't see even what he knows so well, then there is little chance of him ever picturing his son's face, which he doesn't know at all. For the first time since the explosion, he feels anger drag determination along in its wake.

With something for him to do, and a reason to do it, he musters his forces and formulates a plan. Realising that he must start with the familiar, he tries to picture Katell walking into his ward—that determined look, that distinctive tread, that curiously delicate way she has of brushing hair away from her face. A space on the blank canvas of his mind is needed and he fights to clear it, but he can trace nothing more than Katell's outline in his memory. Appalled by his continuing failure, he tries to reconstruct other images but finds that he can't conjure up his father or mother either.

There was a photograph on a red lacquer cabinet that he used to stare at as a boy, a very early photograph of his father as a young man, standing behind his parents in some forgotten studio in western Shanghai. The poses and the clothes were stiff and the expressions unreadable but, to a small boy who had never known his grandparents, the photograph was a link in a chain that could be hauled up from the past. The photograph *was* his grandparents. The studio, with its ridiculous backdrop of palm trees and badly painted chaffinches, *was* the nineteenth century. Now, as he lies in a scratchy bed in a forgotten corner of northern

France, Wang can see that photograph in excruciating detail, but he cannot picture his father on the day he left him.

Leaping from the photograph to the hospital, he tries to see the ward—the wooden bedside cabinets, the birdcage that Blyth used to keep his canaries in, the other patients—but all he can manage is the blandest of images, a children's picture drawn with a very blunt pencil. Kicking against his inability to perform so simple a task, he struggles to extricate himself from the bear hug of despair and hurls himself towards the son he has never seen. He takes his smudged image of Katell, and what he remembers of his own reflection, and tries to find a version of the boy in which he can believe. Reproaching himself for not having traced the pattern of the child's face with his hands, he tries to patch together an image that he can hold onto. But however hard he works at reshaping the faces that cluster in his mind, he can get no further than a smaller, thinner version of Katell herself.

'I've got to see him,' he says plaintively when Katell returns.

Katell nestles François closer. 'You can't see him. I'm sorry, Weijun, but you just can't.'

'I need to see him here,' Wang insists, gesturing to his head, 'but I can't see anything at all. Not really. Not sharply. It's a blur, a mist, a crazy mix of shadows.'

'Then you've got to work at it.'

'My eyes are shot away. How the hell am I going to work at it?'

'I'm not talking about your eyes. I'm talking about what you can see on the inside. You're giving up, but you can't. Not now there's three of us. You're an intelligent man, Weijun. You've got to work at seeing like you used to work at geography and history, or whatever it was you studied in China.'

Ignoring the nurse who has arrived to change his dressings, Wang tries to picture his history and geography teachers but fails.

'English,' he says eventually.

'What?'

'English and French. That's what I worked at when I

255

was back in China. I didn't bother too much with history and geography.'

Katell extracts François from a fold of blanket where he has managed to entangle himself and carries on speaking.

'Like English and French then. You're going to have to treat vision like language. You're going to have to work at translating what you can remember into something you can see. It's going to take work, Weijun, it really is, but you're no shirker. At least, you weren't when you were here before.'

'But I've never seen him,' Wang protests. 'That's the whole point. How can I translate him into sight when I've never seen him?'

Katell gives up trying to wrap the blanket round François and lets it fall onto the bed.

'Then you're going to have to start with what you have, which means the ordinary, the everyday. And it means me too. I'm going to teach you to see what's around you, what you've seen a thousand times before.' Wang lies back, unconvinced. 'We're coming back every day. I hope you're ready for us.'

With a vigour worthy of a military campaign and a slightly manic abruptness, she arrives early next morning to deliver her lesson. Pulling up a chair by Wang's bed, she tousles his hair and launches straight into action.

'I'm sitting on a chair. Describe it.'

Wang groans. He is over the worst of the physical pain, but his body no longer works well and he is permanently lethargic.

'Have we really got to go through with this?'

'Describe it!'

'Four legs, one seat. What else is there to say?'

'This isn't something you can opt out of, Weijun. If you're going to be of any use to your son—to us—then you're going to have to lose your self-pity. Describe the chair.'

There were only a couple of schoolteachers Wang feared— the sort of men who could bring a class to order with a look,

256

who could compel diligence from a distance—but he remembers finding them most chilling when their voices dropped in much the same way that Katell's does now.

'It's brown,' he says doubtfully.

'What sort of brown?'

'Dark—'

A cough makes him think again.

'Light brown, and the legs taper slightly at the top.'

Katell smiles grimly. 'That's more like it. Carry on.'

'It's got a curved back and a square seat.'

'Square?'

'Well, almost square. Squarish. Look, I don't know, Katell. Why don't you tell me and then I can tell you back?'

'Or,' she says, getting off her seat and picking up the gurgling François, 'maybe you can get off your arse and have a feel around.'

Stifling a protest, Wang levers himself up, leans over and lets his hands explore the chair's smooth, hard outline.

'All right, not square but I don't know what you'd call it—'

'You're the one with the words. Give it a try.'

'A blunt rectangle with curved corners. How's that?'

Katell snorts.

'All right then.'

As he strains after something more descriptive, a linguistic substrate is uncovered. Without knowing how he has found the words, or why these particular words matter, he tries again.

'It's square as a cushion is square. It's geometry with the edges knocked off, a poem in wood.'

Katell looks at him quizzically, then remembers that he can't see her baffled expression. 'That's much better, but a poem in wood?'

Wang has sunk back onto his pillow, but she can see from the twitching around his mouth as he suppresses a self-satisfied smile that he is pleased with his description.

'I'd forgotten until you got so demanding,' he says, 'but we had a mathematics teacher once who was a Lewis Carroll fan. He used to quote one of Carroll's poems all the time. I used to know it by heart.'

'Maybe you still do.'

Wang casts the net deep into his pool of memory and, dredging what must be the bottom, pulls a verse haltingly to the surface.

'I often wondered when I cursed,
Often feared where I would be -
Wondered where she'd yield her love
When I yield, so will she.
I would her will be pitied!
Cursed be love! She pitied me ...'

'What on earth are you babbling on about, Weijun? When I was at school we did ordinary, conventional mathematics, not the mathematics you have to think about, not poems about wood.'

'So did we. Mostly.'

'Well, what was it then, that poem? English or pure nonsense?'

'Both,' Wang replies. 'It was a square poem, like the chair. Brown, tapered and poetic.'

Scraping the chair back to the foot of the bed where François can lie more easily, Katell prepares for a long morning's vigil.

'You know what?' she says. 'I think some part of you is getting better already.'

Wang sniffs just loudly enough to express his doubt. 'Some part, but not necessarily the right part.'

'Enough to be rewarded with a kiss,' she adds.

Wang stifles a reply. He doesn't dare open his mouth. As Katell leans over him, he holds his breath in anticipation.

'Kiss Daddy on the cheek,' she says.

'What?' Wang blurts out.

'Oh, all right then. If you won't kiss him then he'll just have to kiss you. Come on, Weijun, give your son a kiss.'

Scarcely registering what he is hearing, Wang holds out his

hands. Cradling François as gingerly as he might an expensive vase, he puts his lips tentatively to the boy's forehead, or where he hopes his forehead might be, and tries not to grimace when the infant starts crying. Murmuring Breton terms of affection, Katell takes the boy back and, when he is settled, reaches back over and pecks Wang on his undamaged cheek.

'That poem,' she says. 'Could you translate it for me?'

In his misery, Wang can hardly shape a reply. 'There are some things,' he says, 'that will always be untranslatable.'

The lessons continue every day. Knowing enough about human fragility to keep the tasks simple, Katell chooses solid, hearty nouns for Wang to describe. He starts ponderously but, within a matter of days, and despite the dull headache that never wholly leaves him, he begins to relish the challenge.

Once he has got beyond what Katell tells him are his first feeble efforts, he manages to construct lyrical definitions of the words he is given. Books are 'red and stiff-spined, with pages that smell of dank libraries'. The piano is 'as heavy as an ox, with a body like a Louis XIV cabinet, and white teeth capped with black crowns'. An erhu has 'a neck like a giraffe's, strings like a woman's hair, and a wooden sound box with a snakeskin belly'.

Katell is patient with him, even when he becomes too tired to think—'cheese: that funny stuff you French eat, looks like nothing else on earth and tastes worse'—but she can hardly let a sentence go by without prompting him to describe what he sees, and always refuses to accept fine words as a substitute for truthful description.

For his part, Wang finds words return to him with a healing force. Unable to force himself to see—though he does everything Katell asks of him—he falls back on the power of language, which returns from the dark places of his mind and the hidden storerooms of memory. He doesn't believe that language can ever be a substitute for the visual world, but it is enough to feel the sweet taste of words in his mouth to know that there is virtue in what Katell is forcing him to do.

With a determination that Fell (and possibly even Katell herself) thinks is verging on the obsessive, Katell steers Wang away from any discussion of what their son looks like. She sticks to her rigid regime of naming the palpable, and when she cannot prevent him from taking some abstract linguistic byway, she turns to the other senses instead, touch above all. At the slightest provocation, she encourages physical contact between Wang and François, wrapping the broken man's arms round the boy, encouraging kisses of greeting and farewell, brushing broad fingers across the baby's features. Holding the boy as tenderly as he can, Wang traces the outline of his innocent face, starting from the crown, back through his brushstroke of hair, over the tiny, flabby ears, and round to the lips, the stubby nose, and the delicate, unblemished eyes that he sometimes dares to hope are looking at him.

Are all babies like this? he thinks. Are they all so awkward and trusting and breakable? Do they all have skulls which feel misshapen and lumpy? Do they all have curious dimples for chins and ridges above the line of their noses? Do their faces all crumple and stretch when they howl for milk and for comfort? Or is it just my son's? Dimly he tries to recall the hundreds of babies he must have seen and ignored in China, and the dozens he must have seen in passing in France. He desperately wishes he had looked more closely. A specially privileged traveller he may have been, but the presence of one special child brings home to him the extent of his visual ignorance.

'What does my face look like?' he asks, when the three of them are enveloped in a reasonably comfortable silence. 'Don't lie to me, don't smooth things over. I know you think I'm not ready for François yet, but you can tell me what my own face really looks like.'

Katell looks anywhere but directly at him. Dreading a question like this, she has prepared all sorts of false answers, but none of them now seem to match the moment.

'I don't see you injured,' she says. 'I just don't see the scarring and the blindness. No, don't interrupt. I'm trying to be honest. I see you whole, as you were when you first came to the estaminet.'

'It's not what I asked,' Wang says.

'I know it's not, but it's still true. You're not a cripple, you're not incomplete—I need to tell you that.'

'Katell, what does my face look like?' he repeats.

She forces herself to look—she has had enough training over the last few weeks—and searches for words to describe Wang's pitted and deformed face.

'It's dark, darker than I remember from before, and it's full of life. Perhaps I notice it more than I did before—I spend so long just looking at you now—but, with your other eye gone, your mouth and artificial eye come into their own. It was odd at first, seeing that enamel eyeball move in my direction when we were talking. It was like being followed by an incompetent spy. Sometimes it wandered towards me, and then it was as if it lost its way. I would move and it stayed still, or the other way round.'

Determined not to let her escape now that she has started to speak, Wang leans closer.

'But what does the rest of it look like? The damaged part? The bit that got blasted away?'

Katell forces herself to look again. She is struggling, but somehow it is a relief too, this opportunity to hang words onto the unspeakable. Shutting out the sound of the ward—two labourers arguing over a game of *xiangqi*, someone slurping his drink—she concentrates on not destroying the trust she has worked so hard to create.

'It's like a map,' she says eventually. 'Or maybe not a map, but one of those papier-mâché models where you can see all the bumps and hillocks. You know the ones I mean?'

'Relief maps.'

'That's it. It's like a relief map of some bit of the country they've been fighting over. You know, Bapaume or Ancre, or somewhere like that. It's like one of those pictures they used to show in the papers, looking down from above, from one of those air balloons or airplanes, you know? It's like a map—what did you call it?—a relief map of one of the battlegrounds. Lots of trenches. Shell holes. Craters in unexpected places. But somehow, despite all the destruction, you can still see where the fields and hedgerows used to be. The pre-war world pokes through.'

Into the silence that rushes after her words, the ordinary world re-emerges—the game of xiangqi, coughs, the rasping sound of caught breath. She looks up bewildered and, seeing Fell behind her, raises her palms in a silent request for help.

'Not France,' he says, 'but China.'

'What?' Katell blurts out.

'Not France. Not the Somme. Guilin, where my mission station was. The most beautiful place on earth.'

'What on earth are you talking about, Fell?'

Fell ignores the question and, checking Wang's pulse and dressings, answers another question instead.

'I'm sorry I shouted at you the other day, Wang, I really am. Too many patients. Not enough doctors. Not enough decent nurses. Haven't seen my family in far too long. It wasn't good enough, I know, but'—he shrugs—'you know what it's like when the nerves start going. I shouldn't have said it.'

'No,' Wang replies, thinking about his face, 'you shouldn't.'

Although Fell tries to resurrect their pre-armistice banter, the cut and thrust of words—or the lunge and parry of language, as he used to call it—is too much for Wang now. Not having a great deal of choice, he tends towards introspection, finding himself adrift in a sea of thoughts when Katell is not with him, as afternoons pass without focus or precision. When definition returns, as it always does, he hates finding that his mind is flabbier than it ever used to be.

'You know what you were saying the other day?' he says, as Fell gives him an injection.

'I doubt it,' Fell replies.

'About my face looking like Guilin.'

Fell taps the side of his syringe and peers short-sightedly at the phial on his trolley. 'Ah, yes. That. Maybe I got a bit carried away.'

Resisting the temptation to rub the spot into which Fell has just stuck his needle, Wang leans forward and attempts to lay his hand on the doctor's arm. 'What exactly did you mean?'

Fell drops the used syringe into a metal dish and sits heavily down on the end of the bed. 'What exactly did I mean? I've been wondering that myself.'

Wang waits patiently. A distant clock ticks, and somewhere outside a thrush's song shoulders itself into the stuffy ward.

'It was listening to Katell that did it. She's—well, she's a good woman is Katell but—it isn't France scratched into your face, but China. You know, the mountains and those enormous rivers that look so insignificant up against them. I don't know how to put it into words like you do but, while she was talking about craters and shells, I was thinking of Guilin.'

Wang hasn't been to Guilin, but he remembers picture books from his childhood that created a fairy-tale picture of China—all pagodas and palaces; emperors and scholars; mountains, rivers and beauty. Before he learned to be contemptuous of these visions of the mythical past, he loved poring over them with his one good eye, imagining himself promenading in the pleasure gardens of Suzhou, smelling blossom in Hangzhou, or climbing Guilin's holy mountains.

'Do you know what I'm talking about?' Fell probes as Wang sits in heavy silence.

'Mountains clustered like limestone pagodas on the banks of the River Li,' Wang replies. 'Fishermen poling punts with bamboo-hung lanterns illuminating their cormorants and their fish. Terraces cut into the hillsides like thousands of pale green wedding cakes.'

'How the bloody hell do you do that?' Fell demands.

263

'I'm not quite sure. I think it may have something to do with wasting my time on Shakespeare as a boy.'

Fell smiles wryly. 'Not a problem I ever had,' he says, levering himself off the end of the bed. He bustles around the trolley for a minute before turning back to Wang, who looks as though he might be drifting back off into sleep or confusion.

'All the way through this damnable war, I told myself I just had to hang on until the end and then I could get back to where my heart is. Well, we got to the end and I discovered two things. That the end wasn't the end, not for me anyway and not for you lot either. And that my heart had split—no, that's the wrong word— that it had expanded until it was big enough to pump lifeblood to my family in Kent and to my adopted home in Guilin.'

He breaks off and runs a hand through his thinning hair.

'There you are, you've got me all philosophical as well, which is a sure sign that I've either had too much to drink or that I need to get back to work. In this case, it's the latter.'

Wang lets him go. He is thinking about China, a country he scarcely knows, a place he will never see again, and he's thinking about what Fell has just said. He wants to tell the Englishman that he too is a man divided, but now that he wants them, words refuse to come.

Chapter 24

'How are the mice?' he asks when Katell returns the next day.

'Escaped mostly,' she says, her mood audibly darkening. 'A pane of glass got broken and there was a mass breakout. By the time I got there, there was only half a dozen of them poking around among my strawberry plants.'

'Dare I ask about the polecat?'

'Probably had a field day with all those mice turning up. I don't like to think about it really.'

Wang's face twists into a smile despite himself.

Katell stares at him, as if unsure how to read his expression now that his features are so gnarled and battered. 'But let's forget about the mice and concentrate on getting you to see again,' she says.

Relying on her to prompt when words fail, Wang describes Blyth and Fell, then moves onto the Chinese labourers he used to carouse with in the estaminet after curfew—Pang Wei, Ma Gaoteng, and the giant, Zhu Qinan.

'Can I tell you what François looks like now?' he asks, after a particularly satisfying session.

Katell hesitates. 'Not yet,' she says. 'I've got to get you outside first.'

Wang lifts his head, surprised. 'Get me outside where?'

'Anywhere, as long as it's out. I can't stand you being in here anymore.'

'I'm not strong enough. Ask Fell. He'll tell you.'

Fell is no more enthusiastic than Wang is, but Katell is

difficult to resist. After much persuading, he helps manoeuvre Wang into a bath chair, but insists on digging out a woollen jumper and pulling it over the CLC uniform. Katell adds a trench coat and a red and green checked blanket.

'How do I look?' Wang asks.

'Bloody awful,' Fell replies. 'Now get out and make sure you don't drop dead on us.'

Wang has been shut up for so long in the hospital ward that he has forgotten how much he misses the outer world—the rasping freshness of the air, the sharpness of the cold, the shock of the first breath. Katell is cautious at first, taking him no further than the Chinese arch in one direction and the derelict workshops in the other but, after that first trip out, she persuades Fell to let them travel further afield. Needing to have Wang to herself, for a short while at least, Katell leaves François behind, sometimes with Fell, who protests loudly but secretly enjoys looking after the baby, but more often with Marie, a neighbour who now helps her run the estaminet.

As she wheels Wang through the countryside in his bath chair, or helps him walk by getting him to lean on her as well as on his stick, she does what she can to distract him from the uncertainties that lie ahead, cutting him off when he mentions the war, and steering conversations away from the future. Instead she feeds him normality, conscious somehow that she is also protecting herself from emotions she is not yet ready to embrace.

She takes him to the estaminet and leaves him in the one comfy seat by the piano where he can hear the swirl of Franco-Breton conversations. Sometimes Dingo or one of the cats nuzzles against him, but Wang prefers to be left entirely alone. He rarely joins in the conversation and never engages in banter. Katell just lets him sit and hopes that will be enough.

There are few British officers in the camp now, and none of the Chinese who remain are well enough to break the hospital's bounds, so she considers herself safe enough from the agitation both groups inevitably bring. When she can, she extracts François from her regular customers and brings him over to where Wang is slumped. At first he is embarrassed but, once he realises that the eyes of the room are no longer on him, when it dawns on him that he has become as much a part of the furniture as the mismatched tables and chairs, he accepts the paternal role that has been given to him and holds the boy. Gradually, painfully to anyone who does stop to watch, he experiments with different ways of keeping François quiet—rocking him gently from one hand to the other, bouncing him hesitantly up and down on his knees, muttering classical Chinese poetry in his ear.

Fell encourages Katell to go further, knowing that inscrutable civil servants in London will start demanding Wang's repatriation as soon as he can fend for himself, and knowing too that, torn away from the only reason he now has to live, he won't survive the long sea journey home. Pushing desperation away, Katell tells him that she is doing all she can and invites him to the estaminet for Christmas.

As he sits in the corner and listens to dozens of villagers become slowly incoherent with drink, Wang takes another swig of the unidentifiable liquor Katell has presented him with and attempts to work himself up into a temper. But he cannot do it—the music is too jaunty, the drink is too sweet, the company is too alluring. With François on his knees, he is suddenly and acutely aware that he prefers the warmth of the estaminet to anywhere else on earth, a realisation that makes him feel, above all else, acutely guilty.

Katell, watching the two of them gurgling to each other, breaks off from her work.

'Do you want to tell me what he looks like now?' she asks gently.

Wang turns his head towards her. 'When he's like this, and I'm here and you are too, I don't need to see him.' He tickles the tiny tummy again. 'What are words worth now when'—he shrugs—'when the world is as it is?'

Whenever Katell can get away from the estaminet, she rushes down to the hospital and bothers Fell into letting her take Wang off his hands. Then, having screened him off from the rest of the ward, she dresses him in several layers of clothes to keep him warm, before handing him an equally well-wrapped François. Sometimes Dingo comes with them, bounding off ahead to chase highly elusive rabbits and returning exuberantly as though proud of his lack of success, and sometimes they go alone. They explore as much of Noyelles as can be reached in a bath chair and then expand their horizons. As they visit the Bois de Nolette and the saltmarshes, Wang's face starts to struggle back towards expression.

'I grew up in one great city,' he says, settling back in his chair with a smile, 'and learnt everything I know in another, but now...'

Katell takes him further into the countryside and tries to teach him the little she knows about the natural world. It isn't easy, especially when François exerts his own particular natural demands, but she does her best to learn with him and thinks that maybe she is making progress. When she discovers that he can identify butterwort, milkwort, and a smattering of other plants besides just by their smell, she knows it for certain. As they explore the farms that lie on the road to Abbeville and lurch into any woodland that has ground solid enough for the chair, Wang staves off the future and acts as though the present might be never-ending. But he cannot forget Guo and, however light-hearted Katell sounds and however distracting François might be, he suspects that Katell can't either. In Belgium or China, or buried in some foreign grave, his rival and victim is sporadically as much of a presence as he was when he was based at Noyelles.

As far as she can, Katell keeps Wang to herself, but isolation is not always easy to maintain. On their way back to the estaminet one day in early February, she stops to change François' nappy and is alarmed to find that an elderly farmer is standing by the bath chair when she returns.

'I've always wanted to know what it's like,' he is saying, as she rushes up with François under one arm. 'Being blind I mean.'

'What's going on here?' she demands, until Wang holds up a hand to quieten her.

'It's something you have to learn to do,' he says.

The old man nods, touches his cap to Katell, and walks off. Katell puts François back on Wang's lap and pushes off more firmly than she had intended.

'You didn't need to speak to him, you know.'

'And you didn't need to protect me,' he replies. 'I may not be able to see but I can still manage my words.'

She isn't sure that he can manage anything any more, but she doesn't tell him. Instead she works harder to keep him away from any conversations she cannot control. As the days grow longer and the inevitable topic of Wang's departure grows closer, she also starts to give him at least the illusion of choice.

'Shall we try the woods today or the fields?' she asks. 'Shall we head north or south?'

She knows what he will choose—he always heads towards the sea, to where he can smell the salt and feel the damp on his face. Despite having lived all her life in the village, she cannot fully understand this obsession. To her, the sea is a backdrop, a low murmur that need not overwhelm the sounds of everyday life, but to him the ocean is a lure he cannot ever quite catch. As Dingo races ahead, his tail thumping the air and his ears flapping with excitement, she takes Wang up what passes for a hill in Noyelles, where she can see both the camp below her and a thin line of water that she knows is the estuary in the distance.

'What can you see?' he asks quietly, holding François tightly against him.

The channel is a mere tracing in the landscape, a thread it is virtually impossible to catch in the greater tapestry, but she tries to give it the significance he seems to need. She describes the way it catches fragments of the sun's brilliance, the way it appears to get snagged in the countryside only to emerge broader and bluer

269

a few yards further off. She tries to pluck words—the sort of words he routinely uses—from the great storeroom of her mind, but she isn't used to using language in this way and finds herself lapsing into silence before he has exhausted his need to see what she is telling.

'What about you?' she asks. 'What can you see?'

Turning his head one way and then the other, as though trying to decide which view to describe, Wang considers his words carefully.

'I can see the camp. Five, ten low blocks, whitewashed and as clean as any army camp can reasonably be expected to be. I can see the pagoda bearing down on the entrance gate—vermilion and saffron yellow with its *hanzi* boldly black—and the bell's clapper hanging like a drunk from a tall building, swaying precariously. I can see the recreation hut, covered with movie posters—Chaplin, Keaton and Fairbanks lined up ready to hurl the audience like petals into the breeze. There are trucks washed up by the side of the roads, like barges ready for the next leg of their journey up the Grand Canal, and men, hundreds of them, milling about, joking, smoking, hitching up their trousers, hawking on the ground, doing bad impressions of their officers, sharing obscene songs.'

He turns back to Katell who can scarcely bear to listen.

'That's what I can see, Katell. I know it's all gone really, but that's what my memory sees.'

'Oh Weijun!' Katell cries, rushing over and giving both him and the startled François a huge hug. 'You weren't even looking in the right direction.'

Wang returns her hug as fiercely as he can. 'The lessons have worked,' he says. 'You've brought me back but, whatever I do now, I'll never be able to see.'

As Katell pushes the bath chair back onto the path, he carries on talking, knowing that if he doesn't say now what he has been afraid to say this past month he will never say it.

'Fell told me what happened at Versailles. They sold us out. Lu Zhengxiang did us proud and stood his ground, but they still sold us out. One hundred thousand of us came to the West, and they didn't even give us our own land back. Thirty nations came to Versailles, and they all got what they wanted except us. Thirty ambassadors signed, and Lu Zhengxiang was the only one who refused. Guo was right—they used us, and now they've sold us out.'

It is the first time that either of them has mentioned Guo in weeks. Sounding his name out loud jolts both of them out of their immediate passion.

'You sound like him,' Katell says. 'So angry. So full of grievances.'

'Is that such a bad thing?' he asks quietly. 'Isn't that why you still love him?'

Katell is silenced by the question. Taking François from Wang's lap, she clutches him close to her chest and walks up and down.

'Maybe it was anger that did for him,' she says. 'Maybe that's why you're here and he's not.'

It is the sadness in her voice as much as the words themselves that silences Wang.

'They're going to send me home,' he says eventually. 'So you've just got to get back to your own life. I'm an albatross round your neck. You don't need me and, now that I'm like I am, I'm never going to be any use to you.'

Katell moves round in front of him. Holding François firm with one hand, she puts her other to his forehead and strokes it.

'It won't be long before they'll say I'm fit to travel,' he says, 'and then I'll be back on the *Empress of Russia*, but this time I'll not see the bright lights or the whales. All I'll see is what I've left behind in France. All I'll see is what I can recall before my memory fades. They're going to send me home, but I don't know where home is any more.'

'You could just choose to stay,' she says.

The words, physical and stark, reach out and strike him.

'What do you mean?' he says.

Katell starts to pace up and down again.

271

'You know what I mean,' she says. 'You know what you want, and you know what I could do.'

'I don't,' he says, trembling.

'I could go to the mayor and apply for the licence. We'd probably have to write to Paris too, but I could do that. Others have. It's not impossible.'

A low throb starts to pulsate through Wang's right ear and then spreads to his left. He feels his throat constrict.

'What are you talking about, Katell?'

She turns back towards him. 'Weijun,' she says.

He lowers his head. 'I couldn't let you do it.'

'Why not?' Katell says. 'They'd do it if that was what you wanted. It'd save them another job. Why go to all the trouble of shipping you home when you could stay here with me and François?'

'But, Katell, how could you look after me and François and the estaminet? You'd be doing all the work while I just dribble in a corner.'

'Will you stop talking like that! You're not a helpless invalid, Weijun. You're not a victim or a wreck, and you're certainly not a drooler.'

'That's exactly what I am! I can't do anything. I'd just sit and eat and terrify your customers. I can't even look after François properly. Just look at me.'

Katell takes both his hands in hers. 'Listen, Weijun. I can't lose Ziqin and then lose you too. And do you know why? Not because I need a man to keep me strong—I've lost one man after another in this terrible war—but because our son needs us both. François needs us. He doesn't care what you look like. He doesn't care whether you can see. He just needs you.'

'To do what?' Wang asks bitterly.

'To be his father, Weijun. To be his father.'

She sounds so angry that Wang tries to nurture a sense of grievance in return. 'He needs his mother,' he says, 'not some cripple in a wheelchair.'

'Don't tell me what he needs, Weijun. He needs not to lose one man after another from his life. He needs me and he needs you. You came back, but if you—if you leave us, we would lose more than you can ever understand.'

'It's impossible. It's ridiculous,' he says. 'What about Guo? For God's sake, Katell, what about Guo? I did what I could in Belgium, Katell, I really did. I searched. I asked anyone who came to the camp. I was in the middle of organising search parties when I—when the shell . . .'

He thumps the side of the wheelchair.

'I could speak to Fell. He'd know what to do now that I've not got any eyes to see. I don't know why I didn't ask him before. I should have really but . . . I'm sorry, Katell, I really am.'

When she replies, she speaks so quietly that he can hardly hear. 'He's never coming back.'

She drops down beside him and puts her hand to his mouth as he starts to tell her that it's not true.

'You know it's true,' she says. 'He's never coming back. But if I've got François, then I've got you, and I've got Ziqin too. But if you go, François loses a father and everything he knows. You carry more inside that dark head of yours than your own little life, Weijun. You are father and lover and every memory I have. If you won't marry me, then they'll have you back on that boat and all China will be gone.'

She kisses him gently on the forehead and takes him briefly in her arms. Then she takes hold of the chair's handles and starts pushing again.

'We need you, Weijun,' she says. 'I don't care how dark it is in there, we need you.'

Chapter 25

Katell doesn't know what Fell means when he tells her in his idiosyncratic French that Wang has sunk into a slough of despond, but when she sees him again, slumped in his wheelchair, a blanket over his knees, she realises that she doesn't need a translation.

'Why don't you read to him or something?' Fell suggests.

Katell has a tatty copy of *La Maison du chat-qui-pelote* in the estaminet and a family Bible, but books have never been a source of consolation for her. Nor has she ever considered reading to him.

'I'm not much of a reader,' she says.

'But he is. I think you're going to have to put your own limitations to one side for the time being, don't you?' He pulls a battered book out of the bedside cabinet. 'This is what he had in his pack when they brought him in. It's not my cup of tea, but he seems to thrive on it.'

Katell flicks through the book, pulls up a chair and, realising she has no choice, waits for Wang to wake up. When eventually he stirs, she gently lays the sleeping François next to him. Wang stiffens and then lets himself fall back onto the pillow.

'I've got a book here,' she says.

'What is it?' he asks listlessly.

'*Henry V.*'

He lifts his head in surprise. 'Where did you dig that out from?'

Katell hesitates. Suddenly she doubts Fell's advice. Having coaxed Wang into an expectation of healing, she doesn't want to ruin it by forcing the past onto him. She's not even sure she can get the words out. Whenever she tries to turn what she's heard or read of English into something worthy of communication, the words sound flat and wrong.

'Shall I read it?' she asks, and for a moment she isn't sure whether she's speaking to Wang or to herself. 'I haven't much English, and some of these words look awful funny, but I can give it a go.'

When Wang nods, she opens the play, flicks through the pages, and hopes to find an easy scene. When it becomes clear that there are no easy scenes, she gives up and chooses a page at random.

'*I was not angry since I came to France,*' she reads haltingly.

She hesitates again.

'Well, go on then if you're going to read.'

She begins again, stumbling over most words and mispronouncing others.

'*I was not angry since I came to France until this instant. Take a trumpet, herald; ride thou*—I don't know what that means—*unto the horsemen on yon hill: if they will fight with us, bid them come down, or void the field; they do offend our sight: if they'll do neither, we will come to them, and make them skirr away*—is that how you pronounce it?—*as swift as stones enforced from the old Assyrian slings: besides, we'll cut the throats of those we have, and not a man of them that we shall take shall taste our mercy. Go and tell them so.* Look, Weijun, are you really sure about this?'

'*Here comes the herald of the French, my liege,*' Wang replies. '*His eyes are humbler than they used to be.*'

She looks at him in amazement. 'How do you know that comes next?' she asks. 'I can't even read the words and you have them by heart.'

'*I come to thee for charitable licence,*' Wang prompts.

'*I come to thee for charitable licence,*' she repeats, '*that we may wander o'er this bloody field to book our dead, and then*

to bury them; to sort our nobles from our common men. For
many of our princes—woe the while!—lie drown'd and soak'd in
mercenary blood; so do our vulgar drench their peasant limbs
in blood of princes; and their wounded steeds fret fetlock deep in
gore and with wild rage yerk out their armed heels at their dead
masters, killing them twice—'

She breaks off again, but Wang finishes the sentence for her anyway.

'O, give us leave, great king, to view the field in safety and
dispose of their dead bodies.'

Katell drops the book onto the floor and wipes her silent tears away.

Wang gently eases himself up. 'I think it's time you took me to the cemetery,' he says.

As she hauls him up the road to Nolette, to the dark field where the Chinese dead are still being interred, Katell does what she can to get Wang to play with François, while Dingo runs on ahead. Ignoring his son, who seems unsettled by his father's strange silence, Wang recovers some sense of equilibrium only when they head towards the mouth of the Somme. Katell realises that she cannot reach inside the more profound blackness that he has pulled over himself and concentrates on pushing the chair instead.

When they arrive at the cemetery, a work party of Chinese labourers is getting ready to leave. One or two of the men call out greetings to their former comrade, but the majority of them steer well clear, as though blindness and disfigurement could be contagious. The head ganger nods curtly in their direction and then fires a series of orders to his men, who collect their picks and shovels and start sauntering towards the exit.

'You need the help?' he asks in broken French.

Tying Dingo's lead to a tree to prevent him from pawing at the newly-dug graves, Katell shakes her head. Wang lifts his chin from his chest. It is a fine Spring day, and the blanket Katell has covered him with almost as a matter of habit has slipped down to his knees.

'So you're a translator?' the ganger says when he spots Wang's armband.

Wang nods.

'Never bothered with the white devils' language myself,' the man continues.

Ignoring the comment, Wang asks, 'Who is it you've buried today?'

'Diao Xufeng,' the ganger replies.

'What happened to him?'

'Stepped on an unexploded shell.'

'Where?'

'Over near Arras. They were clearing the fields while the white ghosts sat on the road and drank.'

Though she hasn't understood a word, Katell can read the tone. 'Stop talking to him,' she demands. 'He's had enough.'

The ganger swears at her.

'It's all right, Katell,' Wang says. 'He's only telling me what I already know.'

The ganger looks curiously down at him, as if bemused to discover that the white woman's language could emerge from such a battered Chinese face. He thinks about asking but bends down to pick up his bag instead.

'Don't let the foreign devil stop you doing what you've come here to do,' he says.

Wang nods again and returns the salute the ganger hasn't yet offered. Katell, who has been attempting to suppress an urge to offer a further piece of her mind, watches as the man walks unhurriedly away and then pushes the chair round the perimeter of the cemetery. She is annoyed with Wang for asking to be brought here and annoyed with herself for agreeing. They walk in as much silence as François decides to permit and then stop in the sunlight while she has a rest.

'How many new ones are there?' Wang asks eventually.

'Four or five,' she says. She picks François up and puts him on the grass.

'Read me the names,' Wang says.

'I can't, Weijun. They're all in Chinese and I don't recognise the words.'

Wang's head falls again. 'Give me a cross then,' he says.

'What, pull it up from the ground, you mean?'

He nods. Katell isn't sure she should be moving even temporary headstones, but she does as he asks and waits for Wang to feel the marks with his fingers. He lets his hands rove over the slight indentations but cannot make sense of what was never intended for blind men. Handing the cross back, he waits for her to thrust it into the soil.

'I came to France as a translator,' he says, once she has crouched down beside him, 'but now I don't know who will translate for me.'

'You do know, Weijun,' Katell says.

He lifts his head again and turns it in her direction. 'Fell told me this morning that they're clearing us out of the hospital,' he says quietly. 'They're closing the place down and sending the last of us home.'

She puts her arms round him. 'Then let me go and see the mayor.'

Wang turns away. 'I thought they would do it gradually,' he says. 'I thought they'd give us time to decide.'

'They've given you time, Weijun. You've just got to say yes, that's all.'

He pulls the blanket up again, though the sunshine is stronger than it has been all day. 'Be my eyes again,' he says. 'Tell me what you can see.'

Katell thinks for a moment and then tells him about the crosses and the few faded wreaths. She tells him where the earth has been gathered into mounds and where it lies tramped and even. She describes the cherry tree that is showing its buds in the south-east corner and the bare field that lies on the other side of

278

the fence. She tries to find words to describe the carvings on the wooden Chinese arch that spans the cemetery's narrow entrance. She tells him everything that can be seen and never once looks away from the ridges and furrows of his face.

'Where are we, Katell?' he asks. 'Is this France or China or England?'

'It's France, silly,' she replies. 'It's Noyelles. It's where you belong.'

Wang sinks even further down into his chair. 'It feels like no man's land,' he says.

They stay so long in the cemetery that Katell accepts a lift home in a military truck that stops for them as they are trudging back through Nolette.

'Where are you going, love?' asks the driver, a gap-toothed Liverpudlian, as he stows the wheelchair in the back among piles of old gun parts and sacks of vegetables.

'The estaminet at Noyelles,' she says, once she has deciphered the question.

'No,' Wang interrupts. 'I want to see the sea.'

'Bloody hell,' the driver says. 'I wasn't expecting that. You sound like the king. Better bloody English than mine.'

'We can't go to the sea, Weijun,' Katell says, putting her hand on his.

'Well, we could do,' the driver says. 'I'm heading to Saint-Valéry if it's really the sea you're after.'

'I need to see the sea,' Wang repeats.

'Righto, guv,' the driver says. 'The sea it is then. Let's get you three up front here. What about the dog? Is that yours too?'

'It's hers,' Wang says.

'Well, it's a fine looking fellow. What sort is it?'

'Enthusiastic,' Wang replies.

'A bit of everything,' Katell says, once Wang has translated the question. 'Part collie, part wolf, I think.'

Once Dingo has taken up his place in the front with his feet on the dashboard, and the others have squeezed in beside him, the truck driver talks incessantly as he takes them through Noyelles, across the marsh road, and up the canal towards Saint-Valéry and the mouth of the Somme. He talks about his missus, about the evil concoction he and his mates brewed up in a distillery they talked their way into in Abbeville, and about the bloody Americans and their plans to carve up the Empire. He talks, then suddenly stops.

'Hope you don't mind me mentioning it,' he says, 'but your face is a bit of state, isn't it?'

Wang nods slowly.

'But you've got a good woman too. That makes all the difference.'

'Thank you,' Wang says.

'That's all right, mate. It's all part of the service.'

He helps them out of the truck at a place where the road draws close to a small jetty, reaching François down to Katell and then fetching the wheelchair from the back.

'You look after yourself,' he says to Wang, as he climbs back in, 'and make sure you keep an eye on the boy.'

He honks the horn as he moves away, turns round where the road widens, and throws them a friendly wave as he speeds off. It seems very quiet when he is gone.

'Take me to the end of the jetty,' Wang says.

Katell pushes into the wind as it sweeps across the estuary and then stands huddled up to Wang with François in her arms as they let the wind attack them. Here, where France gives way to the sea, it is a living force that shouts and hurls and grapples with itself; there is nothing to do but meet it. She watches as Wang lifts his face, then, unable to contain herself any longer, turns away to where the croaking birds are trying to disentangle themselves from the wind's skein.

Wang, too, is trying to catch his thoughts as they swoop through his head, attacking his memory and tormenting him with their intractability. Now that it is no longer possible to avoid, the future seems intangible. Instead, he reaches out to the past and finds a line of faces, like Banquo's descendants, stretching out in front of him—his father, yearning for an elusive modernity; his mother, dead and disappointed; Rong Meifan, looking disdainful. Blind and helpless, pitiful and pathetic, he tries to push them away, but he no longer has the strength. Looking deeper into the darkness, he sees other faces emerging from the gloom—Captain Blyth, General Greenstreet, Guo Ziqin. He tries to reason with them, but they cannot hear. He puts his hands to his face instead and feels its terrible roughness.

But when Katell slowly prises his hands away, he lets her fold them back onto the blanket, and when she lays François down on his lap, he takes him gently. The boy gurgles excitedly and starts to reach for the buttons on the front of his jacket. Dingo barks madly at thousands of spiders of surf.

'Can I read to you?' Wang asks.

'How can you, Weijun? You can't see and I haven't got your book.'

'I don't need the book,' he says wryly, 'and, before you ask, I don't have to translate either. There's a part of the play that's in French. Some of it anyway.'

Katell wraps her arms around him and reluctantly agrees. 'Only if you're sure, Weijun.'

'I'm sure,' he says. 'If I stumble, you can stop me, and if I go wrong, you'll never know.'

She stoops down lower to catch his voice.

'*Les dames et demoiselles pour être baisées devant leur noces, il n'est pas la coutume de France,*' he says. '*It is not a fashion for the maids in France to kiss before they are married, would she say?*'

A wave crashes against the jetty, wetting their feet. Wang lifts his voice against the wind.

'*O Katell, nice customs curtsy to great kings. Dear Katell, you and I cannot be confined within the weak list of a country's fashion. We are the makers of manners and the liberty that follows our places stops the mouth of all find-faults—as I will do yours for upholding the nice fashion of your country in denying me a kiss; therefore, patiently and yielding.'*

He breaks off for a moment and, when he resumes, he speaks in French.

'You have witchcraft in your lips, Katell: there is more eloquence in a sugar touch of them than in the tongues of the French Council.'

'Oh, Weijun,' she says and, making sure she doesn't squash François in her haste, places her lips on his. Then, working her way from top to bottom, she covers every lump and hollow of his face with increasingly desperate kisses until François starts to gurgle in his own untranslatable language.

Wang holds onto the baby with one hand and pulls a grey drawstring bag out of his pocket with the other. He loops the string over his finger, eases François' tiny hands away, and hands the bag to Katell.

'I don't need this now,' he says. 'Keep one ball back and bury the rest at sea. Throw them as far as they'll go.'

Katell peers inside. She's never dared look before. 'They're different colours,' she says.

'I know.'

'But which one do you want me to keep?'

'It doesn't matter now, does it?' Wang replies. 'I wouldn't be able to tell.'

Katell leans down close and kisses him again, then puts her hand into the bag and pulls out a piece of enamel. She stares at it, rolls it in her palm for a moment, and steps up to the edge of the jetty. Without looking round, she pulls her arm back and throws the bag as far as she can. It arcs through the spume and, because she has forgotten to pull the drawstrings tight, the balls spray into the gathering grey. Shielding her eyes from the glare, she looks down at the water. There is nothing to be seen but the leaden waters and the fragile white flecks of the waves as they fray. She steps back and puts her hand on Wang's arm.

'Here you are,' she says, giving him the last artificial eye.

Wang takes it and, keeping one hand firmly on his son, holds up his other hand for Katell to take.

'*You may, some of you, thank love for my blindness, who cannot see many a fair French city for one French maid that stands in my way,*' he whispers.

Katell can see his lips moving but, unable to hear a word he is saying, leans down closer. 'It's brown,' she says. 'I saved a brown one.'

Wang doesn't reply. As the wind lashes him with memories of lepers and lunatics, trachoma and trauma, he grapples with Guo Ziqin and fights back against guilt. When he puts his head up again, the wind catches him. It sounds, he thinks, like a baby wailing in the dark, a broken voice calling from across the world, a call that has to be answered. Pulling away from Katell's grasp, he slips the enamel eyeball into his pocket and, as if finding it for the first time, feels his face with his hand, allowing it to run in and out of the grooves, exploring every contour, probing the place where his eyeball used to rest. As he falters, Katell rests her hand on his and, lifting it to her face, allows it to continue its journey through her tangled hair, over the bridge of her nose, around her eyes and down over her chin to their son's face. Drawing their thumbs across his smooth forehead and caressing his cheeks with their interlinked fingers, they track new paths across the unblemished map of his skin until the wind's assault and the sea's implacable defence fade into the welcoming dark.

Acknowledgements

With grateful thanks to Fionnuala Kennedy and Brianna MacLean for early encouragement, Anne-Marie Doulton for all her input, William Bearcroft for magical advice, Professor Michel Hockx for his linguistic and historical help, and Marie Emery for her French and Breton expertise. I have learned a great deal in the British Library, the SOAS Library, and the Wimereux public library and am grateful to the librarians in those institutions. I was permanently astounded by my family's patience as I trekked across northern France in search of Chinese cemeteries and then shut myself away to write up the results; I thank my wife and children with all my heart. I am also extremely grateful to Jane Spencer for her enthusiasm, sensitivity and attention to detail - it has been great to work with such a wonderful editor and publisher.

About the author

After reading Modern History at Oxford, Roy Peachey went on to study English at the Open University, Lake District Studies at Lancaster University, Theology at the University of Nottingham, and Chinese Studies at SOAS, University of London, where he first learned about the Chinese Labour Corps in World War I. He has written for many national publications and taught at a number of schools across the country. His other publications are *Out of the Classroom and Into the World*, and *Did Jesus go to School? and other questions about parents, children and education. Between Darkness and Light* is his first novel.